HEART OF STONE

What Reviewers Say About Sam Ledel's Work

Worth a Fortune

"The romance burns tantalizingly slowly as Ledel takes the time to thoroughly explore the ways her well-shaded heroines both complement and clash with each other. This remarkable emotional maturity does not come at the expense of heat, however; when the love scenes come, they steam up the pages. It's subtle, lovely, and stirring. Starred review."
—*Publishers Weekly*

"Loved this! It was exciting, down to earth and totally unexpected. Nothing outrageous, just a wonderful connection between two women who find their world has completely changed following the Second World War. I adored the way both of them had to learn new things, take new changes, risks, and try things that weren't known to them, only to find themselves reconnecting in a most lovely way."—*LESBIreviewed*

The Princess and the Odium

"The world-building in the whole trilogy is fantastic, and even if it feels familiar now that we've been navigating it with the characters for a while, it's still surprising and unsettling. All in all, *The Princess and the Odium* is a fitting end to a well-written YA fantasy series."
—*Jude in the Stars*

Rocks and Stars

"I think Sam Ledel told a great story. I adored Kyle even though a few times I wanted to shake her and say enough girlfriend. I wish the ending was a bit longer, but that's the romance addict in me. I look forward to Ledel's next book."—*Romantic Reader Blog*

Daughter of No One

"There's a lot of really smart fantasy going on here. ...Great start to a (hopefully) long running series."—Colleen Corgel, Librarian, Queens Public Library

"It's full of exciting adventure and the promise of romance. It's sweet, fresh and hopeful. It takes me back to my teenage years, the good parts of those years at least. I read this in a few hours, only stopped long enough to have lunch. I hope I won't have to wait too long for the sequel—I have high hopes for Jastyn, Aurelia, their friend Coran, Eegit the hedgewitch and Rigo the elf."—*Jude in the Stars*

"A fantasy book with MCs in their very early twenties, this book presents a well thought out world of Kingdom of Venostes (shades of The Lord of the Rings here)."—*Best Lesfic Reviews*

"Sam Ledel has definitely set up an epic adventure of star-crossed lovers. This book one of a trilogy doesn't leave you with a cliffhanger but you are definitely going to be left ready for the next book. ...As a non-fantasy lover, I adored this book and am ready to read where Ledel takes us next. This book is quality writing, great pacing, and top-notch characters. You cannot go wrong with this one!"—*Romantic Reader Blog*

"If you're a huge fan of fantasy novels, especially if you love stories like this one that contains a host of supernatural beings, quirky characters coupled with action and excitement around every tree, winding path or humble abode, then this is definitely the story for you! This compelling story also deals with poverty, isolation and the huge chasm between the royal family and the low-class villagers. Well, fellow book lovers, it really looks like you've just received a winning ticket to a literary lottery."—*Lesbian Review*

Broken Reign

"Sam Ledel has created a fascinating and at times terrifying world, filled with elves, sirens, selkies, wood nymphs and many more. ...Going on this journey with both young women and their fellow travellers still has this fresh and exciting quality, all the more so as new characters joined the story, some just as intriguing."—*Jude in the Stars*

By the Author

Rocks and Stars

Wildflower Words

Worth a Fortune

Heart of Stone

The Odium Trilogy

Daughter of No One

Broken Reign

The Princess and the Odium

HEART OF STONE

by

Sam Ledel

2023

HEART OF STONE
© 2023 By Sam Ledel. All Rights Reserved.

ISBN 13: 978-1-63679-407-5

This Trade Paperback Original Is Published By
Bold Strokes Books, Inc.
P.O. Box 249
Valley Falls, NY 12185

First Edition: August 2023

Credits
Editor: Barbara Ann Wright
Production Design: Susan Ramundo
Cover Design By Tammy Seidick

Acknowledgments

Thank you to Sandy Lowe for your guidance on this story's beginnings. Thanks to the BSB team for your hard work and dedication to helping us, the authors, tell our stories and share them with the world. And as always, a big thank you to my fabulous editor, Barbara Ann Wright. We'll always have the fruit leathers.

My deepest appreciation to my family, friends, and partner. You listened to my early ideas, nodded along even if you had no idea what I was talking about, and continued to encourage me along this journey. Big love to you all.

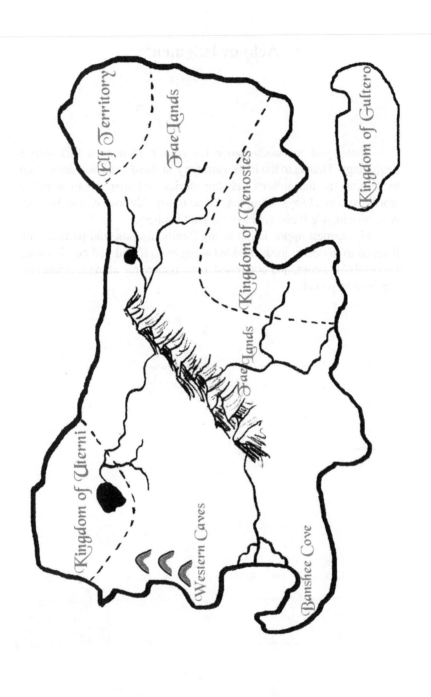

Prologue

Maeve stepped carefully toward the riverbank, excitement spinning around her. The local fairies had spoken of nothing but their annual festival for two moons, and she'd spent the last week dreaming of the beautiful lights dancing in the sky.

At only eight, her mother would never allow her to attend. Maeve had asked, but her plea had fallen on resolute ears. "You know we can't go to that, Maeve."

"But they're fairies," she had replied, an emphatic stamp accompanying her words.

Her mother hadn't even turned from the hearth where she'd stirred rabbit stew over the fire in a small cauldron. "It's at the river. It's too close to the kingdom."

"But—"

"No." She'd thrown a hard look over her shoulder. "That's the end of it."

Maeve had stomped off in a huff, shoving through their front door and toward the corner of their fen. There, a series of lush ferns grew, the perfect place to pout in peace.

Now, her heart thundered in her chest, not only in anticipation for the fairy festival but in trepidation at having defied her mother. She'd waited for her mother to fall asleep in a chair by the fire. Sweat had trickled down her spine as she'd worked to quietly unlock their door. With a final glance, certain her mother was asleep, Maeve had slipped out.

"She never lets me go anywhere," she muttered now to the muddy grass along the river. For a moment, she shivered at the sight of the pointed petals of the red flare lilies scattered across the water. Their mahogany leaves seemed to point accusingly. She turned her gaze skyward. Fading sunlight stretched over the land in a dim screen of yellow. Maeve smiled at the first fairies gathering overhead.

A snapping branch caught her ear. Without thinking, she turned to find the source of the noise. An old man in Uterni's colors stood on the other side of the bank, twenty yards away. Maeve's breath caught when his gaze met hers. She knew immediately it was too late.

His mouth slackened. He clutched his stomach, then his chest, a pained moan escaping his lips.

"No," Maeve whispered, ducking. She wanted to go to him, to help him somehow, but his haggard face turned ashen. His body stiffened, and he fell out of sight into the brush.

Trembling, Maeve glanced up at the gathering fairy lights. She swiped at tears, then looked again to where the man had stood. "I'm sorry," she whispered, feeling the fae and wildland creatures watching her. Slowly, she retreated as voices sounded from the distant bogs just outside the village.

Stumbling over gnome hills and pushing through thick flora, Maeve tearfully returned to her fen. All she had wanted was to see the fairy festival. She hung her head, more tears falling. Her mother had been right.

I wish she wasn't. She wished her life wasn't confined to the fen. She wished she hadn't hurt the old man. She wished, more than anything, that she was different.

CHAPTER ONE

I think it's ready." Maeve carefully tugged the trio of flat, palm-sized servings of acorn bread from their baking stone near the edge of the fire burning in the hearth. She placed them on a smaller brown rock and carried it to the wooden table in the middle of her cluttered kitchen. She stepped back, admiring her latest batch of savory sustenance. Hands on her hips, she asked, "Care to try one?"

Her companion snake, Rowan, slithered lazily onto the table, draping over an empty cauldron so his back half lay between a pair of dirty cups and a half-eaten apple. His slender silver body, peppered with black patches that formed no distinct pattern, moved steadily closer to the hot bread. His thin pink tongue flickered out, taking in her latest feat.

He lifted his head and met her gaze. "Well?" she asked, staring into his round black pupils. He blinked.

She grinned. "I knew you'd like it. Now, let's see." Quickly, she adjusted the handkerchief to keep her hair from her face, then picked up the closest piece, carefully holding the bread like a disc, the pads of her fingers and thumb beneath it. She took a bite, closing her eyes and savoring the hint of sweet in the dough. "Yes, this is definitely one of my best. It was the honey I added to the acorn flour." She took another bite and scanned the dozens of clay jars and woven baskets littering this table, along with the smaller table next to the fire. "I think I'll try adding elderberries next time."

Rowan's tongue flickered.

"Don't be greedy," Maeve told him. He turned his head, showing her only one eye. She laughed. "Of course I'm kidding. Have as much as you like." Finishing the bread, she muttered, "Not like anyone else is here to eat them."

She brushed crumbs from her worn, forest green tunic. Sipping from a cup half-full with water, she tried to ignore the familiar sense of sadness that crept upon her. Only recently had she begun to feel such longings, as she'd decided to call them. For years, she'd been perfectly content in her quiet life.

Rowan slithered across the table, knocking over a stack of berries. Maeve had found him when she was fifteen while collecting fresh fruit. He'd been coiled beneath a rowan tree just outside the border of her spring fen, the low-lying grassland at the base of a hill. Having never seen a snake before, she'd screamed, which had prompted the poor creature to coil tighter in fright. Realizing he was as afraid as she was, Maeve had left him alone. Over the next few days, however, she'd spotted him again, each time a few yards closer to her home. One day, she'd stepped outside and bent to pick up a new baking stone from the collection near her door, only to yelp at the sight of the two-foot spiral of silver unraveling in greeting.

Having a snake follow her home was the most exciting thing that had happened to her, maybe ever. She'd named him and let him stay until he was the closest thing she had to a friend.

She washed her hands in the water basin below one of the windows that looked out into her small corner of the realm. She stared at the monotonous wall of green, all thirty-two shades—she'd counted—and tried to shake this sense of longing from her limbs. She knew what it was about, this feeling. It had to do with living alone since her mother's disappearance fifteen years ago. It had to do with the absurd number of bread loaves sitting on the table behind her. It had to do with the fact that her only friend was a snake.

She knew she might be mad. She knew talking to a snake was likely not what everyone else in the realm did. Not that she'd met anyone else. She just had a feeling.

After stoking the fire to rekindle the yellow flames, Maeve crossed the only room of her modest home, the earthen floor compact beneath the soles of her hand-me-down, ankle-high boots. She paused to stand before a tall foggy mirror leaned against the wall. Her mother had found it on one of her outings to the river when Maeve was young. Sometimes, people from Uterni used the empty land as a dumping ground for old and broken things. This cracked mirror was one. Its edges were uneven around the glass; what was once probably an ornate frame was now gone, the ancient wood eaten away by time. Still, the glass was in decent condition, and in it, Maeve scrutinized her figure. The mirror was almost as tall as she was, though she didn't know if she was short or tall compared to others. She had to step back and hunch to see all of herself. She reached beneath her short tunic to the waist of her pants. Standing sideways, she frowned.

She ran her hands over her wide hips. Like her height, she wasn't sure whether her figure was like that of others. Personally, she'd always likened her body to that of a pear, with its wider lower half that seemed to pinch at the waist that went straight from hips to bosom. She shrugged, brushing off the shoulders of her tunic. She felt healthy. That—as her mother used to say—was what mattered.

Stepping closer, she played with the edges of her hair. Most of it fell to her shoulders, coming to rest above the fair skin exposed by the wide neck of her tunic. Some thick pieces, however, lay in jagged sections an inch above the rest, the result of her own attempt at a haircut. She'd tried braids, buns, and even letting her golden locks swing free, but ultimately, her hair only seemed to fall in her face and obstruct her vision. It grew fast, so on a monthly basis for the last year, she'd taken a sharp knife and started chopping. It wasn't like there was anyone other than Rowan to see her. What did it matter if her hair was uneven?

She was on her own and had been for a long time. That was the spark that ignited these recent longings. Every day for years now, she'd been alone. She knew she had to be. Her mother had explained everything. Despite that, Maeve—now in her twenty-fourth year—found herself longing for something, or someone, to come along.

A raven cawed overhead. She looked to the sloping thatch ceiling. She traced the beams to the carefully laid stones and boulders that comprised the rounded walls of her home. Between some of the stones was a layer of peat or moss, but most of the boulders were so closely placed, not even a whisper of wind could breach them.

A familiar *thud* sounded just outside her door. Maeve lingered a moment more at the mirror. Reaching up, she wiped a crumb from the corner of her mouth, then held her own gaze. Her gray eyes were the only pair she'd seen since her mother had gone. She wondered at the swirling silver around her pupils until Rowan gave a low hiss.

"All right, I'm going." She gave him a short wave before walking past two wooden chairs, one of which held a thick layer of dust, past a low-framed bed shoved into the corner, a single woolen blanket tucked neatly around it. Rowan was at her heels when she pulled open the door. Evening light of an early spring day greeted her as the sun sank behind the high, thick tree cover lining her overgrown fen. The greens, browns, and grays all seemed to meld into one in the dawning twilight. A single fairy nest glowed to her right.

She bent to collect the basket of goods that had been left for her. It seemed to contain the usual assortment of plums, gooseberries, and flaxseed. As she held a cluster of raspberries, examining the ridged exterior of the fuchsia fruit, Rowan wrapped around her right leg, then leaned his head to hover over the basket as if to get a better look.

"Always so nosy," she teased. Replacing the berries, she rummaged until she found the folded piece of pale parchment. "Let's see if there's any news."

Unfolding it, Maeve was greeted with the familiar slanted writing of her caretaker. At least, that was what she'd dubbed the mysterious individual who, once a moon, left her baskets like this one. They were her lifeline to the outside world and kept her in enough supplies to get through the days. At first, she hadn't known what to make of the monthly offerings. When she was younger, a small part of her had hoped it might be her mother leaving these gifts, but that had been a silly childish wish. Her mother was gone. Even if she was alive, it wasn't likely she was free and living among the kingdom. A small part of Maeve hoped she was out there somewhere. But that small part grew fainter each day. Over time, Maeve had accepted her lot in life. Her curiosity about who left the basket waned as she simply took the stranger's benevolence with resigned gratitude.

This month's letter read:

M,
I couldn't get honey this time, apologies. I hope the raspberries will make up for my shortcomings.
A banshee was caught on royal grounds. The wood nymphs snared two humans last moon.

Maeve scanned the lengthy list of fae-happenings. After a short briefing on the elves to the east, she frowned as she read:

No, M. Nothing of your mother.
I'll try again on the honey next time. Stay safe, and don't wander far.

She read the last line aloud, happy the writer couldn't hear the disdain in her voice. She shoved the note back into the basket. Rowan slithered down and stretched along the grassy edge of her home. She looped her arm under the basket's woven handle and leaned against the wall beside him.

She was grateful for the Caretaker. She didn't know what she'd do without his supplies. She was a mediocre hunter, more of a trapper, really. She wandered to the river, fifty paces from her fen, when she needed water, but that was as far as she could go, something the Caretaker seemed to know. He had to know her or of her life. One idea was that this person was some acquaintance of her mother's, perhaps somebody who'd taken pity after learning she had a daughter she'd left behind. Maeve closed her eyes, picturing the curled edges of the "M" in shimmery black ink.

She'd been named after her grandmother, whose mother had caused such turmoil—inflicted so much pain and ruined so many lives—that she'd banished herself to this tiny pocket of the realm. Here, she couldn't hurt anyone with her powers, the powers she'd passed down to her daughter and her granddaughter after that, until they'd reached Maeve.

Each woman had lived a life of isolation chosen by and for each of them. But as Maeve's mother had said, it was the only way to keep innocent people from being hurt, to keep others safe from creatures like them. Being the great-granddaughter of the infamous gorgon Medusa didn't leave her any other choice. Momentarily, the old man's face, gray as stone, swam before her. Just as he had when she was a child, he fell hard near the river, the sound reverberating. She shuddered.

The sky deepened to crimson. Maeve turned. "Come on, Rowan."

At least she had him, she thought, as he slithered inside behind her. It could be worse. She could have been hunted like her great-grandmother, or she could submit to the crushing loneliness that sometimes roared like a blazing fire. That was what her grandmother had done. Maybe her mother was smart, disappearing before either could happen. But then, Maeve thought about the stories, the awful, heart-wrenching stories her mother had told her before she'd left. If her mother had left willingly, why would she endanger the lives of any human whose path she crossed? Maeve might never know why or how her mother left. It was one of many things she couldn't think about, or she'd go mad.

No, it was better to be grateful. It was easier not to ask questions or wonder why things were the way they were. She'd learned long ago what happened when she pushed the boundaries of her life. It was better to stay where she was and be safe. It was too dangerous out there.

She was too dangerous.

Chapter Two

K eeva pulled back her shoulders, glancing to find her woven leather belt had tangled itself at her side. She adjusted it quickly, resuming her stance: feet shoulder-width apart, one hand gripping the large bow in her right hand, her left on her hip. She lifted her chin, the final touch of her victory pose. She'd perfected it over time, as she'd had ample opportunities to do so.

A few feet away, her twin brother, Donovan, snorted. She smirked in reply, silently reminding him of last month's spear throwing tournament, where she had also claimed victory.

They stood on raised wooden planks that formed a path, beginning where she and half a dozen other archery contestants waited. The planks created a track wide enough for a wagon to pass atop. It snaked over the bog, stretching nearly fifty yards ahead where a keen-eyed fae stood analyzing a large, red-ringed target packed tight with twenty arrows. Each was fletched with different colored feathers. Hers, the red ones, sat inside the bull's-eye alone. The analysis of the target was merely a formality.

The large crowd of villagers twenty yards behind them murmured with anticipation. She glanced over her shoulder at the men, women, children, and fae. Most were clad in the kingdom's colors, many wearing dark brown cloaks to shield against the wind. She'd hoped her mother would have made it down from the castle, but Keeva saw no sign of her.

The sound of a horn turned her attention back to the fae—a purple-skinned half nymph—as he held up his hands to silence everyone before saying, "This year's winner of the spring equinox's archery contest is…" He paused, and even Keeva held her breath. "Her Royal Highness, Keeva Glantor, princess of Uterni!"

The spectators cheered. A clamoring of bells and drums started. To her right, her brother groaned and rolled his eyes.

"Maybe next time," she said, not even trying to hide her triumphant grin.

To her left, her best friend, Naela, shook her head. "Couldn't you have gone easy on us? Just this time?" Her large, catlike brown eyes held a playful shine, though Keeva caught a hint of disappointment in her tone.

Donovan stood beside her as the other contestants grumbled and dispersed. "Not in her blood to go easy."

Keeva shrugged. "He's right." At the acquiescent look on Naela's face, Keeva reached out. "Hey, we still have your lessons tomorrow. Same time?"

Naela waved a dismissive hand as she moved past, her cloak billowing behind her, revealing the guard uniform she wore as the captain of the royal regiment. "Same time. I'm gonna go commiserate with the other losers." She turned back, and her eyes brightened as she addressed Donovan. "You coming?"

"I'll be there in a minute," he replied, collecting some of the arrows at his feet, his thick blond ponytail falling down his back.

Naela nodded and disappeared into the crowd that had rearranged itself on the edges of the muddy marshland. Her no-nonsense best friend was already back to making sure the young guards she oversaw were in line and given their orders to patrol the edges of the tournament, mainly in case the villagers grew rowdy after a day of free-flowing mead. Half the remaining spectators stood on the trackways, while others seemed content to dirty their boots, as was the custom in their rain-soaked, bog-filled kingdom.

Keeva handed her bow to a stable hand. "You should go with her," she told Donovan. "Naela likes you, you know."

He raised his brows, his green eyes lit with seemingly genuine surprise. "You think?"

She sighed dramatically. "Everyone in the castle seems to know. Everyone but you."

He was watching where Naela had stood but shook his head. "No way." Squared up with her, he loomed in height and width. They'd been born two minutes apart, and at first glance, it might have been easy to tell they were siblings, but she saw in him her fair skin, bow-shaped lips, and pointed chin that would reveal the subtleties of twindom. He accepted the camel-colored cloak from his page before pinning it at his left shoulder. "Besides, I received another letter from Etaina."

Keeva fastened her own cloak over her dark green tunic, fiddling with her leather bracelets before scoffing. "You're not still interested in that woman, are you?" Each of Etaina's letters were the same since her brother had received the first one three years ago. "She sounds…" Keeva searched for the best way to describe the flighty, ignorant whimsy that the daughter of a Gultaran magistrate wrote with.

"Beautiful?" Donovan replied, his strong jaw set in a smile. "Brilliant? Bold?"

"I was thinking more naive or uninformed."

He shoved her, but she punched his large bicep in retaliation, which he hardly seemed to notice as they made their way toward the royal grounds. "She's not a commoner, Keeva. She's well-bred."

"You make her sound like a piece of livestock," she replied, nodding graciously to the villagers shouting congratulations.

Donovan said something, but she couldn't make it out over the sound of the crowd as more discordant music began. They climbed the muddy hillside above the bog and archery field. "I don't see why you waste your days on a Gulteran court member on the other side of the realm when Naela is right here. She's my best friend, and she's great. Plus, she's mad about you," she added as they reached the top of the hill where the court members gathered, clear of the rowdy villagers below. Keeva almost said, "I'd give up my saol for someone to look at me like that," but stopped herself, not wanting to give her brother the satisfaction.

Light music played across the hilltop. "Perhaps I like speaking to somebody outside our walls," Donovan mused. "Etaina is different. She gives me perspective from the mundane."

Keeva frowned at the strange tone in his reply as they made their way to the group of archery contestants standing in a tight bunch. Her brother smiled broadly, greeting and applauding each of their efforts. He was the epitome of pleasant no matter where he was. Keeva stood beside him, a tight smile on her face as Donovan gave her a look telling her to table the Etaina topic for later.

"Congratulations, Your Highness, on another win." Grun, one of the sons of her father's advisors said before downing a cup of mead.

"Thanks." Keeva accepted a drink from Donovan, who snatched one for himself from a passing staff member carrying a tray of frothy beverages.

"What is this, win number eighteen in a row?" Naela asked, brushing back her black hair that fell in tight ringlets around her oval face.

Keeva grinned. "Come on. I can't help it I'm good at this stuff." She ignored Naela's eye roll before Donovan started a conversation about next week's festival. Keeva let her mind wander while her brother held their group's attention. She closed her eyes briefly, taking another sip of mead. She loved the feeling after a win. It was like she floated above everyone and everything else.

The competitions were her favorite time, her escape. Sure, it didn't hurt that she had a natural talent for things like archery, slingshot, and horseback riding. It also didn't hurt that she usually won. She didn't mind admitting that she liked the attention. The fawning handshakes and admiring gazes were different from the revered looks she got roaming the castle. Donovan garnered the friendly banter of castle staff. These events gave her a chance to stand out. They also gave her something else to think about besides her royal obligations, her monotonous routines, and most of all—

A loud cry came from the crowd as a fire-breather finished her routine behind them. Looking over the top of her cup, Keeva met Donovan's gaze. Maybe it was because they were twins, or maybe it was because they'd spent so many years together in the castle, but it was like she could hear his thoughts and imagined the silent conversation:

"You're worrying about it again, aren't you?"

"How can I not, Donovan?"

"It's not good for you, Keevs. You end up throwing yourself into stuff like this."

"I'm dedicated."

"You're going to wear yourself down."

"I'm fine."

Standing across from her in their huddled group, Donovan's gaze was worried. She turned her cheek to him.

"Keeva?"

"What?" She'd been so lost in thought, she hadn't followed any of the conversation.

Grun frowned. "I was asking if Queen Asta is any better."

Keeva swallowed hard, the mead lodging in her throat. She caught Donovan's gaze, and he faced Grun. "Our mother is fine," he answered for her. "That is kind of you to ask."

Their group fell quiet. A familiar deafening hum, like a perpetual wave crashing upon the shore, consumed Keeva's mind. Grun ran a hand through his wavy locks, seemingly lost for words. Fortunately, through the rising hum, Keeva heard the familiar, hoofed tread of her parents' magistrate. Standing on her toes to peer over the heads of the court members, she spotted him. "Tacari."

Tacari smiled warmly as the court members parted, letting him through. His hollow wooden staff echoed off the trackway alongside him. The pair of four-inch, three-pronged antlers atop his head made him the tallest on castle grounds by far. Over everyone else, she could see his serene face framed by a rusty red beard that was shaved close to his round cheeks and ended in a point beneath his chin, which always reminded Keeva of a satyr. When she'd told him this, he'd politely corrected her that he was only one-quarter satyr. The rest was a mix of wood nymph and human, as was evident by the lean torso beneath the open, tanned hide vest. Loose pants with their kingdom's colors of forest green and camel-brown woven at the cuffs fell to his shins, where the rest of the satyr was obvious in the black hoofs.

"Your Majesties." He bowed to her and Donovan, then nodded to their group. "Your mother and father would like a word."

Keeva's mood sank like the heavy silence following Tacari's request. "I'll see you at dinner," she said to Naela, whose dark eyes seemed to say she understood the change in her demeanor, one of many reasons Keeva treasured their friendship.

She waved to the others before falling into step with Donovan behind Tacari. They walked to the castle in silence, Keeva's mood going sour with each step. They were leaving her happy place and going back to the stacks of herbs and endless potion bottles that didn't work to help her mother's health. Her gracious, strong-willed mother, who had been the victim of a weak body since birth but who had surpassed every apothecary's expectation by living into adulthood. She hadn't been the woman many expected the young King Ragnar to choose, but they were in love. Her status as queen afforded her the resources she'd only dreamed about as a villager. The remedies helped, but three winters ago, she'd taken gravely ill. As the years passed, her time in this realm grew even shorter, and each season seemed to yield a new malady she had to battle. Now, after nearly three decades not just as a queen but a loving parent, she wasn't getting better.

They passed through the castle gates and the main hall, where staff scurried about prepping dinner. After winding through a series of dark hallways, they stood outside her parents' chamber. All of the joy, all of the elation Keeva had felt minutes before vanished. As Tacari knocked, Keeva closed her eyes to steel herself. She hated this. She hated the way this part of the castle, this chamber, even this door made her feel. She hated that no matter how many competitions she won, no matter how many hours she spent losing herself in training, she always ended up back here.

Keeva braced herself and took another deep breath as Tacari pushed opened the chamber door and led them inside.

CHAPTER THREE

K eeva was bombarded with commotion within her parents' chamber. Inside the vast, stone-walled room—half the size of the main hall—stood nearly a dozen court members and staff. Each one seemed to flit from one side of the cavernous space to the other so that they looked like a group of hummingbirds hungrily searching behind tall chairs, stacks of books, and washbasins for their next task.

"Oh good, you're here." Keeva and Donovan's father, King Ragnar, threw them a glance over an unfurled scroll. A gnome sat on the table to his left, organizing a stack of hand-drawn maps and treaties. His two lieutenants stood conversing behind him beneath a pair of torches near a window that looked out at the choppy northern sea.

"How did the competition go, darlings?" From the left side of the room, their mother, Queen Asta, sat up in the large bed, its tall posts boasting intricate carvings of geometric patterns that were found on many of the gold and green tapestries hung on the surrounding walls.

"Keeva won, of course." Donovan was already at their father's side, peering over his massive shoulder to read. He undid and retied his long hair into a ponytail, one of his "thinking habits," their mother called it. His face fell in concentration as his eyes roved the scroll their father held closer to the candlelight for him.

Keeva moved to stand beside the bed as her mother said, "Why am I not surprised to hear that?" The amused tone made Keeva swell with pride as she met her mother's hazel gaze. Her mother was always her greatest supporter, and even now, Keeva clung to her words of affirmation. Her tall frame seemed to be swallowed by cushions and furs that kept her upright. Her fair skin looked pale, but she seemed lively tonight, which was a good sign.

"I've been training an extra hour each day," Keeva said as a maiden pushed behind her to adjust the furs strewn over the bed before replacing the pan of warm coals near her mother's feet.

Her mother's gaze landed on her a moment. Keeva self-consciously ran a hand up to tuck hair that was no longer there behind her ear. She'd cut it short a year ago but only recently decided to crop the right side until it was nearly shaved around her ear, liking the imbalance with the inch-long curls on the rest of her head.

"When did that happen, the magenta?" her mother asked, her eyes narrowed on the locks Keeva swiped her hand through.

"Do you like it? I was deciding between this and deep blue."

"I prefer it to the green from last winter," her father grumbled without looking up.

She laughed as Donovan said, "She found a nymph to help her with the coloring."

"It's lovely, sweetheart. Very…vibrant." Her mother returned to the large text in her lap that resembled the five others strewn across the bed.

Keeva made room for herself among the clutter and plopped near her mother's feet. The lieutenants excused themselves while the maiden who had replaced the coals offered Keeva a goblet of wine. Over the top of it, she watched her mother's face. Wide-set, slightly down-turned eyes sat over high cheekbones. A pointed chin and bow-shaped lips were the only traits she seemed to have passed on to her children. Keeva and Donovan both had the tall, strong stature of their father, along with thick blond hair and green eyes. Keeva had never liked being compared to her brother, who was always just a little taller, just a little stronger than her.

"How are you feeling?" asked Keeva, smoothing the blanket next to where her leg rested.

"I'm fine, sweetheart. Getting a bit of a headache reading all these." Her eyes stayed on the page.

Keeva caught Tacari's gaze where he stood on the other side of the bed, shuffling through more papers on the side table. His raised brows told Keeva her mother was once again putting on a brave face.

"We need to talk about the next lichen shipment." Her father's tone implied their mother's health was not a topic to be breached, and they had other matters to attend.

"My conversation with the farmers gave the impression they'd have the final bushels harvested in two days." Donovan grabbed a handful of berries from the half-empty tray of fruit on the desk. "They're working hard to be ready in time."

"Very good," their mother said. "Keeva, did you speak with the shipmen? What did they say about the arrival time?"

She turned and faced the room, fiddling with the sword-shaped earring that dangled from her right ear. "The ships are ready. They anticipate good weather to the east. They should make landfall in Venostes in two months' time."

Her father nodded, adding a note to another scroll. "Excellent."

"I am grateful to those men and women taking to the seas," her mother said, reaching for a blank scroll. "I couldn't imagine spending that long on the water. The very idea makes me faint."

"Nor could I," Keeva said. Uterni was the northernmost kingdom in the realm. In the days of the first kings, Uterni's founder had settled in the northwestern corner of the land, a large lake and the distance from the other kingdoms an apparently great appeal. Keeva never understood why he'd chosen the marshy grasslands full of bogs and perpetual mist. It seemed utterly unappealing as a place to call home. The people of Uterni had adapted, of course, utilizing the soggy landscape to their advantage and inventing ways to live off the land they were given. The bogs were a great source of material, the lichen that grew atop them able to be converted into dye for clothing. That was Uterni's main export, traded for the wool of Gultero and the many herbs and food from Venostes that Uterni lacked.

While their isolation had its benefits—they'd never been invaded or even threatened with attack—it also meant all imports took an eternity to reach their shores. The treacherous selkie waters lay just off the western coast, and all three kingdoms steered clear, choosing the safer but longer route around the eastern coastline.

Keeva finished her wine, running a finger across the half dozen bracelets that lined her wrist. The warm liquid gave her the courage to query her mother's health again, and she mulled over the best way to ask. She knew that if she lifted the blankets and furs, she would find her mother's legs swollen, their undersides pocked with bedsores. She could see the edges of an iron bedpan tucked under the wooden bed frame. When her mother raised one arm to brush aside the light brown hair cascading down one shoulder in a long braid, Keeva saw the many scars from the apothecary's bloodletting. The long tunic sleeves, the layers of comfort, the rotation of staff were all a ruse to give the illusion that everything was fine.

When her parents mentioned news from the east, Keeva's ears perked up. "What did you say of the elves?" she asked, always interested in the ethereal fae who lived on the other side of the realm.

"They're sending representatives on the new moon," her mother said, a thin hand lifting to cover a sneeze.

Her father scratched his cheek, scruffy with the edges of his beard. "We'll have to begin preparations."

"Keeva and I can take care of that," Donovan said, tossing her a smile.

"I think your true calling is a feast planner, dear brother."

"I think you may be right," he countered. "I do love being in charge."

Rolling her eyes, Keeva asked, "What's their reason for visiting?"

Her father leaned back in his chair, his burly arms reaching up to rest behind his head. He was a well-built man, but the passing years were evident in the bags under his eyes. His tendency to indulge at dinner revealed itself in the stomach protruding under his tunic, the belt stretched tight around his thick waist. "Something to do with Venostes," he said, his small kind eyes twinkling as he took a drink from his goblet.

"Again?" Donovan asked, rolling up a scroll and handing it to a page.

"Now, Son, it's undignified to pass judgment," their father said, a gruffness to his deep voice as he scratched the top of his head.

Their mother added, "The Diarmaids have their own way of doing things, just like we do."

Keeva shot her brother a look. She could imagine him saying, "We do it better," and she would have to agree. Though she'd never met the royal families from either Venostes or Gultero, her parents had educated them on their neighbor's laws and customs. She remembered being confused by the southern kingdom's shocking intolerance. She'd been raised in a castle full of people from other lands. Fae lived among the human villagers. Tacari was one of many fae who worked alongside them. She and Donovan had been teenagers when her parents had explained that Uterni was a sanctuary for many fleeing the south.

She was proud to be part of a royal family who helped those forced to leave their homes for fear of persecution…or worse. She had been taught history, but it was still difficult for her to fathom the seemingly cruel monarchies on the other side of the Mountains of Ionad. How could a king and queen who'd sent her mother remedies turn around and punish women who bore children without a husband?

Pondering this, Keeva jumped as a freckle-faced maiden appeared at her mother's bedside. Atop the wooden dish was a small vial of clear liquid. "Your medicine, Your Majesty."

Her mother, eyes on a map of the western caves, took the vial and downed the contents. She made a face, coughing. "Gods, that's awful." A thin sheen of perspiration lined her forehead. Briefly, Keeva caught the flash of pain in her eyes. A moment of what seemed like exhaustion passed over her smooth face and settled on her shoulders, small beneath her tunic.

Looking around, Keeva tried not to feel spiteful at the never-ending work that went on in this chamber. Her parents had always been busy, diligent leaders, determined to maintain an efficient, smoothly run kingdom. However, as the years passed, Keeva had begun to see the constant flow of work for what it really was: a distraction to keep her mother's energy up. It was also a distraction for them. If she, her father, and Donovan kept themselves occupied every hour of every day, there would be no time to worry about her mother's health.

Most of the time, Keeva could abide by the unspoken rule of ignoring her mother's ailing state. She could attend a court meeting, see to the stable hands, and make sure the village grievances were heard. More and more lately, though, Keeva's patience wore thin. She tried not to dwell on the fact that her mother was dying. It was why she threw herself into her training, spending hours in archery or staff practice with Naela. It was why she was always challenging Donovan to a spell-fire duel. Anything to fight the inevitable fact that sooner rather than later, her mother would be gone.

CHAPTER FOUR

The gentle trill of a thrush woke Maeve the next morning. She stretched, reaching over her head and pressing into the smooth stone wall. The small bed creaked in protest as she sat up, searching the earthen floor for Rowan. She scanned the spaces between her and the far wall lined with cauldrons and ladles.

"He's probably out sunning himself." She shook off the rough blanket to stand. A square-cut window, slightly larger than a melon, sat above where her bed stood flush against the western wall.

Standing, she peered out to the tangled branches of elder trees, their pale yellow flowers in bloom among the lush leaves. All around the fen stood a mix of elder, rowan, and oak trees, along with shrubs, ferns, and knee-high grass. She knew every inch. A jay flew to its nest, and she smiled, watching the tiny pair of baby birds lift their chirping heads in search of food.

"Another day." Maeve made her bed like she did every morning. After washing her face in the water basin near the hearth, she started her routine.

The more time passed, the more Maeve took comfort in the familiarity of her days. Each morning was the same: she started a fire; enjoyed a plate of berries, soft cheese, and several slices of bread; then she grabbed a bucket and went to fetch water from the river. Outside of her shady, flora-filled space, Maeve inhaled the scent of muddy earth lining the marshy lowland that lay between her dwelling and the outskirts of the kingdom of Uterni. The river was a sort of border between the two, and it was as far as she ever went. She knelt and dipped the bucket into the steady rush of clear water. Beyond, the land grew marshy until it transformed into stretches of moss-filled bogs that surrounded the castle and its village to the north. Maeve had never seen the bogs, or the castle, up close, but her mother had described it all to her when she was young, and Maeve could imagine it well.

Placing the bucket beside her, Maeve closed her eyes. If she listened closely, she could hear the faint buzz of the village coming to life, waking up to another day. She thought she heard the deep distant call of a horn when a smooth cool surface slithered over the back of her calf where she knelt.

"Good morning, Rowan."

He slithered to the edge of the bank and took a drink. A rustling in the low brush on the opposite riverbank made both of them pause.

"Time to go," she said, standing and sloshing water over her boots in the process. Quickly, she returned home. Rowan slithered speedily ahead, leading her back. The noise had probably been nothing, a hare or a river nymph. But it could have been children from the village who had strayed too far into the untamed marshes. She couldn't risk it.

Pushing aside a low branch, Maeve exhaled at the sight of her home. She smiled at the flattened grass forming a well-trodden path to her front door. A thin layer of smoke hovered above her thatched roof, a gray cloud having escaped through the layers of reeds and tree limbs that created a ventilation system, yet they still managed to keep her dry enough during heavy rains. A collection of firewood sat neatly near the cutting stump where an ax lay atop it. Through a circular window to the left of her front door, she could see the flicks of yellow flames from the hearth.

Rowan found a large flat rock and stretched out. The bucket swaying at her side, Maeve's eyes danced over the structure she'd always called home. Her safe space. She scrutinized the basket of acorns she needed to crack and wash. Next to that stood a thin pair of birch trunks. Between them, resting in their lowest branches, she'd laid a longer branch for four hares she'd trapped along with a trout from the river. She'd had ample time to perfect the snares on the edges of her land.

A blue butterfly fluttered past as she made her way inside. "What'll it be today, Rowan?" she called to him through her open door. "Another batch of acorn bread or a barley loaf?"

She blew a strand of hair from her face and poured the water into a large clay bowl. Most of the items she owned had been her mother's, some even her grandmother's. Occasionally, she'd find an abandoned flask or broken fishing net in the river. Once, she'd even found a bow and shield. The bow had been broken and the shield cracked, but she'd loved imagining who they might have belonged to, a soldier in the Uterni army, perhaps. Maeve had snatched it from the river, eager to have a keepsake from a world that was only a mile north but seemed farther away than anything.

Pushing up her sleeves to sort through the items from the Caretaker, she threw a glance to the back corner of her home. Among the broom and rags were her found treasures: the end of a spearhead, a dozen or so wagon wheels, a mismatched pair of knee-high leather boots, and her personal favorite, a woven belt patterned in green and brown.

Sometimes at night, when she'd treated herself to a glass of brandywine from her meager supply her mother had kept in a barrel outside, she took the belt down from the hook where it hung on her wall. Before the mirror, she wrapped it around her waist and imagined she was a member of Uterni's village. She let herself dream that she was like the people and fae who called the kingdom home. She pretended she had real friends who could talk back to her. She imagined somebody looked at her in a way she knew was impossible.

Sometimes, when the moon was high, she ached to belong somewhere, anywhere. Maeve ran her fingers over the frayed threads and wondered what it was like to be accepted, to be welcome rather than feared.

Every time she gave in to her fantasies, reality always reared its head. She knew she could never be a part of any community. If she tried, she'd be putting everyone at risk.

Ensuring the dark magic inside her would never hurt a soul, she only went as far as the river. It kept her from unleashing a second wave of terror on the realm like that of her ancestor.

She sighed and began to roll out a new sheet of dough. She couldn't take back the awful time that her great-grandmother had wreaked havoc on the land. As her descendant, it was Maeve's responsibility to make sure it never happened again. She had been taught the safest thing was to live a life of quiet. A life of solitude.

❖

That night, the nearly full moon sent beams of pale light through the window above Maeve's bed. She sat with her back against the wall so the moonlight could assist her reading. She took a bite of acorn bread and turned the page of a book. It was an old text, frayed paper and faded ink. It contained the history of Uterni, and the pages were filled with information on the first king and how he had come to settle the northern kingdom.

A soft crackle from the fire made her glance up. Rowan was curled at the base of a table leg, his eyes closed. Returning to her book, Maeve read for the hundredth time about the kingdom's resources, its laws, its people. As she read, she recalled a memory from long ago, when her mother was still there.

"I don't know why you love that book so much," her mother had said one morning as eight-year-old Maeve had sat with the book inches from her face, attempting to absorb all of the information.

"I want to know what it's like."

Her mother's gray eyes had met hers. Her hands had worked deftly to crack acorns, methodically separating the shell from the savory nut they would later clean and crush for dough. The look in her mother's eyes had been one of wonder and deep sadness. At such a young age, Maeve had struggled with their life confined to the fen at the bottom of this hillside. She didn't understand why her mother had always made sure the door was locked at sundown or that Maeve didn't wander off. Growing up, she had yearned to visit the village that was so close, she could hear the festival drums each solstice. Her pleas had been met with warnings of the dangers that came with leaving and the horrible consequences of meeting somebody who wasn't like them, somebody they might hurt.

Presently, Maeve sighed, adjusting the candle settled on a metal tray to her right. Eventually, she had decided that if she could never see the village and its inhabitants for herself, she could at least learn everything about it.

A snap, like someone stepping on a fallen branch, made her look up. Keeping her place in the book with one finger, she carefully shifted to her knees. From the foot of the bed, she grabbed a triangular shard of glass resting atop the blanket. Holding the larger end that was safely wrapped in cloth, she arranged herself so that when she looked into the broken piece of mirror, she could see outside. Aside from the moon and fairy nest glowing faintly, there was no light. She waited a few moments, scanning the dark patterns of the flora that acted as a border to the rest of the world.

Returning to her book, she plopped cross-legged on the blanket, keeping the glass close. She was rereading the section on the royal family when the same snapping sound broke the quiet night. This time, it was followed by the unmistakable sound of footsteps.

Maeve closed her book and blew out the candle. She pulled the curtain over her window and checked the door. Finding it locked, she stepped quietly to the other window that looked out over most of her fen. Rowan had uncurled himself and slithered toward her. Listening with her back pressed beside the window, she waited. Soon, she was able to make out three sets of footsteps.

"Over here," a man's voice called, disturbing the peaceful night air.

"I knew it was true. My uncle said she lived on the other side of the river." This was said by a woman, a young woman, Maeve imagined.

"He was right," the first man said. "Let's get closer."

Maeve could hear the trepidation in the third person's voice, another man. "What if…what if she's there?"

"Boran, that's the point," the first man said, prompting a cackle of laughter from the woman.

At her feet, Rowan gave a low hiss. She raised a finger to her lips, silencing him. She crept back to her bed, snatched the mirror shard, then returned to watch the reflection, careful to keep herself hidden in the dark window.

Three figures revealed themselves through the final line of brush before the open air of her fen. The first two were holding hands, stumbling over one another as they walked, giggling. The third, a young man of maybe twenty, with dark skin and short black hair, followed. He was the only one to have conjured a companion flame, the soft yellow bouncing beside him. To his credit, Maeve saw the reluctance in his slow stride, the way his head swiveled, taking in her sacred space.

The first man, who seemed a little older, with creases in his fair skin, shouted, "We've come to see the witch!"

More laughter before their footsteps slowed. Maeve ducked from the window, listening as one of them began to rummage through the cauldrons she'd left outside to dry.

"Come out, witch," he yelled again.

"Yeah," the woman called. "I want you to turn him into a toad."

Maeve rolled her eyes. She glanced at Rowan, who had picked up his head and seemed to be glaring at her through one eye.

"I know," she whispered before reaching up to grab a length of rope. It hung overhead at the foot of her bed, running between the roof and topmost boulder of the wall, then outside to stretch across the low-lying limb of a nearby oak tree. From the branch hung an assortment of metal bells. Maeve gave the rope three tugs, and a series of sharp, jarring clangs rang out.

"What's that?" one of them asked.

The others seemed to wait. Maeve could imagine their wide eyes, searching the dark, trying to find the source. Once again, she leaned and looked at the mirror's reflection out into the night. They'd drawn closer. Their Uterni colors were visible, though their worn, patched tunics indicated a lower status.

"Go home," she whispered, hoping to convince them to leave her alone. Her eyes trained on the glass, she grimaced as they stepped nearer. She reached for the second rope. Watching the mirror, she waited until the older man was aligned with her chopping stump. When he was, she used two hands to yank the rope hard.

A surprised squawk told her she'd been successful.

"Dain," the woman shrieked as her partner's foot was snared and him upended. Maeve adjusted the glass, smiling at his flailing, hollering figure while the others struggled to help.

"Get me down," he barked, spinning helplessly by his ankle. The youngest pulled a dagger from his boot. The woman grabbed it and reached up. After several frantic moments, Dain was loose, falling hard to the ground.

"I told you this was a bad idea," the soft-spoken man said, taking back the blade.

"The stupid witch," Dain shouted.

Maeve's eyes widened as he found a large rock and hurled it toward her window. It smacked just to the right against the outside wall.

"Don't. You'll make her mad," the woman hissed.

Finally, they retreated. For added measure, Maeve gave the bells another ardent ring. The frightened cries grew distant until they were gone.

Exhaling, Maeve slid to the floor. Rowan hissed, his tongue flickering twice. "You're telling me." She wiped sweat from her hairline. She felt perspiration gather under her arms, even behind her knees. "Now I need another wash," she said.

It wasn't often people came upon her home. She, her mother, and her grandmother had all gone to great lengths to ensure they were isolated, tucked in a dense, tree-covered place away from everyone and everything. Most residents of Uterni didn't travel beyond the river. Only a few times in her life had someone found her. Usually, people saw a home so far from the rest and interpreted that whoever was living inside wanted to be left alone. Sometimes, though, they were people like the ones tonight: young, obnoxious, looking for some sort of thrill. She'd been taught humans liked to do such things. For them, she had the bells and snares. Her mother had set most of them; Maeve only made repairs or adjusted things now and then.

The closest anyone had ever gotten was three steps from the front door. When she was six, she'd been playing outside when her mother had come running back from the river. Her blond hair had been wild, strands flying out from under the brown handkerchief she always wore.

"Get inside!"

Maeve had hurried to stand, her mother scooping her up until they were on the other side of the locked door.

"What is it?" Maeve had asked.

Her mother had shushed her. A bellowing voice like that of a lion called, "You've got to help me." Maeve had heard the quiver in his voice. "I know what you are. I know what you can do."

Maeve's mother had pulled her close.

"Please help me. I've lost my wife and child and I—" There was a clamoring like he had stumbled over their pots. "I can't go on."

Maeve had shivered. "Mother—"

"Quiet, darling."

"Look at me." The man's voice had taken on a frantic pitch. "Please. Why don't you help me? Look at me!"

Maeve hadn't understood then. She'd heard the man's broken cries but hadn't grasped their meaning. She hadn't understood why her mother had kept them below the window, out of sight.

The man had succumbed to loud, heavy sobs. Together, they'd listened to his cries for what seemed like hours. Eventually, they'd heard him go.

"Mother, what did he want?" Maeve had asked.

Her mother had faced her. Maeve was struck by the shine in her eyes. "He was very sad. Sometimes, people who are very sad try to find ways to make their sadness go away."

"But how?"

Her mother's gaze had held hers. "You know what we can do. You know why we keep to ourselves." Maeve had nodded, trying to understand, but she couldn't quite connect the man's desperation with their power. Then, she was startled when her mother had reached up, framing her face. "Maeve, you must never look. Do you understand me? No matter how sad someone claims to be, no matter what they say, you must never give in to their wants. It's too dangerous." Her mother's hands had gripped her tight. "You must never look."

Presently, Maeve placed the shard of glass on the floor. Closing her eyes, she tried to clear her mind. Her mother's warnings were always with her; they were the ringing of the bells among the trees; they were in the books she clung to for a taste of the outside world; and her mother's words followed her, tethering themselves to her feet, always ensuring Maeve never strayed far.

Those villagers couldn't know. Hardly anyone knew about the gorgon in the fen, deep in the lowlands of Uterni. It was safer. Maeve's power, like that of her mother's, was too awesome, too horrifying. A single look was all it took to end a life. The old man from the river haunted her every day, and the idea of that awful deed happening again frightened her every second. It had been her great-grandmother's curse. Her grandmother, as a result, had become so consumed with helplessness that she had taken her own life. Maeve's mother had taught her life was possible but only if it was a careful one. A life of quiet. Of isolation.

She guessed the villagers tonight had heard about a strange fae in the kingdom. Stories were inevitable. While the stray nymph or dryad sometimes wandered through, they seemed to realize that the occupant behind the locked door didn't want to be disturbed.

"Humans are obstinately curious," her mother had told her. "They can't help themselves. We must be ready when their zealous appetite for discovery brings them here."

So they'd laid snares. Set up a system of warning to deter unwelcome visitors. Maeve felt well-equipped to handle herself. She'd done all right so far.

Rowan slithered across her ankles.

"Humans," she said, tossing him half a smile, though unease lingered around the edges of the room. Slowly, Maeve rose, forcing thoughts of the intruders from her mind. Then she relit her candle and returned to her book.

CHAPTER FIVE

Together, Keeva and Donovan walked the dim passageway to the southern end of the castle. Between the low ceilings and small, infrequent windows to keep the blistering winds out, their long stretch of stone-laden home always seemed dark. They turned a corner, Keeva's gaze raking over the familiar woven tapestries lit by flickering torches along the walls.

"She's getting worse," she muttered only loud enough for Donovan to hear, tossing a glance over her shoulder at the duo of servants following ten paces behind.

"I thought she seemed all right," he replied, receiving a scathing glare. He held up his large hands defensively. "Better than yesterday, I mean."

Keeva took a deep breath as a guard stood at attention on their way to the southern tower. Another visit to their parents' chamber gave them a new list of tasks to complete. Her mind worked to prioritize each one, preparing herself for the toil the coming days would bring. Her body, however, seemed to be in contradiction with her mind's ability to compartmentalize. It droned with distress. She knew keeping herself and Donovan busy was a means to distract them, a way to keep them away from their dying mother.

"I need to practice," Keeva said, taking a left away from their chambers and making Donovan stumble to chase her.

"We just had a tournament. Give yourself a break." She caught her brother's gaze but continued. As the door leading to the armory appeared at the end of the hall, he added, "Your *body* needs a break."

She ignored him, annoyed at his awareness of her strict training regimen that, as of late, had become intense. A day after the archery tournament found her biceps still tight as the new soreness settled into her arms. It ran through her triceps and shoulders, the lingering effects of weeks of practice leading up to the event. Add to that her lessons teaching Naela, and her arms were feeling strong but tired.

Keeva shoved through the armory door, Donovan behind her. The discordant sound of wood clashing against iron struck her ears from across a large room lined with wall-to-wall stands hosting fighting staffs, long and short swords, and dozens of bows resting beside quivers packed tight with arrows. As she and Donovan—who was now boring his disapproving gaze into the side of her head—passed a woven basket of retired shields waiting for repair, they found the source of the noise.

Naela was in mid-combat against one of the other children of the court, a young woman Keeva knew as the daughter of one of the leaders in the Uterni guard. Moving to stand just outside of the designated training area where straw had been laid beneath a reed rug, Keeva leaned near the staffs, watching.

"Someone's been practicing," Donovan said next to her, folding his large arms over his muscular chest. An impressed glint shone in his eyes as they trained on Naela.

Keeva had to agree, though her best friend's combat skills had always been impressive. As the daughter of a lieutenant and general of the Uterni guard, Naela had been raised amid talk of weapons and strategy despite no one having attacked Uterni before. Naela's mother, General Adna, had taught her daughter how to fight as soon as she was old enough to hold a staff.

The row of torches danced, seemingly as enthralled as Keeva and Donovan at the show of prolific skills. The orange light gave Naela's dark brown skin a soft glow and lit her dark eyes. Keeva grinned at the joy she saw in them as Naela spun, twirling the staff overhead before swinging it down, using one end to take out her opponent's feet. Upended, the girl hit the mat hard. In one motion, Naela leapt atop her, the shining cap at the end of her staff hovering above her opponent's throat.

Donovan clapped. Seemingly surprised, Naela looked up, her shoulders rising and falling quickly. "Well done," he said as Naela stepped aside. A blush had risen in her face, and she dipped her chin as she helped her fellow guard to their feet. Keeva tried not to laugh at her inability to hide her feelings. Donovan was an oblivious twit for not seeing what was right in front of him.

As the young guard bowed and left, Naela adjusted the grip of her staff, her breathing steady once again. She tore her gaze from Donovan, who was already across the room, fiddling with a pair of sais.

"Late-night practice session?" Naela asked.

Keeva grabbed one of the staffs reserved for her, a five-foot-long pole of solid, polished oak with a black onyx head. It had been a gift for her twenty-sixth birthday and one year later, already featured shallow grooves where she'd gripped it during rounds of training.

"Keeva's request, not mine," said Donovan, twirling the small sais mindlessly.

Naela's eyebrows rose. "That's four nights in a row, Keevs."

Not liking the wary tone they had taken, Keeva took the staff to the far corner where three bales of hay were stacked. "It's just a cooldown. I'm still sore from the tournament." She rolled her shoulders, then took her attack stance, the staff looming at her target.

Donovan said something, but Keeva didn't hear him. She let her mind drift until she found the clear, empty headspace that was getting harder to find. It was the state she normally accessed easily, especially when she was training or in a competition. It was when she could let go of all the nagging burdens of royal life that only grew in scale the older she got. She understood she and Donovan would eventually rule, but she'd always imagined it would be much later in life. It would be after her parents were gray and old. It would be after Donovan grew out of his daydreams and asked for Naela's hand. And—Keeva thought as she began a series of strikes against the hay—it would be after she'd found someone to rule alongside her, someone to love.

When she'd satisfied her need to hit something, she stepped back, taking a shaky breath. It was quiet for a moment. A *whoosh* broke the still air. Spinning, she met the sais mid-flight, catching the blade with the solid surface of her staff.

"Just making sure you're still here." Donovan smiled, but she wasn't having it.

She huffed. "I'm here." She dislodged the sais. Naela glanced between them. Feeling agitated, Keeva tossed the blade back with more force than intended.

"Whoa." Donovan stumbled, catching it before it could nick his arm. When Keeva didn't apologize, Naela shifted awkwardly until Donovan said, "Message received. I know when I'm not welcome anymore."

Keeva turned away, staring at the middle distance. She gripped the staff tight, feeling guilty she'd let her emotions get the better of her. Then again, she knew these were the two people used to her inability to deal with certain things the way other people might. Things like feelings.

"Don't stay up too late," her brother said before leaving.

Naela swapped the staff she'd been using for another, this one a darker wood with intricate leaf carvings down its length.

When the silence dragged on, Keeva finally said, "She's getting worse."

"Is she still taking her medicine?" Naela stepped closer, and Keeva cracked a smile as they both took opposing stances, staffs ready in the middle of the makeshift arena.

"Some herbal concoction from Venostes," Keeva said, biting her lip at the familiar tensing of her muscles as she quickly analyzed Naela's position: her boots pointed at an angle and the bend to her knees that creased her brown leather pants. The pleated belt at Naela's hip swayed as she raised her elbow, pinching the material of her tunic sleeve.

Lunging forward, they spoke between well-trained strikes.

"The herbs aren't helping?" Naela asked.

"No more than anything else."

"My aunt found an old text."

"How exciting."

Naela laughed at Keeva's sarcasm before knocking her back a step as she spun to avoid a strike to her left leg.

"Fine," Keeva replied. "A book?" The retaliatory blow narrowly missed as Naela jumped nimbly out of the way.

"It speaks of the Otherworld."

"My mother isn't in the Otherworld." Their staffs clashed. "Yet."

"I know, Keevs." Naela pivoted. Both of their breathing came fast. "The book mentions a way into the Otherworld. A way you could get in to"—she swung hard—"speak to someone."

Keeva eyed her and stepped back, poised in an attack stance. "To what? Bargain?"

Naela's look told Keeva she knew it was desperate, but they'd tried everything. Keeva knew it was only a matter of time before her mother was gone. "The gods are known for making deals."

Keeva lunged, the blunt end of her staff grazing Naela's side before she knocked it away. "I'm a Glantor, Naela. The court would have my neck if they knew I'd gone to make a deal with a god."

There was a noise like a snort before another crack of their staffs. "You wouldn't be the first royal to do so."

"Just the first to get caught."

More strikes, the wooden clang reverberating around them as they moved with practiced ease. Naela said, "Just look at it, okay?" They both spun, coming to meet face-to-face, their knuckles grazing as the head of their staffs pressed into one another. "You may find something new."

Keeva met her gaze. She admired the tenacity in her eyes, the hope that always swirled in the dark brown irises. Of course, Keeva knew Naela was trying to give her something else to do, something other than pushing her body to its limits. She recalled the time three months ago during a bad spell of her mother's, when she had thrown out her shoulder in a night of nonstop training. Still, Keeva didn't want to believe that Naela, just like her family, didn't agree with her choices.

"Please, Keeva." Naela pushed against her. Perspiration dripped down Keeva's spine. Naela's forehead shined as they both began to shake, neither willing to give.

Releasing her arms, Keeva relented. "All right."

Naela smiled, tossing the staff to her other hand. "I'll have my maiden bring it to your chamber tonight."

"Not tonight," Keeva said. At Naela's curious look she added, "Tomorrow morning. I'm too tired to read anything tonight."

"Fine." Naela gave her hip a bump, then wrapped an arm around her. "I expect a full report in three days' time."

"If you say so." The taut ache in Keeva's muscles sent a sensation of pleasure through her, and she leaned gratefully into Naela. She let the feeling chase away the dull thud of frustration that everyone in her life seemed to be judging her decision to train as hard as she was. "Come on. I heard they're serving raspberry cream for dessert."

They replaced their weapons and left, the guards closing the armory behind them. Keeva tried to release the tension in her body, willing herself to leave her worries in the glinting shine of the armory swords.

CHAPTER SIX

The next morning, Maeve stepped outside into fog. The clouds had drifted down into her fen after a rainy night, shrouding her home in a gray mist. She felt mixed emotions when the realm seemed to ally itself with her way of life. On one hand, the skies adding another layer of protection from the rest of society was a welcome act of comradery. Meanwhile, another barrier between her and anyone else felt like a crushing reminder that she was alone.

Rowan didn't seem to care for the damp chilly air. After cleaning the overturned items left from the intruders the night before, Maeve came inside to find him curled below the hearth, his head tucked close for warmth.

Making space between a plate of apricots and berries, Maeve pulled up a chair to the table. She found her quill beneath a cauldron filled with remnants of a stew and rummaged through a stack of books for a clean scrap of parchment. Dabbing the quill into her slim supply of ink, she wrote a reply to the Caretaker:

Thank you for the raspberries. I'll find it hard to ration them until next moon.

She paused, contemplating whether to mention the incident from last night.

Can you send more rope? Not much, only three lengths. I fear tree-dwellers are getting to my snares before I can get to them.

Not a complete lie. Her ropes *were* worn, but she could get by for another season. Maeve had woken up with the nagging feeling that those villagers from the night before might come back. At least, the one called Dain seemed upset enough to do something human. Another snare or two wouldn't hurt.

The next lines she wrote without thinking, the same words that she'd ended the last seven years' worth of letters:

Your continued efforts in the search for my mother are appreciated. It pleases me to know you care enough to keep looking.

She closed the letter, rolling up the paper. Grabbing an apple slice, she wandered outside. The sun was trying vainly to lighten the grim day. She inhaled the moist air and admired the tranquility of an intruder-free fen.

Peering into the mass of branches of the surrounding trees, she spotted the flash of black hidden among the lush leaves dripping with moisture. "There you are." She finished her apple, then pressed her thumb and forefinger to the corners of her mouth and gave a high, short whistle.

The raven cawed. A flutter of wings sent a drizzle of water to the ground. The Caretaker's messenger swooped down. Maeve raised her left hand, the end of the rolled parchment skyward. Claws first, the raven snatched the scroll, and she watched it fly to the edge of the tree line, then circle back. Another caw and it flew higher, disappearing over the horizon.

❖

Sipping from her goblet, Keeva turned another page in the book Naela's maiden had brought to her after dinner the next night. On her stomach atop the bearskin on the large bed, she skimmed the drawings and ancient text for whatever new thing Naela was certain she'd find.

"Nothing so far," she mumbled after another sip. She had read nearly three-quarters of the large, leather-bound book and found nothing relevant to helping her mother. There were seemingly endless stories of the gods creating the realm, how Dagda—king of the Otherworld—had built a passageway through the bogs of Uterni to his eternal kingdom.

All this, Keeva already knew. She'd attended plenty of Remembrance ceremonies for prominent court members. Each one ended in the traditional journey; after a funeral pyre, the remains of the deceased were laid in the bog so their soul could move on to the peaceful fields of the Otherworld.

The text featured tales of trickster gods, benevolent spirits, dryads, muses, none of which seemed like a good source of help for an ailing queen.

Keeva knew her mother was dying. She knew she would be gone one day. But she also knew that it was too soon. Her mother couldn't go yet. Keeva wouldn't let her.

"Potions for altering one's mind. Curses of the dying. The Well of Slaine. Ugh." Keeva downed the last of her wine, tossing the jewel-encrusted goblet onto the pile of cushions nearby. "I can't use any of this." Rolling onto her back, she stared at the ceiling, running a hand through her hair. "Father would kill me if I did anything that might look questionable in the eyes of the court." Fae and their magic were helpful, but some of the magical beings were still wary of humans. Deals struck between the two were often filled with tension and unkept promises. Uterni was a kingdom built on tolerance and acceptance. If she made and then was forced to break any deal with a fae, it would be ruinous for her family's reputation as well as dangerous.

She rolled back over, thumbing through to the first pages. "There's gotta be something."

A large scripted letter caught Keeva's eye. She flipped back, flattening the book's spine to better see. On the left page was a name.

"Epona." Keeva didn't remember her from her childhood lessons. "Well," she said, smiling as she quickly read, "looks like I found something after all."

"Are you crazy?" Donovan stared at her from across the long oak table in the main hall. The next morning had brought sunshine to the gray highlands, and beams of light shot through the circular windows behind her brother, framing him and a few other court members in a pale glow. The air was crisp, and a fire crackled on the other end of the vast room.

Keeva replied between bites of pork sausage. "Maybe, but you know that already." The late morning bustle of the castle helped muffle their voices to the other late risers just now getting to breakfast. Still, Keeva kept her voice low, throwing a glance at her father at the other end of the table. "Well," she asked, "what do you think?"

Donovan sipped his juice, eyeing her. "I think your brains have given way to brawn."

Her magenta saol leapt to life in her right hand. She chucked it over the sprawling selection of meats, cheeses, and fruits. Donovan blocked it, sending the spell-fire to a nearby torch. Those sitting nearby grunted in amusement. Their father didn't glance up.

"Fine," she said, "I don't need your help."

He leaned forward, his large forearms coming to rest behind his empty plate. "Keevs, there's a reason not much is written on Epona. Only a handful of people have ever seen her. Those who do, well…" He made a slicing motion across his throat.

Keeva ran her forefinger along the edge of a knife. "Only because they weren't smart."

"And why would they be?" he fired back. "Only desperate people seek Epona."

She glared.

"Why do it, Keevs? What's the point?"

"Donovan, she's the gatekeeper. I know there's not a lot of information." She held up a hand before he could interject. "But she's the one who keeps the door between our realm and the Otherworld secure. She's the one you see before passing over." Keeva's voice rose, and she inched closer, elbows bumping into platters. "If I can talk to her, tell her who our mother is, how important she is to Uterni, maybe she'll give her more time." She averted her gaze a moment, hoping he didn't catch the real reason she wasn't ready to let her mother go.

He stared. When he leaned back, his arms crossed and his chin low, she let his silence fuel her determination. Then, seeming to read her thoughts, they turned in unison to the far end of the table. Their father conversed with Naela's parents, both looking fresh and ready in their guard uniforms. Keeva's gaze fell to the empty chair beside him.

Donovan sighed. "Keevs—"

But she was already standing, the abrupt scrape of her chair drawing inquisitive eyes. "Like I said, I don't need your help."

With a final glare over her shoulder, she stormed out, itching for something to hit.

❖

"I thought I'd find you here."

Spinning around, Keeva found Naela framed by two of her guards at the entrance to the armory. She nodded to them, and both men retreated to the hallway, leaving them alone. Yanking out the trio of arrows from the target roped to the bale of hay, Keeva averted her gaze and took another ready stance where she'd already shot ten rounds. The soreness in her arms was beginning to wear on her, but she nocked her next arrow anyway.

They stood in silence, Naela moving to better see as Keeva lined up her shot. The arrow hit the edge of the outermost ring. "I don't like it when people stare," she grumbled, nocking her next one.

Naela snorted. "That's a load of troll dung. You love when people watch you compete."

"That's different." The second arrow landed closer to the center but still one ring off.

"If you say so."

The final arrow landed in between the first two, quivering on impact. Keeva rolled her eyes, but it was half-hearted. "I guess you came for the book report?"

Naela smiled and helped extract the arrows. Handing her one she said, "You guessed right. From the looks of you, you've been in here since breakfast." Naela crinkled her nose, sniffing. "Yep, since breakfast."

"Hush," Keeva said, but she had succeeded in making her crack a smile. "I did find something in the text you lent me." She returned the arrows to their quiver, and together, they walked to the shelves. Keeva replaced her practice weapons.

"That's great." Naela squared to her, searching her face. "Isn't it?"

"Yeah." Keeva frowned. "I just...don't know where to start."

"Well, tell me what you found, and we'll work through it together."

An hour later, Keeva and Naela were back in Keeva's chamber. Naela sat on a spare throne chair. Her legs—tucked into dark leather pants under a forest-green tunic with the captain's token pinned under her left shoulder—dangled over one side as she leaned back comfortably. Keeva paced across the wide room, tossing her saol between her hands.

"If Epona's the gatekeeper, wouldn't she be near the bogs?"

"I don't know," Keeva replied. "It makes sense, but no one has ever seen her there."

Naela's brow furrowed, a worried look gathering in her eyes. "You don't think you'd need to go...*in* the bogs, do you?"

"Gods, I hope not. I don't think I could." Keeva had seen one too many people try to gather minerals from the depths of the bogs. They never resurfaced.

"But that's the passage to the Otherworld in our kingdom. At least the only one I know of." Naela hummed to herself, her lips pursed as she stared up at the ceiling. "Did you talk to Donovan about this? He always has good insight."

Keeva threw back her head dramatically. "Yes." Her entire life, people sought a second opinion from Donovan. Despite their equal knowledge of the kingdom, its politics, economy, and history, it was him they turned to. She never seemed to be enough. "My brother is an idiot. He won't help."

"He won't or, he's concerned for your safety?"

"Same thing."

Naela shook her head. "Siblings. I'll never understand."

"Lucky you."

Leaning down, Naela gathered the large book and tugged it into her lap. "There's got to be more. Something we're missing about how to find Epona."

Keeva paced to the open window. Standing beside it, she closed her eyes and let the night wind hit her face. She tried not to compare the raging sea to the unrest in her own mind. Her mother had missed three of the four meetings her family had yesterday. She could hardly get out of bed, she'd been so weak. Keeva hated to see her mother unable to even unfurl a scroll. Even more, she hated to imagine the day when she couldn't share her latest triumphs with her mother.

Naela's voice pulled her from her thoughts as she read from the text. "'Epona travels by horseback. On rare occasions,' it says, 'she gives out fruit, grain, and bread to people as she wanders, waiting to welcome the next soul into the Otherworld.'"

"That's oddly generous, considering she's waiting to escort the dead," muttered Keeva.

Naela chuckled, then frowned. She looked up. "I wonder what kind of fruit?"

Keeva met her gaze. "Why would that matter?"

"Well, if we know what kind of fruit she hands out, we could locate the shrub or tree it grows from."

Keeva grinned. "Where her fruit grows, she goes."

"Exactly." Naela matched her smile.

"Can I trade Donovan for you?" Keeva asked.

"We did that years ago, Keevs." She winked, and they both laughed. After a moment, Naela's gaze returned to the book.

Keeva could see she wanted to say something. "What is it?"

"Well, I do think your brother could help us with this."

"Naela—"

"He's always in the market meeting with vendors. He must know more than we do about the orchards and groves in the kingdom." She grimaced. "I'm afraid my people skills aren't as good. I've met with maybe three vendors in three years. If the young guards could keep themselves in line, I'd be able to spend less time wrangling them out of skirmishes with locals. The downside of peace. Nowhere for those youngsters to direct their egos."

Keeva flopped onto the floor, her back resting against the foot of her bed so she faced Naela. "Always the people pleaser, my brother." She rubbed her forehead, feeling the ends of her hair between her fingers. "Fine," she finally said. "We can see if he'll help. But only mention the fruit. Keep Epona out of it."

Naela nodded and fell quiet as she once again scanned the text. "I'm going to ask my aunt some more about this," she said, closing the heavy book and tapping the cover. "She knows a lot about local legends. Hangs out in leprechaun lodgings more than she's in the castle."

"Okay." Keeva felt agitated and brought her knees up to her chest. She ran her hands over her pants, pressing into her quad muscles to relieve some of the tension in them.

"We can't do anything yet," Naela said. "But soon. I'll do some research tonight and talk to Donovan tomorrow."

Keeva was thinking about her mother. She stared past Naela, imagining she could see through the many rooms separating her chamber from her parents'. She pictured her mother hunched in a chair, weak but still working diligently to run their kingdom. She imagined her on her side, her cheeks hot with fever but still seeing to the castle's endless list of needs. Keeva hated how unfair things were. Why her mother? Why take the queen before her time? Uterni needed her.

I need her.

"Keeva?"

"What?"

Naela was already in the doorway, the book beneath her arm.

"Sorry. I...I was just thinking."

The look on Naela's face was sad, but she smiled hopefully. "Go take a hot bath and relax, will you?" Then, she added playfully, "I refuse to be best friends with someone who smells like the bottom of a bog."

Sharing a laugh, Keeva waved good night. A bath would do her good. She needed to clear her head. She needed to focus. A clear mind was key to helping her mother, and the early stages of a plan began to form as she headed for the washbasin.

CHAPTER SEVEN

The early morning sun broke in golden shafts over the treetops. Maeve rose early to collect gooseberries from their shrubs before the woodland creatures that lived along the edges of her fen could beat her to it. Outside, the air was thick with moisture from the night's rain, and mud stuck to her boots as she wandered toward the eastern border of her home. Rowan slithered alongside, his sleek body cutting through the damp earth layered in decades of fallen leaves that now cushioned her steps as thick loam. Morning jays jeered from their nests, invisible behind the many tree limbs stretching overhead. Maeve strode lazily, an empty woven basket perched between her right hip and arm.

"What shall we make with our new items, Rowan?" she asked, glancing down as she ducked beneath a low-hanging branch. The scent of the ripe fruit wafted to her as the brambles came into view. Rowan stuck out his tongue, moving quickly to dive into the thick roots at the shrub's base. "I was thinking a hearty pie would be nice." Maeve smiled, imagining a day spent kneading dough and creating a filling with the plump gooseberries that greeted her now. She reached out, taking a few of the berries between her fingers. Their skin gleamed with dew, the round supple texture firm to her touch.

There was a rustling deep in the shrubs, and she heard the familiar sound of Rowan diving across the earth. "I see you've found breakfast," she teased, catching a glimpse of his head darting between leaves. A small squeak confirmed her suspicion, and she sighed contentedly and began to pluck the berries, adding them to her basket. The familiar routine, one she'd done each spring for as long as she could recall, eased her mind, and she fell back into memories:

"Maeve," her mother's voice said, conjuring an image that formed beside her, coming to life like a strange sketch, like one's reflection upon the water. "You must be mindful in which ones to pick." Her mother held up a pair of gooseberries, one in each hand. Her gray eyes met Maeve's; her fair eyebrows raised expectantly beneath a pile of blond hair that was twisted with a series of pins atop her head. A plain brown handkerchief kept the unruly strands back, much like the one Maeve wore for the same purpose.

Maeve, only eight, scrutinized the berries. "They're the same."

"No," her mother said, her voice kind, but a hint of impatience evident. "Look closer. What do you see?"

Itching to return home and start the day's tasks of cleaning and baking, Maeve pouted. "They're both green."

Her mother's lips twitched in a smile. "Obviously, sweetheart. Look again."

Sighing, Maeve leaned down, purposefully drawing her nose nearly into her mother's hands. She knew she was testing her mother's patience, but she loathed these "lessons," as she'd decided to call them. Why couldn't her mother simply tell her what she needed to know? It drove Maeve mad.

Glancing up, she guessed, "The right one is darker?"

"Good," her mother said, giving a satisfied nod. Then, she handed both to Maeve, who took the berries carefully between the thumb and forefinger in each hand. "What do you feel?"

Still pouting, Maeve gently squeezed each one. She raised the left. "This one is too hard." Her mother watched her, waiting. Her smooth, oval face revealed little emotion, but her gray eyes seemed pleased. "So," she said, waving the berry in her right hand, "this one is ready."

"Excellent," her mother replied. "Remember, we mustn't rely only on what we can see. Our other senses are just as strong, sometimes stronger. Everything has its right time, like these berries." She turned, motioning for Maeve to join her as she deftly plucked several from their stems. "We don't want an overly tart pie, now, do we?"

Maeve shook her head, grateful to return to the task at hand instead of fielding more questions. She worked slowly, not yet as skilled as her mother, who seemed to know instantly which berries were ready to join the collection in the basket placed between their feet. "Mother," she said, feeling a berry and deciding it wasn't ready yet, "did Grandmother teach you this? When the fruit is ready to eat?"

Her mother continued to pluck the fruit, her eyes focused on the green shrubbery. Maeve wasn't sure if she'd heard and was ready to repeat her question when her mother finally spoke. "No, I taught myself."

"Oh." Maeve watched a butterfly flutter overhead. "But she taught you how to make gooseberry pie?"

Even then, Maeve could tell when her mother's mood shifted, which it had done then. Again, her mother worked to collect more berries before answering. Maeve watched as she hiked up the sleeves of her brown tunic when she faced her. "She did teach me how to make pie. And then, I passed that knowledge on to you." Her mother's eyes scanned Maeve from head to toe as if looking at what she wore for where to improve Maeve's skills in sewing. Her eyes lingered on a patch Maeve had stitched on the knee of her pants.

"I like gooseberry pie," Maeve said, feeling squirmy under such scrutiny.

The reply seemed to please her mother, who wiped sweat from her forehead before she tucked loose blond strands behind her ear. "I'm glad."

Maeve smiled back, happy to have returned her mother's mood to its normal state. She had known that asking after her grandmother often caused this downturn in demeanor, but Maeve was curious. She had a right to be, she figured, when asking after her own family. Over the years, she'd had to pry information from her mother about her ancestors. She'd learned that they were all creatures of the sea. During the first new moon of winter, when the world was darkest, each gorgon had journeyed under the cover of night to the tumultuous northern waters. A drop of their blood mixed with the changing tide was enough to conjure new life. Thus, Maeve's grandmother, mother, and she were born.

She also knew her grandmother had died young, leaving her mother to fend for herself. Still, Maeve never understood why her mother always seemed angry about that fact. She hadn't worked up the courage to ask why. She figured they had all the time in the realm to discuss such things.

They worked in companiable silence, plucking more berries as the morning sun drifted higher. A snapping branch at their backs made both of them turn. Finding nothing over her shoulder, Maeve looked to her mother. Her gaze was dark as it bored into the folds of green layered thick between the trees. When a raven cawed overhead, her mother's eyes widened, and she grabbed the half-filled basket, spilling a few of the ripe berries.

"It's time to go."

"But…" Maeve gestured to the berries, leaning down to scoop up the ones that had fallen.

Her mother grabbed her wrist, making her wince at the pressure. "Now."

They hurried back to the fen, Maeve on her mother's heels. Daring a glance over her shoulder, she thought she saw something, a flash of white moving behind the screen of leaves. *Panic rose in her small chest, and she followed her mother back into the safety of the fen.*

Now, Rowan slithered out from under the same shrubs, their roots gnarled with time. The memory lingering like fog, Maeve looked once again over her shoulder as she had sixteen years before. This time, there was no flash of white, and any raven's caw would only be that of the Caretaker's messenger. Maeve had never known what had frightened her mother so much that day. She had figured it was the threat of villagers, some unsuspecting human accidentally stumbling upon them, prompting her mother to get them inside lest they hurt somebody.

She had not allowed herself to dwell on memories like this. They only brought confusion and sadness. She watched Rowan emerge, slithering contentedly. Shuddering, she wondered now if her mother's fear that day had been for something else entirely. That flash of white had to have been something. One year later, her mother was gone. Something she didn't understand had happened that day, something real enough to scare her mother.

Maeve frowned, staring into the bright green gooseberries piled within the basket. Briefly, she let her mind conjure old questions, ones buried deep under days spent making snares and traps and endless pieces of acorn bread. As they resurfaced, she wondered if whatever her mother had seen that day had to do with her disappearance.

Her mother had taught her how to keep their home safe. She'd taught her how to remain hidden, how to survive in a world that was frightened of their power as gorgons. Even now, she often felt angry at the curse, as she felt it was better named. What besides a curse could force her to live alone with no hope for any semblance of companionship?

Rowan hissed. Maeve shook her head. "Of course I am grateful for you," she said, wondering if she'd said her thoughts out loud. She looked up, peering through the flora. For a moment, she hoped for a disturbance in the trees. A sign of life. A presence other than her own. She closed her eyes, tilting her head toward the sunlight that grew stronger as it rose in the sky, pouring over the trees. The warmth reminded her of the hearth burning bright after her mother would replenish it with fresh logs. The feeling coiled around her like smoke, warm yet insubstantial. Maeve had given up searching years ago. She'd gotten used to things as they were. Still, in quiet moments like this, as she continued the rituals passed down from her mother, she couldn't help but yearn to know the truth of why she'd gone.

Like always, though, Maeve squeezed her eyes closed as the question grew larger in her mind. "No use looking behind," she said to Rowan. He flicked his tongue in agreement. She sighed loudly, making a fairy nest buzz overhead. "And certainly, no use dwelling on what could be," she said. She shook her head in the effort to clear her mind of its clutter. She couldn't allow herself to ask questions.

After her mother had gone, she'd spent a year in agony, tearing the fen apart, searching for answers, trying to understand where she could have gone or what could have happened to make her leave and never return. The days had been awful, filled with constant sobs that racked Maeve's young body, filling her mind with dread, confusion, and hurt. As time passed, and she learned nothing, Maeve knew she had to move forward. It was the only way.

"Come along, Rowan." He hurried ahead, leading her back.

Gorgons couldn't seek companionship. They couldn't live among the kingdom. And they certainly couldn't ask questions. Questions only caused her pain.

Chapter Eight

K eeva woke to a solid series of knocks upon her chamber door. Groaning, she rolled onto her side, grimacing at the pain in her legs. They felt heavy after she'd spent half the night in mock staff combat with a handful of the young guards in training. The midnight hours had turned into a blissful blur of staffs clashing, limbs glistening with sweat, and a reminder that she could still best even the strongest burgeoning guards.

Now, though, her body held a deep ache. She stretched, sitting as she called, "Come in."

The steady *clop* of Tacari's hooves echoed on the stone floor as he entered, his walking staff in step alongside him. "Good morning, Princess. Your family awaits your presence in the south tower meeting room."

Leaning forward to grab her toes, Keeva relished the tight stretch in her calves. "I take it I slept through breakfast?"

Tacari grinned. "I thought you might." He revealed a fresh roll and a bowl of cherries that he placed on the table next to her bed. "Returning to your chambers when the moon was in her descent." It wasn't a question. He raised a brow as she gratefully shoved the bread in her mouth. "Another training session so soon?"

She sighed, falling off the bed and scampering behind a tall chair to find the tunic her maiden had laid out for her the night before. She quickly tore off her sleep tunic for the fresh one before running a hand through her hair. "Not you, too, Tacari."

"I'm only expressing concern for you, Keeva." He studied the window as she hastily splashed her face above the water basin. She shot him a look for dropping her title and all pretense. When she didn't answer, he lifted one hoof, pawing at the stone floor a few times, his signal that he wasn't going to put up with her nonsense, as he liked to call it. His concern, she knew, was genuine. He was practically family and treated her as such. He had worked alongside her parents as their magistrate ever since their coronation. He'd been present for Keeva and Donovan's birth, and was often the only one in the castle she and her brother would obey when they were children.

"You know the exercise helps me." She kept her eyes on the clear water in the basin as she washed her hands.

"I know you believe that. I'm sure it does, to an extent." He held up a large, fur-covered hand when she started to protest. "I only remind you that your royal duties mustn't be neglected. Your mother—"

"Needs help, I know." She bit the inside of her cheek. Must she be reminded of that before she'd even had breakfast? Grabbing a handful of cherries, she motioned for Tacari to follow as she started through the open chamber door.

He fell easily in step alongside her. "Your list for today," he said.

Keeva took the scroll from him as they rounded a torchlit hallway. Guards stood at attention every fifty paces. She unfurled the scroll and read. "I'll take care of all of this," she said, eyeing the long list. "Don't I always?"

His ears twitched as he lowered his voice. "With all respect, you seem…weary."

"Weary?" she retorted, catching the eye of a guard who had been watching them. She lowered her voice. "I'm the strongest I've ever been in my life."

"You also were late to the last three meetings. Not including this one."

"My handmaiden doesn't start until midday. Her father is ill and—"

"You are the princess, Keeva. You have a responsibility."

"I know, Tacari." Frustration pooled at her hands, her saol flickering. She clenched her fists to quiet the spell-fire. Feeling the need to explain, she added, "Sometimes, I have trouble sleeping." She knew it was an excuse, though not a complete lie. She hated how observant everyone seemed to be when it came to her daily schedule. "I'm fine," she said with a glare for good measure.

They passed the main hall where castle staff was clearing the long table. A quartet of minstrels and musicians practiced a song near the large fire. Her gaze fell back to the scroll. "Is this what the meeting is about?" She nodded to the bottom of the list. "The elves have called an audience?" She began to recall her father mentioning this a week ago.

Tacari nodded. "The elf queen has paid Uterni a visit."

Keeva raised a brow. "Queen Sina? She hasn't been here in years." Taking a right past the armory, Keeva hurried down the hallway leading to the southern tower. The guards opened the doors for them, and Keeva found her family already seated at a gleaming oak table in the well-lit, warm meeting chamber.

"Her Highness, Princess Keeva," Tacari announced.

She rolled her eyes at his formality. Seven castle guards, lined in a half circle around the room, bowed.

"Sorry I'm late."

Across the room at the far end of the table that could easily seat twenty people, sat only three. Her parents were side by side at the head. Keeva noticed her father had donned his woven, copper crown and his nicest, fur-trimmed robe. When she was younger, she had teased him that he resembled a great bear in such an outfit. The passage of time had only solidified this. Beside him, her mother sat tall. Her pale skin glistened with a sheen of sweat. She looked frail, but the raised tilt of her chin told the room she was still capable of tending to matters of the kingdom. Keeva was glad to see her smile when she looked up from the scroll she was reading.

"Hello, darling." She, too, wore her simple crown and elegant, dark green robe. Even Donovan had slicked back his hair into a ponytail, with braids along his temples. A handsome tunic with a tall collar framed his strong neck. Keeva wished she had thought to grab her crown, at least, before rushing from her chamber. Why hadn't Tacari mentioned this was a meeting requiring such accoutrements? Perhaps it was his way of teaching her not to oversleep, not unlike when she'd missed lessons in her youth, and the armory door had been locked, the key secured around Tacari's neck. At least her maiden had decided on one of her nicer tunics that, fortunately, matched her mother's.

Taking a seat in her high-backed chair catty-corner to her mother, Keeva caught Donovan's gaze.

You look like something the horse dragged in.

Shut up.

He smiled, pointing to his own chin. *You've got a little something.*

She reached up, swiping the back of her hand across her face. Cherry juice spread down her wrist. *Thanks.*

Gods, she felt completely out of sorts. Taking a deep breath, she caught the scent of henbane from her mother, no doubt taken to get through this meeting. It was barely covered by the slightly stronger odor of mint.

Keeva smoothed her tunic, running a hand through her hair once again and adjusting the leather bracelets on her wrists. "How are you feeling?" she asked her mother. Several staff members came and went from the room in a flurry, handing her father pages of scrolls.

"I'm feeling fine, sweetheart." Her mother cut her gaze to Keeva. "Tired, that's all." She squinted, scanning Keeva's face. "Late night?"

"I was training."

Keeva was grateful when a page entered and announced, "Queen Sina, leader of the twelve clans."

Standing, the royal family waited as the elf queen was led into the room.

"Queen Sina, welcome." Keeva's father bowed, and the rest of the room followed suit.

Queen Sina was surrounded by four elven guards. Each of them wore ankle-length tunics, a soft shimmering turquoise that reminded Keeva of the sea on a clear day. They all had long white hair that fell to their waists. Their skin was shockingly smooth, the shades varying from eggshell white to deep umber. They moved in unison, four stalwart corners standing tall.

"King Ragnar. Queen Asta. Lovely to see you both again."

Keeva had always found Queen Sina's voice to be in contradiction with her appearance. She was tall, taller than even Donovan. She had a figure that resembled an hourglass, which her light blue tunic clung to tightly. Biting her lip, Keeva forced her gaze to meet the elf queen's. Her steel gray eyes were kind but clouded. Queen Sina's femininity dripped from her long sharp nails and the high cheekbones set in an oval face, yet the voice that fell from her full lips was husky, like sand scraping over stone.

When a seat at the far end of the table was pulled out for her, she sat with perfect posture and said, "I apologize for the hasty nature of my arrival. I wasn't scheduled to be here for another week. I would have sent word, but it was urgent."

"Nonsense," Keeva's mother replied. "You and your people are always welcome in Uterni."

The four elven guards showed no emotion as they readjusted to flank their queen on either side of her chair. Sina smiled. For the first time, she acknowledged Donovan and Keeva. "Your Majesties."

Keeva and her brother nodded their greetings. Queen Sina leaned back, her towering pile of hair arranged elegantly like some shining, silver beehive. It bumped against the top of her seat. She gripped the ends of the armrests, her long fingers seeming to search the very grains of the wood. Keeva glanced at her parents, wondering if they noticed this show of tenseness.

Her father said, "Please, to what do we owe the pleasure of your visit?"

"I trust you received my latest correspondence?"

"We did."

"Then, you are aware of our, shall we say, strained relationship of late with the Diarmaids?" Sina's voice lilted in the way many of the elves' voices did, like a song.

Her parents chuckled. "The Diarmaids seem to thrive on such relationships," her father replied. "What exactly have they said?"

"It's not what they say," Sina replied, "but what they do."

All of them raised their brows. "Oh?" her mother said, sounding as intrigued as Keeva felt.

"We're all aware of the Fae-Diarmaid Treaty, signed after the royal family expanded their territory, and my people were relegated to the northeastern corner of this realm."

Keeva didn't miss how Sina's voice turned sharp at the last words, the faintest hint of malice adding a hard edge. Shifting, she caught her brother's gaze. He looked as uncomfortable as she was beginning to feel. Everyone knew that neither Gultero or Uterni had done anything to stop the Diarmaids from claiming more land for themselves. All of the kingdoms had long ago staked their claims, but the Diarmaids were the ones who seemed to always seek more. Of course, Keeva reminded herself, they were the most powerful of the three kingdoms. Gultero was a small island, and Uterni was so far north, they were often ignorant of much of what was happening in the rest of the realm.

Both depended greatly on the resources of Venostes, the central force between them.

She and Donovan had been infants before the treaty, but by the time word had reached Uterni of what was happening in the south—young king Grannus and his queen pushing the allotted boundaries of their kingdom—Keeva's parents had felt the only option was to take a stance of neutrality since the damage had been done.

In a show of benignity with the fae—mainly the elves—whose land had been taken, Keeva's parents had opened their doors to those who had been forced out. Growing up, Keeva had been taught that even still, many fae were angry not only at the Diarmaids but at the other kingdoms for not doing more to help protect their native lands.

"It was a dark time. My people lost their homes," Sina was saying, pulling Keeva from her thoughts. "Nevertheless, we are resilient. We have always been and always will be great, regardless of the limitations placed upon us." As she spoke, she reached up to clutch the end of a necklace Keeva was surprised she hadn't noticed. A thin vial rested at the end of a silver chain, nestled against the queen's bosom. Blue liquid shimmered within the glass. "But now," Sina said, drawing Keeva's gaze upward, "I fear the humans seek too much."

The air in the room had grown thick. Keeva swallowed. Her parents sat quietly, seeming to weigh their words. Her mother's lips were pursed while her father tapped pudgy fingers atop the table.

"Have they sent soldiers to your territory?" Keeva asked, not able to sit in the silence.

Queen Sina turned, her sharp eyes peering into her. "Not yet."

"With respect, Your Majesty, the Diarmaids are our allies." Her father's deep voice was kind, but Keeva could hear the incredulity slip through. "They are *your* allies. The treaty has been upheld since its instatement. I see no reason why it would be breached suddenly."

Half moons crested in the elf queen's cheeks when she smiled. "Is it not in the nature of humans to want more?"

Inhaling sharply, Keeva frantically threw her gaze around the table. The elf queen had just insulted them, had she not? Keeva wasn't sure how her mother could smile at such a comment, but she did before saying, "It is also in the nature of humans to honor our word."

It fell quiet again. Queen Sina held her parents' gazes.

Her father leaned back, opening his arms in a showy gesture. "I'm not sure I understand your concern. Perhaps there are some adventurous villagers roaming the edges of Venostes, stepping where they shouldn't. But I see no reason—"

"There's more."

Keeva's father fell quiet. They all waited, watching Sina sit eerily still. Keeva had always liked the elves. They were self-reliant, confident. There was also something just beneath the surface of their eyes Keeva could never pinpoint. Typically, she found the quality alluring. Now, that same elusiveness bore into her family and left her unnerved.

"I've heard whispers of a dark force. It is in its infancy, only now crawling out of the shadows, but it is slithering along the corners of the realm."

"A dark force?" Donovan asked, leaning forward to rest his forearms against the table's edge.

Her mother frowned. "I don't understand what this has to do with the royal family."

"The force has roots in Venostes."

Keeva's father brushed a hand through his beard, a vee between his bushy brows. "Your Highness, how can you know this?"

Queen Sina squinted, drawing the smooth skin around her eyes into the faintest of lines. Keeva wondered if she was annoyed with them. This was not the same elf queen she remembered from a solstice festival four summers before. Then, Keeva had known a pleasant, if reserved, monarch who partook in Uterni's frivolity. Now, she seemed anxious, her hands still gripping the edges of the chair's armrests as her gray eyes met theirs with a preoccupation that startled Keeva. Finally, she said, "My kingdom received a visitor from Venostes. He warned of the darkness. He claims he can aid in its vanquishing."

"Who is this visitor? A representative of the court?"

"The situation is new and fragile," Sina responded tersely, and Keeva met Donovan's gaze, noting how she skirted the question. "The man is powerful. His wind magic is unlike anything we've seen in decades. My people are already afraid. They've been through so much in only my lifetime." She trailed off, her gaze distant as she once again fingered the end of the vial. A guard coughed, and she looked up. "I will do what I need to in order to protect my people."

"Queen Sina," her mother said, using a handkerchief from inside her cloak to quickly swipe the perspiration from her forehead, "it sounds as if you're implying the Diarmaids have a hand in this new darkness, as you call it."

The elf queen sat quietly for a moment. "From where the darkness spreads is not the question we should be asking. How to keep our borders safe and our people secure would, I hope, be your main concern."

"Of course," her father said brusquely. "But if we can learn more about the source of this potential threat, we could help."

"You can help by continuing to ally your kingdom with mine should we need to take up arms."

Keeva's eyes went wide at the idea of war. She swallowed as her mother replied, "Our allegiance to you is never in question."

"Even if it means fighting your fellow man?"

The crackle of torchlight was the only sound. A few of the guards shuffled their feet. Keeva glanced at one of them, knowing the information in this room wasn't supposed to leave but would fly like a hawk around the castle once they were adjourned. She would have to monitor the gossip over the coming days. Biting her lip, she glanced back at her parents. They seemed to be having a silent conversation, furtive glances shared between them.

Finally, her father said, "Uterni has long been a kingdom that believes in a just and fair land. We harbor those who have fled unjust hardship, we welcome those who seek a better life. We do not, however, draw lines against our southern neighbors. We value the security you have helped to provide to the east, but we cannot promise alliances in war."

A sound like a grunt came from Sina, and a small smile lifted her face from the shadows it had fallen into. She stood.

Quickly, Keeva did the same. Donovan stumbled to his feet at the abrupt end to their meeting.

"Your chambers are prepared in the east wing," her father said, and Keeva could tell he, too, was thrown by the elf queen's behavior.

"Thank you."

The four guards once again took up their corners around their queen. Then, they exited the meeting room without a glance back.

CHAPTER NINE

By midday, Keeva had spoken with the local fishermen to analyze the anticipated summer supply, she'd met with the blacksmith to check how the new guard swords were coming along, and she had just finished walking the trackways with the village's chief woodworker to assess the planks in need of repair.

She was tired and—after saying good-bye to the kindly old man who recommended two months' time to replace a dozen planks that were more rot than wood—eager to return to the castle. Brushing her brown cloak behind her, she hurried along the trackway that wound over the bogs between the outskirt of the village and the royal grounds.

The bright sun sat hidden behind a screen of gray, a crisp wind tugging at her tunic and pants. Keeva swept her gaze over the sporadic tufts of grass that varied in color from pale yellow to a sickly reddish-green. The patches poked up from the sticky earth as the grass, much like the planks hosting their raised trackways, seemed to search for higher ground. Behind her lay the highland littered with low, thatch-roofed homes comprising the village and beyond that, Uterni's wildlands and border. She watched a dragonfly zip over the soggy stretch of bog. It landed atop a cropping of lichen. Moments later, a toad she hadn't noticed croaked, his tongue like a slingshot as it snared the dragonfly. She shivered at the sight.

"Careful, the bogwitch will reach up and pull you under."

Keeva turned to find Donovan at her side. He wore an identical cloak, his large frame making the planks groan beneath his leather boots.

"I'm sure she'd spit me back out," Keeva retorted.

"Sour again?"

She met his gaze, lively and bright against the gloom. His crown was gone, and the good tunic from the meeting yesterday had been replaced with an only slightly less fine one of forest green with a gold trim on the cuffs and collar. "Only tired," she said.

He hummed, eyeing her but not saying anything as they started in unison away from the marshy, mud-filled land and toward the rocky cliffsides bearing their home to the north. After a moment, he said, "Queen Sina is scheduled to leave tomorrow. Though, after the meeting yesterday I'm surprised she didn't leave immediately. Rather icy, wasn't it?"

Keeva nodded. The meeting had certainly unsettled her. She had already had three conversations with castle staff who had spread rumors of an uprising. "What did you make of her words?"

"Disconcerting." He spoke low before smiling at a gaggle of youths helping to herd a group of goats. They all giggled. "She didn't seem herself."

"No, she didn't." Keeva kept trying to reconcile this version of the elf queen with the one from years past. Of course, she could relate to such a preoccupied state of mind. Between her endless list of mundane responsibilities and worrying about her mother's health, her thoughts were in a constant state of tumult.

"The Diarmaids are greedy," her brother was saying. "Etaina speaks often of how stingy they are with newly acquired riches."

She was half listening but gave a snort at the mention of his continued interest in the Gulteran woman. She decided not to say anything, and he continued, ignoring her.

"Still, I've no reason to believe they would seek to push the elves' border farther away."

Glancing sideways, she found his thin lips downturned, a small crease in his forehead. She spoke his thought out loud. "It doesn't make sense."

"No, it doesn't."

"Mother and Father didn't seem as concerned," she said after a moment. They stepped off the planks and onto the dirt path leading to the front gates of the castle.

"No." His gaze flickered to her, his concern obvious as she worked to focus her thoughts, but walking into the castle now brought back the moments following their meeting: staff flying to her mother's side as she slumped in her seat; her father's frantic eyes as a maid revived her with a rag of cold water; then her mother being led back to her chambers, unable to join them for dinner.

"Keevs." Donovan nudged her, but she hardly noticed as they strode through the main hall. The usual bustle seemed muted. "Perhaps we should talk to her before she leaves."

She looked up from where she'd been watching her steps. "Queen Sina?"

"She was holding back."

"I agree."

"After dinner, then?"

"Once most of the court has retired." Her steps faltered. "Gods, I forgot I'm supposed to meet Naela after dinner." Naela was spending today out in the village with her aunt, learning more about Epona.

"Another training session?" asked Donovan, taking a seat at the dining table.

At this hour, the main hall was in transition, the vast, brightly lit room full of servants clearing dishes from late breakfast goers while others rekindled the massive fireplaces and prepared for the evening's dinner.

When Keeva joined her brother at the table, they were each presented with a goblet of wine. Since Donovan's initial ardent rejection of her idea to find Epona, she hadn't brought the subject up again. Instead, she was only more determined to handle this without him. "Can't get enough," she lied, pulling her chin close and hiding her face behind the cup. Perhaps he would find out anyway. But she couldn't stand the look on his face, another set of eyes wondering about her choices. Another family member who disapproved of her actions because they didn't benefit the kingdom. At least if he thought she was only training, his disapproval stayed in the same place. He could maintain his status as the gold-star prince.

He shook his head, and she knew what he was thinking before he said it. "You're pushing yourself too far."

"I'm fine."

He watched her, chewing on a stray piece of bread that hadn't been cleared yet.

"Anyway," she said, "I'll find Sina this evening before I train. She always walks the halls before retiring."

Donovan still seemed irked at her but took the change of subject in stride. "If I can join you, I will. But we both know she's always had a liking for you more than me." He winked, and she was grateful for the return to his joking self. She chucked a raspberry at him for good measure.

❖

"Queen Sina?" Keeva's hamstrings protested as she ran to catch up to the elf queen whose long stride was swift as she left the main hall after dinner. Two elven guards spun to face Keeva, crossing thin spears to block her from getting closer.

"Princess Glantor." She smiled, though her eyes seemed clouded. "Please send my gratitude to your cook for that lovely parting dinner. The olives were particularly exquisite."

Keeva laughed, then, realizing the queen was serious, nodded. "I'll be happy to." She glanced at the guards, and Sina seemed to catch on to her silent request.

"It's all right," Sina said, waving her hand. The guards relaxed, joining the other two on either side of the queen. Standing so, Sina gleamed in her shimmering tunic like the bright point of a star in the dark castle corridor. Even the torchlight seemed to extend its flame, reaching toward her glow.

"May I join you?" Keeva asked.

Sina blinked but nodded. Keeva slid into the space next to her, and they walked down the hall toward the southern wing.

"Your Majesty," Keeva started slowly but faltered as she tried to express her apprehension from the previous day's meeting.

"You wonder why I'm so concerned about a distant kingdom and talk of darkness that may be only lore."

"With respect—"

"That is an overused phrase," Sina interjected. "And often means quite the opposite of what is intended." Surprised, Keeva's mouth fell open. Sina, meanwhile, gave a small smile. "I'm sorry. I know I haven't been myself since arriving."

"You seem…" Keeva searched for the right word. "Preoccupied."

Sina's long fingers found her necklace, fiddling with the vial as they walked. "It's my job to keep the twelve clans safe." She paused, facing Keeva. She held the vial above her chest. "Do you know what this is?"

"A necklace?"

Sina explained, "It's water from the Lake of Achmann. You know of it, I trust?"

"Yes. It's an elven lake."

"It's *the* elven lake. The only one that remains of our waters."

Keeva frowned. "I don't...your waters?"

"When the elves lived among all the land of this realm, each river east of Ionad was ours. The water was sacred, pure, and powerful. It was our life source." Her proud gaze turned forlorn. "As our land was taken, the rivers were poisoned by man, tainted with their touch and no longer able to sustain my people. The Lake of Achmann is the only source of these waters that remains." She clutched the vial fiercely, her eyes closed briefly before she opened them and held Keeva's gaze. Feeling awkward under it, Keeva motioned to continue walking. "It's up to me to ensure our waters remain safe. It's up to me that our borders are secure, which proves difficult when members of man encroach upon my people's homes more and more each passing year."

"But the treaty is in place."

"Yes."

Trying to show support, Keeva offered, "It's a lot, Your Highness, the weight of responsibility placed upon a monarch. I understand—"

"You cannot possibly understand." Queen Sina halted at the corner of a passageway, turning as shadows played across her face, making her seem somehow taller and fearsome.

"Queen Sina, I am a princess. I know what it's like to feel the pressure of the kingdom."

The elf queen held her gaze, though Keeva felt her looking beyond, almost through her as she continued like she hadn't heard. "You cannot possibly comprehend leading people who have seen pieces of their homeland stripped away every generation. You cannot understand what it's like to be a proud fae forced into an unlivable part of the realm, relegated to a mere corner of tarnished earth to live, feeling trapped like some beast."

Heat rose up Keeva's neck as Sina stared down, her eyes refocused, boring into her. She stammered. "You're right. I can't...I can't understand that, but..." She licked her lips at Sina's expectant brow. "I can imagine."

Sina studied her, then swiftly resumed walking. "Perhaps," she said. The guest chambers came into view. Keeva had to admit she was glad to see them. When they were nearly to the door, Sina said, "Unlike the Glantors and the other royal families, I do not have the luxury of ignoring potential threats. We don't have the resources of your kingdoms." She glanced at her guards, adding resignedly, "We don't even have the resources of my predecessors. We don't have geographical advantages like your towering cliffsides and bogs." She took a long breath. "We don't have a lot." Keeva could only nod. The elf queen lifted her hand to her chamber door, her gaze staring into the wood as if searching for something before saying, "I will do what it takes to keep my people safe."

Sina was right; Keeva didn't understand. She couldn't understand the desperation and fear gleaming in Sina's eyes. With a wave of shame, she hoped she never would. Swallowing her guilt, she said, "We will keep our ears to the ground for news of this dark force. We are with you."

The chamber door half-open, Sina turned, half of a smile on her face. "So says the family Glantor?"

Keeva balked. She shouldn't speak for her parents. Her father had explained they couldn't side with the elves in war. But what possibility was there, really, of war? This was unrest, nothing more. And in unrest, she would hope her mother and father would agree. "So say I," she said firmly, straightening.

With that, Queen Sina motioned for her guards. Keeva couldn't read the look in her eyes. It startled her, but the smile she wore seemed pleased. Then, without a word, Sina closed the door, leaving Keeva alone and wondering if she'd just made a promise her family wouldn't be able to keep.

CHAPTER TEN

Later, Keeva was still in her day tunic and boots, staring out her chamber window when a quick knock was followed by Naela bursting into the room wearing a satisfied grin that exaggerated her dimpled cheeks.

"Gods, it's cold out there." She shivered, closing the door behind her. "I thought it was nearly summer."

Keeva pulled her gaze from the distant cliffs, a series of jagged shadows under the nearly full moonlight. "This is as warm as it gets."

"Don't remind me." Naela untied the neck of her cloak and swept it off, placing it on a chair near the wall. "Have you any wine?"

Keeva nodded, moving to pour a goblet from the remaining cask on the round oak table that sat atop a black bearskin in the middle of her room.

"Thanks," Naela said, taking the drink. She eyed Keeva over the rim. "You all right?"

Glancing up, Keeva realized she was still holding the cask, her arm frozen as if to pour again. "Oh." She set it down. "Sorry. I've got a lot on my mind." She continued at Naela's expectant gaze: "I spoke with Queen Sina earlier."

Running the pad of her finger beneath her lips to catch a drop of the red liquid, Naela said, "My parents told me about the meeting. They say she was completely paranoid, borderline mad, even."

"She's not mad," Keeva replied too quickly.

Naela raised her free hand, palm up. "I was only repeating what I heard." Keeva sighed. Naela, meanwhile, took a seat in one of the high-back chairs, the leather hides of its backing giving with a creak of the wooden frame. "Anyway." She took another sip. "I've got some information for you regarding our mysterious Epona."

Keeva blinked. Her interaction with Sina had taken residence at the forefront of her mind for the last hour. She'd nearly forgotten about the woman who might be the only one able to help her mother. She pulled up a chair excitedly. "Did you find her?"

"No. But," Naela said, leaning forward to catch Keeva's disappointed gaze, "I spent all day with my aunt. Between her home and the leprechaun lodging, I'll be lucky to ever get the smell of mead out of my hair." She shook her head, the black spirals bouncing.

"Did she tell you how to find Epona?"

"She had some suggestions. As did many of the patrons at the lodge. Odd bunch, they are."

"That's great." Keeva felt her chest tighten in anticipation. "We can make a list of possible locations, then compare those with the places where the fruit she dispenses grows. We'll narrow our search between them and find her in no time."

Naela smiled. "We need to learn where those groves are first. I've neglected asking Donovan. Though, I still think he's the best resource in that regard."

"What else did your aunt say?" Keeva didn't want to dwell on the idea of needing her brother for this, even indirectly. "Any advice on gaining favor with Epona? Everyone has something they want, something we might offer her in exchange for help."

"No," Naela said, setting the goblet aside. "Though, I'm not sure what the Otherworld gatekeeper could really desire." Keeva pondered the thought when Naela added, "My aunt did extend a word of caution."

"Oh?"

"There are stories. Always are. My aunt told one in particular of a man named Svenheld who went in search of Epona and her key." Keeva sat, pulling one knee close to listen. "She told me how people have tried for centuries to trick or trap Epona. Svenheld, after hearing of those failed attempts, decided to try something different. He wasn't going to use magic or deception. He would simply wait." Naela crossed one leg in her chair, her forearms on the armrests as she recounted the tale. "Svenheld's brother was very ill. He knew his brother would be gone soon, so he decided that he would wait for Epona when she came to collect him."

"Not a bad idea," said Keeva.

"Not at all. When his brother passed one winter's night, Svenheld was there at his bedside. When the village was asleep and he himself nearly so, that's when he heard the hoofbeats."

"Epona's horse."

"Svenheld sprang up to find the spirit of his brother outside and astride the giant steed behind Epona. Silently, he followed them into the wildlands near Uterni's border. After walking for hours, Svenheld watched as Epona dismounted, leading his brother to an ancient tree that stood as tall as a giant."

"What happened?"

"He called to her. Epona turned, seemingly surprised at the mortal whose sad eyes pled as passionately as his words. 'Spare my brother,' Svenheld said. 'Please, he's all I have.'" Naela's face fell, and Keeva listened, enraptured. "Epona ignored him. She ushered Svenheld's brother through a door cut into the trunk of the mighty ash. A door she unlocked with a key that hung around her neck."

"She didn't show mercy?"

Naela shook her head. "Svenheld was distraught at her indifference. In a rage, he lunged when Epona's back was turned. He reached for her key, desperate to keep his brother in this realm."

Keeva's breath caught, sympathizing with this poor man's actions.

"The moment his fingers gripped the key, the earth broke open. Angry smoke and screaming fire erupted before him, drowning his senses in agony and chaos. The wails of the dead shrieked in protest across the land." Naela's voice rose a pitch as she continued. "Then, Dagda himself rose up, summoned from his throne by Svenheld's act. The king of the Otherworld struck him down on the spot, and the gatekeeper led not one but two men through the door that night."

A strong wind blew in from the window. Keeva shuddered. "Gods, Naela." She drew a deep breath, then said more to herself, "It's only a story."

Naela leaned back, taking a deep breath. "A right scary one, don't you think?"

Keeva replied, trying to hide the wavering timber her voice took on. "A tale with a lesson meant to frighten children."

Naela watched her. "Maybe. Still, Keevs." She pulled her chair closer. "We need to be careful with this."

"I know." Keeva pinched the bridge of her nose. "Besides," she said, shaking her shoulders as if to shed the lingering sensation of dread the story had left, "the circumstances are different. This is a matter of the royal family. I'm not implying Svenheld's brother wasn't important," she said at Naela's raised brow, "but this is my mother. Queen Asta Glantor. A kingdom needs its leader."

Naela looked at her a moment more before fiddling with the sleeve of her tunic. Keeva knew her mind. She could hear her thoughts, could hear her thinking that while losing a ruler was hard, it was something that always happened. Kings died. Queens passed on. Even a prince might meet an untimely end. It was a fact Keeva knew, but it was not something she was ready for when it came to her mother. She was too young. There was still so much to do. It wasn't time.

"Well," Naela said after a minute, "I'm with you, nevertheless. We've survived our adventures up until now." She grinned. "What's one more?"

Keeva laughed. She was right. She and Naela, along with Donovan, had snuck out of the castle more times than she could count. Her parents trusted them but would surely be cross to learn how often the three of them spent time at the tumultuous seaside practicing spells or camping out near the wildlands during festivals. There was even the one time she and Naela had dressed up as guards—the latter having swiped armor from her parents' room—and joined a patrol squad simply to know what it was like.

"Thank you, Naela," Keeva finally said, feeling warm with memories.

Naela stood. "Don't thank me yet. We've got to narrow down potential locations first."

"Soon, though."

Naela's gaze seemed to understand that she wasn't asking. Keeva's mother was running out of time. They needed to act. "One week. We'll start our search after the half moon."

Keeva nodded.

"Now, I've got to find that brother of yours."

Keeva followed Naela to the door. "It's rather late, don't you think?"

Naela dipped her chin, a futile effort to hide a smile. Her eyes held a hint of mischief. "Not when I bring him his favorite dessert that I'll ask the cook to leave before he's gone to bed."

"Gods," Keeva said, shaking her head, "my brother really can't see what's right under his nose, can he?"

"You've got to lead a man to water, Keevs," Naela teased, pulling on her cloak at the open door.

Keeva sighed. "It doesn't seem to matter either way, does it?" She flashed back to three summers before when she'd tried, and failed, to court a dashing young woman who worked for the Uterni shipyard. "Women aren't much easier."

Naela laughed. "You just need to find the right one." Her gaze turned thoughtful, and she opened her mouth to speak.

Holding up a hand, Keeva cut her off. She knew Naela was going to begin another tirade of relationship advice that Keeva was not in the mood for. Gently, she shoved Naela through the doorway. "Another time," she said, and Naela frowned. "Good night. And thanks again for today."

Naela turned, pouting good-naturedly. "You can't hide from love forever, Keevs."

"I promise, if I ever find it, I'll sprint at it head-on."

Naela chuckled and waved her off. Keeva, smiling, closed the door behind her.

Chapter Eleven

That night, Maeve dreamt of the day her mother had gone. Maeve had been at home, working diligently to sew a patch in her tunic. Her mother had gone with the sun to fetch water from the river. At midday, Maeve's stomach had rumbled. She'd glanced up from her work and frowned. Her mother hadn't returned.

"Mother?" she'd called, her nine-year-old voice barely carrying to the far side of the warm room. She glanced to each window, then to the door, its lock firmly in place. Maeve had slowly stood, placing her work carefully in her chair. She'd called again, this time louder. "Mother?"

Silence.

Maeve hadn't known what to do. She'd returned to her stitchwork. She'd found a handful of berries to eat. All the while, she'd stared at the door. Her mother had told her never to open it unless she'd heard their signal. Four quick knocks. No matter how long she'd stared at the door that day, though, the sound had never come.

It wasn't until the next morning that Maeve had worked up the courage to open the door. She'd peeked out, trembling, fearful of the familiar sounds of her fen. Each fairy buzz, each cackle from a magpie had left her unnerved. It had taken an hour to tiptoe to the river.

At the top of the bank, she'd found the bucket her mother had used to fetch water. Faint footprints were stamped into the mud, but they were sullied with the night's rain, and Maeve couldn't distinguish them from the animal and nymph prints nearby.

"Mother?" she'd called again, holding the bucket close to her chest. Tears brimming, she'd shouted again, "Mother!"

Maeve jolted awake. Her breath came fast, and she clutched a hand over her chest. Moonlight streamed through her window, still and ignorant to the stifling dread heavy on her shoulders. The feeling stayed with her through the day. The old man's face reflected at her in every cup of water. Dain shouted from the shadows.

Anxious, Maeve checked her snares three times that day. Something was coming.

❖

When their mother didn't join them for breakfast the next morning, Keeva went to her parents' chamber after leaving a plate of poached pheasant eggs and berries untouched.

"Come in," her mother called, the feeble lilt making Keeva rush into the room and hurriedly close the door behind her to keep out any drafts. Once inside, she found an uncommon sight: her mother alone. "Sweetheart, good morning."

Keeva worked to hide her surprise but had a feeling her mother noticed as Keeva's lips parted at the sight of her shockingly pale face and gaunt cheeks. Had she really declined so much in just a few days? That combined with the lack of diligent castle staff and maidens made Keeva feel oddly adrift as she crossed the vast space. "I came to see if they can bring you anything from the dining hall." She sat at the foot of her mother's bed where piles of sheepskins lay under even more bundles of scrolls and kingdom documents, like the one her mother held unfurled in her lap.

"Oh, no, thank you, darling." She finished reading and looked up. The shadows beneath her eyes made her seem more phantom than human.

"Are you sure?" Keeva asked. "I can call down for some lamb or even a fresh loaf of bread. You should eat something."

Her mother smiled, her eyes twinkling. "Maybe later."

Not sure what to say, Keeva rubbed one hand up her left arm, running her fingers over her biceps, which were feeling sore following last night's archery practice. After Naela's visit, she'd been wound up with the potential hope of finding Epona and couldn't sleep. She'd spent the night with a quiver and her favorite bow to quell her restless mind.

"How was your training last night?" Her mother always seemed to know what Keeva was up to, despite being confined to her room most days.

"Fine," she answered, fiddling with the end of her dagger earring as she caught sight of the fresh scars on her mother's arms from another attempt at bloodletting. "Any new remedies?" She gestured to the bedside table. It seemed Tacari had been there, as the dozens of vials were arranged by both color and height.

"A few." Her mother was still watching her.

Keeva nodded, chewing her lip as she summoned the right way to phrase her uncertainties and explain the sense of foreboding that overwhelmed her each time she walked by this room. "Mother…"

"Do you plan to go into the market today? I hear people are complaining about the rising cost of meat. We should speak to the vendors as soon as possible."

"Of course." Keeva took a breath.

"And remind your brother to see to the herders. He needs to remind them to not let any of their flock stray. Sheep keep wandering to the border and are being snatched by banshees. Gods know why."

"I will. Mother, I—"

Suddenly, her mother's eyes closed. Her chapped lips pursed, and she winced.

"Mother, what is it?" Keeva moved closer, taking her hand. It was scorching hot to the touch, and at this proximity, the high fever set in her mother's cheeks was evident.

"Pain. It's only pain."

"I'll order more henbane." Keeva could smell it wafting from her mother's sweaty skin, the pretense of mint gone. The stench was like dead earth. She clenched her jaw and tried to breathe through her mouth.

Her mother, the wave of pain apparently gone, returned to her scroll, her hands trembling. "Another thing, make sure that you remind your father he needs to speak to the stablemen. The horses are entirely too—"

"Mother." The sharp edge to Keeva's tone surprised even her. "Stop."

For another moment, her mother's gaze remained on the parchment. She closed her eyes, and Keeva feared she had passed out until she spoke, her voice low. "Keeva, these are important matters to attend to."

"You know I understand that."

"Do you?"

"Yes. Mother, how can you say that? I understand my responsibilities to the kingdom. You have taught us that since we were children."

Her mother slowly leaned back, her tired eyes scrutinizing Keeva's face. "Yet, lately, you seem to be throwing yourself into training and combat magic more and more."

"It helps me," Keeva replied, cutting her gaze to the floor where old rags sat waiting for collection. "You know that."

Her mother set the scroll aside. "You know I don't oppose your training. You are strong. Stronger than I ever was." A small smile lifted her lips. "Neither of my children inherited a hint of my athletic ability, thank the gods."

"Then, I don't see what's wrong with my training regimen."

"You're not a soldier, sweetheart."

"No, but what if one day, we need to lead our people in battle? I should be prepared." It was a stretch of an excuse, Keeva knew, but was easier than admitting the truth. The truth that involved countless sleepless nights and body-numbing combat sessions until the preoccupation sitting before her rested its endless stirring in her mind.

Her mother raised one thin brow. "Uterni is a safe kingdom. We have never gone to war, and gods willing—"

"Never will," Keeva finished in a tone reminiscent of her teenage self. She grimaced. "I can handle things," she said. "But you..." Reaching again for her mother's hand, she stared at their palms pressed together. When had her hands outgrown her mother's? Keeva flashed back to when she was a child clinging tight to her mother's firm grasp as they traipsed through the castle halls together. "You are working too hard. You should rest."

"And what do you call this?" She gestured to the bed, her sleep tunic, and the messy braid resting on one shoulder. "I can't ignore the needs of the kingdom, my darling."

"You also can't ignore your health."

Her mother tilted her head, then squeezed Keeva's hand. They'd had this conversation several times over the past year. "I've been sick a long time, my love." She hesitated, then retracted her hand. "My time has simply run by with swifter feet." Keeva felt a response form, felt the words crawl up her throat, but they were lost on her tongue as her mother's eyes gleamed, and she shook her head. "Which is why it's so important for you to keep up your end of things. You and your brother must be certain of yourselves in decision-making when it comes to the village and affairs of the court. In time..."

"In time, you will still be here leading our people alongside Father."

The candle nearby flickered. Silence hovered over them. "Keeva."

But she shook her head. She knew what her mother was going to say. She refused to hear it. She couldn't. "It's not time," she whispered, her gaze focused on the soft brown fur of the bearskin. When her mother moved to speak again, Keeva's sadness turned to anger. Her voice rose. "You can't continue to pile these trivial chores in front of me and Donovan. It's what you've done for years. You and Father both try to keep us ignorant. I hate it."

Her mother's eyes widened. The chamber door creaked open, and her father entered, rubbing his stomach and looking satisfied after breakfast. "Oh, hello, Keeva."

Her frustration rising, Keeva kept her focus on her mother. "I know what you're doing. You fill our days with endless lists to keep us busy and blind to your suffering. You don't want us to see it. I understand." Her voice grew heated, and her father paused near his desk, watching. "But keeping us in the dark is cruel. You should let me help you." Gathering her mother's hands again, Keeva pleaded. "You cannot deny that this isn't right. The gods were wrong in giving you this illness to fight, a leader tethered to her room when she is needed among her people. Mother, you are brave and kind and strong and..." Her voice broke. "You have to let me help you."

Tears brimmed in her mother's eyes. "That is not your job, my darling."

The words burned Keeva, as if her mother had singed her with spell-fire. "Not my job?"

"You are the princess. You need to focus on the kingdom."

"But I'm your daughter," Keeva shouted.

The room felt heavy. Too thick, like the dreadful, mud-filled bogs outside. Her father stepped closer. "That is no way to speak to your mother."

Keeva glared at him over her shoulder, tears stinging. She wanted to be commanding like Donovan in court. Her mother's suffering, though, always made her feel raw, exposed. It left her feeling like the child she used to be, needy and defiant. "Please." She gripped her mother's hand, unable to look.

"You want to help me." Her mother's voice pulled her gaze.

"Yes."

"Then be the princess our people need."

Her sharp inhale cut between them. Keeva pulled back her hand. "Very well." Standing, she turned to go.

"Keeva—"

"I will see you at dinner," she called, not bothering to even look at her father. She couldn't stand to. How could her parents deny her desire to help? How could they continue like enchanted, mindless fools spinning through their days, unwilling to look at the fact that her mother was dying and needed something—anything—to change.

It was then that Keeva decided she couldn't wait any longer. She would meet with Naela that night. They would call for maps. Then, when the half moon rose, they would go in search of Epona.

❖

The following days, Keeva kept her nose down, which she could tell was disturbing most members of the court. Her loud, confident demeanor—the princess with hair as bold as she—had slunk away. In its place was a traditional monarch who seemed preoccupied with the day's trivial pursuits. Her greeting to her father each morning was so muted, in fact, Tacari asked if she simply hadn't noticed him seated at the head of the table when she sat at the opposite end, as far from the empty chair staring back at her as possible.

When the half moon perched in the night sky, Keeva rose the next day and walked to the dining hall midmorning. She scarfed down breakfast, brushed by Donovan without a greeting, and raced to the kingdom's port to take care of her morning meetings. She stood along the wooden docks, the air packed with the scent of damp sheepskin being hauled ashore. She listened but hardly heard the merchant as he spoke. Nor did she hear the fishermen an hour later, nor the butchers, nor the parade of young guards as they marched past in a training routine.

When her final meeting ended just after midday, Keeva had to keep from sprinting out of the market. She was nearly to the castle gates when a voice called out. Suddenly, Naela was at her side. Keeva couldn't hide her relief, and it spread across her face in a smile. "Is it time?"

Naela wrapped an arm around her, leading her into the castle. "I've gathered our things for tonight. Everything's ready."

Keeva felt as if she could fly to her chamber but worked to keep her face calm. If her parents were content to sit back and do nothing, she would wield that torch and carry it for them. Someone had to.

Chapter Twelve

A nother week gone, and Maeve was pleased that Dain had not returned. Still, she had a feeling that he might. She hoped she'd have her new supply of rope before he decided to come back. She was more than capable of handling herself, but she didn't care to think about what she'd have to do if he tried something stupid.

In the meantime, she carried out her routine. She made two loaves of acorn bread and gathered more nuts for the next round. Springtime was in full swing, which meant rain nearly every night. This kept Rowan inside most of the time. He stayed behind when she went to the river at dawn for water, preferring the mostly dry and warm air inside her home. This morning, she was glad he hadn't accompanied her. At first, she was afraid more villagers had snuck out to the river, and she worried she'd see somebody she shouldn't when the surrounding brush jostled. Hastily, she retracted her water bucket only to discover a pair of water nymphs frolicking nearby.

Fae were immune to her powers, so she let herself gaze upon the fit petite forms of the nymphs. On land, their shapes resembled humans, except for their hair, which fell in gorgeous cascades down their backs. The blue water seemed to run like a waterfall, and the hypnotizing motion allured Maeve. She crept back a few feet, but the nymphs were caught up in each other as they danced along the opposite river bank, oblivious to her presence. Her eyes traced up their female forms, and Maeve bit her lip at the sensation that sprang up in her stomach when one of the nymphs turned, exposing her nude torso.

Embarrassed, Maeve looked away, but only for a second before cutting her gaze back to catch both nymphs giggling and disappearing behind the low-hanging leaves of a willow tree. Maeve stared at where they had been, continuing to imagine the nymphs and letting her mind wander. Then, she sighed and returned to her fen.

Days later, Maeve munched on one of the loaves of acorn bread for dinner. She had added a generous slab of cheese and, feeling frivolous, poured herself a cup of brandywine. Tucked snugly into her bed, she tossed a bite into her mouth, brushed off her fingers, and sipped contentedly while she browsed her well-worn Uterni text. Night had fallen, but she'd lit half a dozen candles scattered through her home. Those combined with the low fire in the hearth provided ample light.

Wound under the kitchen table, Rowan curled tighter, emitting a low hiss. Maeve looked up. "What is it?" She stilled, listening. An owl hooted, and the wind rustled the leaves outside. The rain had stopped an hour ago, and a faint drip fell from the outer edge of her roof onto the ground outside. Otherwise, she didn't hear anything. She met Rowan's gaze. "You're imagining things again," she told him. His tongue flickered, but she returned to her reading, pulling the blanket up around her knees.

She appreciated her companion snake, but sometimes, he was too vigilant. Like when he accompanied her to the river, he always seemed to be on edge, his body tight and ready to return as soon as her bucket was filled. She valued his keen sense of movement, but he could be entirely too uptight. If he were human, she imagined he would be somebody with wide eyes always darting around and fingers that constantly wrung together, worrying about each minute sound. She laughed at the image as Rowan rested his head atop his coils, staring at her.

She shook her head and took another drink. This time, a distant *snap* caught her attention. She paused, listening. Rowan hissed, and she held up a finger. *I don't want you to be right.* Nearly a minute passed, and there was no further noise. She exhaled, but a louder rustling broke through the brush outside.

"A deer, surely," she whispered as Rowan slithered forward, his head lifting as if to scan the higher ground he couldn't see. She stepped off her bed and crouched near the door. Her heart sank at the familiar sound of footsteps, more than she'd ever heard before.

Nightingales sang from their nests, and Maeve could hear the protest of her fen as the intruders approached. Branches snapped beneath heavy boots; the padded feet of animals scurried as they found their burrows; the fairy nest buzzed louder.

"Maybe it's just a group of children," she said, though the parched feeling in her throat told her that was wishful thinking. Quickly, she blew out all but one of the candles, leaving it on the table before moving to stand beside the window to the right of her door. She pressed her back and palms against the stone, her cheek resting on the wall as she listened.

"This is where the witch lives."

Gods. Dain.

There was a sound like several voices congratulating each other, and Maeve's spine pricked with anxiety when she tried to pinpoint how many people Dain had brought with him. She heard the familiar voice of the woman, high and loud. Swallowing, she crawled over to her bed and grabbed the same shard of glass she'd used to see outside before. Moving back to her standing position, she took a deep breath as the sounds grew closer. Then, she held up the glass and looked.

Maeve's stomach dropped. There were at least seven, maybe more, villagers standing just inside the edge of her fen. She found Dain, one of the tallest, standing at the front of the group. Half of them carried torches that threw shadows over their cloaks and faces. The same woman now gripped a staff, and two of the other villagers carried crossbows. Each wore a look like a rabid wolf that had just found its prey.

"Come out, witch!" Dain's words were echoed by the others, followed by raucous shouts and angry jeers.

Swiftly, she grabbed the rope and pulled, prompting the bells to clang. A few of the villagers shouted in surprise, but she grimaced when Dain called out to them. "It's merely a trick, a spell of the witch's conjuring."

More cries, then the woman called, "Let him go." Maeve's jaw clenched, and she re-scanned the glass. One of them had fled, but that still left more people to deal with than she cared for.

Dain kept the group on the edge of her fen, away from the chopping stump where her main snare lay. She had two others set up: one near her door and the other on the opposite side from where they stood, shouting at her home.

Rowan slithered up her leg, wrapping around her calf and knee. He hissed angrily. "Well, I don't know what to do, either." Maeve tried to keep her voice low, but when she checked the glass again, the group was now only twenty paces from her front door. They were laughing. One picked up a cauldron and chucked it toward her baskets of acorns, scattering her collection across the grass.

She stood, terrified. She'd never had to deal with this many people before. Her mother had prepared snares, showed her how to frighten away humans if they got too close. But the most they'd ever had to deal with was three, like the time when Dain had first appeared. She didn't understand him. Why was he so angry with her? Why did he insist on saying she was a witch?

"Maybe if I tell them I'm not, they'll leave me alone," Maeve said. Rowan gave his head a slight shake. "What other choice do I have?" Steeling herself, she stood closer to the window. Cupping her hands but keeping her eyes trained on the lone candle flickering atop the table, she shouted, "Please, leave me alone! I'm not a witch."

"Liar," one of the villagers called back.

She recognized Dain's voice next. "She snared me. She caught me to flay me alive and would have eaten me for breakfast if I hadn't escaped!"

"No," she shouted. "That's not true. I just want to be left alone."

"Only witches live alone."

"Now that simply can't be true," she said under her breath, grimacing to Rowan. Her heart was beating so fast, she clutched her chest in a fruitless effort to quell its rapid pace. Her breathing came quickly, then in short, harried bursts. Her chest felt tight. Gods, what was she going to do?

With a trembling hand, she held the shard up to see the group, now a mass of leering and looming shadows in the dark night. Dain's voice bellowed maliciously, "What do we do to witches in this kingdom?"

The woman sneered and shouted, "Burn her. Burn the witch!"

CHAPTER THIRTEEN

That evening, after dinner, Keeva bid good night to the court members lingering over another goblet of wine. Boisterous laughter filled the dining hall as minstrels began a song. She was in the hallway, mentally preparing for the excursion with Naela, when a strong hand grabbed her shoulder.

"Where are you off to in such a hurry?" asked Donovan before tossing a bite of candied apple into his mouth.

"Training."

"For what?"

"Whatever I want."

He laughed. "Fine. Keep this up, though, and your legs will be bigger than mine." He paused to admire his own.

She punched him in the bicep. "I can dream."

A lady of the court scampered around the corner, tripping on her dress. She simpered when she saw Donovan. "My lord, may we have the honor of your presence? The court is dying to hear the latest from Gultero."

He smiled genially. Out the side of his mouth, to Keeva, he said, "My latest letter from Etaina is an epic. I made the mistake of mentioning it to Tacari. Now, everybody wants to hear it."

"Have fun with that." She moved to go.

"Don't train too hard," he called, and she ignored his curious gaze trailing her.

Waving, she hurried to her room. She was passing her parents' chamber and noticed the door ajar. Slowing, she stood so the wall shielded her and leaned forward to peer inside.

Her father sat on the bed next to her mother. A maid replaced the bedpan while an alchemist Keeva recognized muttered something under his breath, his gray beard trembling with his chin as he handed her mother a vial. She turned her cheek at the remedy.

No, thought Keeva. Not yet. When her father took the vial and attempted to offer it, Keeva's heart sank when it was again refused. Her mother leaned back tiredly, her cheeks flushed and her hair matted to her forehead.

Disbelief burned until rage filled Keeva's fists. She clenched her jaw, unable to fathom her mother's unwillingness to try. *Very well. If you won't fight, I will fight for you.*

In her chamber, Keeva donned her travel cloak and checked the window overlooking the lower castle grounds and its surrounding walls. She waited until she saw the blue flame, Naela's signal. It was time.

They walked directly south, cutting through the village to the path leading to sparse woodland that eventually transformed to lush highland forest. Under a waxing moon, Keeva and Naela walked over large boulders, careful to avoid gnome hills, and wound between row after row of towering alpine. Their wide trunks were four times the size of them combined, with layers of strong branches hosting green needles that enveloped them in their heady scent.

Their saols accompanied them, each conjuring of spell-fire bobbing at their feet as they neared the border between the village and the wildlands. Here, the land dipped in a series of shallow ravines.

The bogs behind them, Keeva pulled her spell-fire into her palm, holding it out to better see in the dark night. "Which way do we go once we hit the river?" she asked.

Naela pulled out a scroll from her satchel and drew closer to use Keeva's saol to read the map. "I think we go right."

"You think?" An owl hooted, and she grimaced when it made her flinch.

"Well, that's what the map says. The grove of plums sits in the southeastern corner, about two miles on the other side of the river. We agreed that's our best option to find Epona." Naela scrutinized the map as Keeva scanned the dark wildlands.

She could hear the steady flow of the river ahead. Despite the darkness, she knew that the flora would soon become so overgrown on the opposite bank she might need the blade tucked in her boot to break through it. She wished she'd brought her spear. The moon shone bright, casting its glow over the land. A fairy nest buzzed sleepily twenty yards away. Otherwise, it seemed most creatures had found their dwellings. At least, she hoped they had. "Come on," she finally said. "We should keep moving."

Naela met her gaze as she tucked the scroll away. "Scared?" she teased.

"Hardly. I just know you need your beauty sleep. Don't want to keep you out too late."

"Very funny."

They continued. A wolf howled in the distance. Upon reaching the river, they paused ten yards from the water.

"Gods," Naela said. "I knew people sometimes left stuff here, but this is…"

"A lot."

For nearly fifty yards in either direction lay items strewn about that could have only come from the village. Old boots, broken wagon wheels, even a handful of old spears she recognized from the armory lay in forgotten heaps, some stuck under the muddy bank or floating listlessly in the water itself.

Naela walked closer, bending to grab something. "This isn't even very old." She held a shield, the strong wood painted in Uterni's colors. She ran one hand along the surface. "There's only a single crack. This could have easily been repaired."

Frowning, Keeva placed her hands on her hips. She couldn't believe the amount of goods before them. Her own people treated their possessions like this? Simply because they were worn or in need of repair?

"Think you should mention this to your parents?"

Keeva nodded. "First things first," she said, stepping carefully over a series of cauldrons, "we've got a gatekeeper to find. Come on."

A short while later, the sight of several lines of gooseberry bushes woke Keeva's spirits. They had to be getting closer to the groves. Naela had consulted the map several more times, though when she turned it sideways, Keeva's confidence dropped. Still, she had faith they could figure this out. They always did.

But when—an hour later—a twisted ash tree appeared before them and the same line of gooseberry shrubs stood at their right, Keeva stopped. "Naela..."

She sighed. "I know. I think we're lost."

"We've got to be close."

This time, Naela left the map in her satchel. She stared into the trees, searching. After a glance at the sky—broken pieces of dark blue between lines of tree limbs—she said, "Half a mile more. The grove has to be there."

A nightingale trilled as if to agree. Keeva glanced to her left as it took flight, diving from its nest and disappearing into shadow. Her saol swung around to follow her gaze. When it did, a flash of light in the distance caught her eye.

"Do you see that?"

Naela was scraping tree sap from the bottom of her boot when she looked up. "What?"

Keeva kept her eyes on the columns of trees. "A light. Like... torchlight?"

"A saol? Maybe somebody's foraging at the river."

"The river's behind us, Naela." Keeva turned, incredulous. "I thought you knew where we were going."

Naela shrugged and gave a sheepish smile. "I'm trying my best here."

A new noise broke the quiet night. It was followed by the unmistakable sound of angry voices. "I don't think those are foragers."

"Maybe they're squabbling over something?"

"Perhaps," she said.

Naela shook her head. Keeva recognized the expression of a jaded captain of the guard who was all too familiar with breaking up arguments. She motioned for Keeva to follow. The light flashed again. This time, it didn't dim, and was accompanied by the smell of smoke.

"Fire," Keeva said slowly, quietly. It took a moment for the word to register even in her mind. Turning, she met Naela's gaze before it widened to match her own. "Fire!"

They took off. Side by side, they flew through the dense forest, the soft grass lifting their feet and carrying them between the trees. Keeva tried to orient herself, but it proved useless. Instead, she focused on the growing light that seemed tucked behind a mass of dark green one-hundred yards ahead. When the ground sloped downward, Keeva faltered, flailing her arms to keep her balance. Naela handled the change in stride, racing ahead. The earth grew damp, and the trees hung low as if peering down to watch the new arrivals to this part of the wildlands.

Finally, breaking through a stretch of thorny bushes, they bounded out from behind a line of trees into a fen. A fen on fire.

Catching her breath, Keeva stood beside Naela, slack-jawed. Six people were gathered around a modest home sitting on the opposite side of the marshy clearing. Several small fires stretched skyward near them. A haphazard bonfire had been made, what looked like several baskets tossed into the flames. What might have once been a collection of poles hosting catches from a hunt and a pair of trees were also bright and crackling under hungry flames. A man in the middle of the group held a torch and was stalking toward the house.

"What are they doing?" Naela asked, breathless. They hadn't been noticed, standing below the dark shadows cast by the tall trees near the fen's edge at the base of the hill they'd descended.

"I've no idea." She met Naela's gaze, and they nodded, hurrying forward. Right before the flames from the man's torch could meet the ready wood of the home, Keeva shouted, "Stop."

Two of the group turned, their faces distorted in livid jeers. It was too dark to make out who they were at this distance, but she could see all of them wore Uterni colors. A woman standing near a chopping stump eyed them suspiciously. Keeva watched them from the dark rim of the fen. Simultaneously, she spotted a tankard of what she hoped was water sitting behind the corner of the home.

The woman shouted, "This is none of your concern."

"None of my concern?" They couldn't see her. They didn't know who she was. Naela's gasp reminded her of that. In unison, they stepped closer.

Save for the man still holding the torch, all of their faces dropped. "Your Majesty!" One even fell to his knees, sweaty forehead bolted to the damp earth at the sight of Naela in her guard's breastplate next to a member of the royal family.

"What is the meaning of this?" Keeva asked the man, whom she decided was their leader when the woman cut her gaze to him. Her own flickered to the fires that were growing, albeit slowly. Now that she was near the center of the fen, she realized that, like the heavy leaves and dew-covered grass, nearly everything was damp. She hoped the wood of the home was, too, in case this man decided to be stupid.

He spoke in a near whine, his tone indignant. "We're helping to rid the kingdom of a pest, Your Highness."

"By fire?"

"I see no better way."

"Why are you attacking this home?"

He sneered, then touched the end of the torch to the corner of the dwelling, singing the edges. "She doesn't belong here."

Keeva's throat went dry. "She...somebody is *in* there?" Her shout made all of them jump. Racing forward, Keeva shoved past the man to the front door. "Hello? Is somebody there?"

"I'm here." The woman's voice was timid.

"You need to leave. Your home..." Keeva said, glancing at the flames behind her as Naela grabbed a bucket of water and—shoving the man aside again—poured it onto the edge of the house. "It's not safe."

It was quiet for a second. "I can't."

"You can't?" Keeva didn't understand. Why wouldn't this woman simply walk out the door?

"She's afraid because she's guilty," the man said.

Naela, adding another slosh of water to the house, spun around. "I knew I recognized you. Dain Caba. You were arrested last year for breaking into the old widow's home."

He flinched at the recognition, stepping back. "This *thing* attacked me." He pointed at the home. "I'm only gaining my revenge."

The woman's voice came from inside, near an open window Keeva hadn't noticed. "I was defending myself from him. Please, I just want to be left in peace."

Confusion grew in Keeva. She saw it reflected in Naela's face as she said, "We don't burn people's homes down simply because we don't like them." Her voice was dubious. Meanwhile, taking this as an opportune moment, three members of the group ran for the border of the fen.

Keeva turned back to face Dain. After noting the fire on the house's edge had been extinguished, she pulled herself up. Doing so made her as tall as him, and she marched forward until she was in his face. "As your princess, I order you to stand down." This close, she could smell sweat and the dirt clinging to his tunic. She could see the red hairs sticking out of his chin and cheeks. His eyes were dark and wild. Keeva didn't blink. He sneered and after what seemed like an eternity, dropped the torch.

Naela reached into her satchel and pulled out a stretch of twine. Stepping behind Dain she said, "You're under arrest for arson and attempted murder."

"What?" He reared, but Naela was strong and held him in place. Tugging his arms behind him, she muttered a spell, and the twine wrapped itself around his wrists. "You can't do this," he barked.

"No," Keeva said. "You can't do *this*." She gestured to the fires still burning.

A rustling at the edges of the fen where they'd entered caught Keeva's eye. A burst of gold spell-fire broke through the trees, and the woman of the group was blown back into the fen. Two others tripped backward after her. A large figure strode through the trees, gold saol at his side.

"Donovan?" she and Naela said in unison.

He lugged a fourth ruffian under his arm. "Do these belong to you?"

Naela laughed as she pressed her knee into the back of Dain's leg, making him walk. "I'll handle this," she said and led Dain toward Donovan and the others cowering near the fen's edge. "Go see about that, Keevs." She nodded toward the circular home with the thatch roof, and Keeva saw the curiosity in her brow. The same curiosity that stirred within her.

Keeva stared at the front door that was slightly off-kilter on its hinges. Dozens of questions swirled in her mind as the fires crackled at her back. The woman hadn't spoken in a few minutes. Was she okay? Was she still in there? Perhaps she'd fled out the back. What had happened to make Dain so angry? Though, Keeva imagined, it probably didn't take much. Dain was the sad type of man who found fault in others when he didn't get his way. She stepped sideways toward the open window. Who was this woman? Why was she alone in the wildlands?

"It's all right," Keeva called, moving toward the window. The inside of the house was dim. A single candle seemed to be lit but nothing more.

Before she could stand in front of the window, the voice inside called in warning, "Don't."

"I'm sorry?"

"Please," the woman said. "Don't come any closer."

"I'm not going to hurt you."

It was quiet a moment. "I…just…thank you, for your help."

"You're welcome." Frowning, she tried to peer above the windowsill. An old curtain flapped, obstructing her view. "Is that water in that tankard back there? I need something to put the fires out."

More silence followed. She was beginning to wonder if this woman was all right. She'd just been attacked. Her house had been set afire. Maybe, Keeva reasoned, she was in shock.

A bucket of water appeared on the windowsill, balanced precariously. "You don't have to help," the woman said, still a faceless voice in the dark.

"I'm sure you could handle things," Keeva replied, trying to keep the sarcasm from her tone. There had just been six very angry people here, ready to burn this woman to the ground. She'd met some villagers whose families had died, leaving them alone. Over time, they'd been transformed into stubborn individuals, denying assistance, too lonely in their grief to accept help from anyone. Maybe this woman was like that. If she was alone. Keeva had no idea if there was anyone else inside as she took the bucket and dowsed the trees. The charred tree bark hissed in relief as smoke spiraled skyward. When she set the bucket atop the open window, she said, "I'm afraid those trees are lost. Along with the baskets they tossed into the other fire." She glanced back at the tall flames.

"Just leave it," the woman called. "I'll tend to it."

Again, the curtain fluttered. Keeva spotted the hearth, dull with embers. She thought she saw the woman inside, then realized it was only an old mirror and her own reflection.

"Are you sure?" she finally asked. Keeva didn't know if it was this woman's insistence on hiding or the soft tremble of her voice that drew her closer. She placed one hand on the windowsill. "I'm happy to stay and help you put things in order." She glanced to the other side of the fen. Donovan and Naela had all of the mob in custody. Dain still struggled while the woman shouted obscenities. When he realized she was watching him, Dain glared. It took her a moment to realize his gaze wasn't directed at her but at the home behind her.

Who is this woman?

Her hand felt cold. Jerking her head around, she found a long silver snake slithering across her knuckles. Screaming, she jumped back. The snake recoiled, lifting its head to hiss. "Gods!"

"Please," the woman said again from inside. "It's safer if you go. Thank you again for your help."

"I…" Keeva stared at the window. She was at a loss as the snake continued to hiss from his perch, one black eye watching her, warning her to stay away from the window. It was all so absurd, so surreal. "Very well," she finally said. She started to say something else but had no idea what she could say. *Be careful. Stay away from men like Dain.* None of it made sense. Stepping carefully back, Keeva gave the dark window one last look, hoping to catch a glimpse of the mysterious woman inside.

CHAPTER FOURTEEN

Maeve waited for the sound of retreating footsteps. Where Dain's group had burned her belongings, there was a resounding hiss, and she guessed the princess had found the only rainwater-filled cauldron that hadn't been kicked over.

The princess. Maeve's breath was still coming too quickly as she snatched up the glass shard she'd been too afraid to even look at before. She crept onto her bed and crouched below the window. With a trembling hand, she angled the glass and peered out into the night in time to catch the fading figure of the princess convening with a woman dressed in a guard uniform and a very large man leading Dain and his cronies away. She could just see their figures through the haze of smoke that had filled her fen now that the fires were extinguished. Between two of the gray clouds, the guard pushed Dain forward, moving back up the hill. Maeve's heart beat wildly, her limbs shaking from what had just happened. Her gaze lingered on the princess, a shadow with fierce magenta hair that stood out in the dark. Suddenly, she turned.

Maeve dove onto her bed. Only when the rustling of brush was followed by a solid minute of silence did she exhale. Still flat on her stomach, one cheek smashed awkwardly into her pillow, Maeve grimaced as Rowan slithered across her legs. He moved onto the floor and seemed to glare with one beady eye. Feeling ridiculous, though she wasn't sure why, Maeve sighed. "Don't give me that look."

Rolling over, she placed one hand on her heart. Her entire body vibrated with remnants of fear from Dain's attack. His fury echoed between the silent walls of her home. She'd never heard such rage from one man. All for what? He'd been ready to set her ablaze because she'd snared him? Could his pride truly be so fragile?

Closing her eyes, Maeve took a deep breath. She lowered her hands, resting both on her stomach. She felt her abdomen rise and fall as her nerves quelled their unrest. She'd been so frightened by Dain and his group. More than that, she'd been frightened of what she had thought, for a brief moment, she would have to do.

But she hadn't needed to. Somehow, for some reason, the princess had stumbled upon her fen at just the right moment.

"The princess." Her eyes fluttered open. The command in her voice had held such authority, its cadence quick and direct as Maeve had listened on the other side of the door. She'd been so taken aback by Dain's reproach, the stark contrast in the princess's words had left her reeling.

She faced Rowan, now coiled next to her bed with his head raised as if scanning for other intruders. "She probably thinks I'm mad." Replaying her stilted replies, how she had scrambled to shove the bucket of water out without being seen, how she'd forced the princess of Uterni to stay away. "Gods, maybe I am mad."

"How did you find us?" asked Keeva as she, Naela, and Donovan emerged at the top of the hill above the fen. Beside her, Naela pulled Dain along. He walked at the front of the chain of offenders Naela had strung together with the enchanted twine. Donovan kept his eyes on the woman of the group, who kept trying to light her saol to burn through the bindings.

"Naela asking about the fruit groves was a pretty big clue," he said over his shoulder.

Naela, a step ahead of him, shot him a look before meeting Keeva's gaze. "I was completely subtle, Keevs. Your brother has always been good at putting two and two together."

"More like one and one. Honestly, Keevs, did you really think I wouldn't see through the questions after your preposterous plan to find—"

"I get it," Keeva fired back. She didn't want to mention Epona in front of all of these villagers, even if they were half-dazed as they trudged forward. A royal seeking aid from any sort of magical being raised unnecessary questions. "Still," she said, stepping around a large boulder as mud stuck to her boots, "we got lost. How'd you know where we were?"

"I followed you to the river," he said. "I lost your tracks near some gooseberry bushes but saw the smoke."

Keeva knew his instincts were the same as hers. Their parents had instilled the importance of helping others in both of them from a young age. As children, they'd stood with their parents in the market, helping clean the mudslide debris that had filled the streets after a torrential storm had destroyed many of the vendors' livelihoods. They'd been some of the first ones on scene when three village children had fallen into the bog. Keeva, Donovan, and their father had helped the families use ladders, spears, and ropes to rescue them before they could succumb to the merciless and murky depths. They knew their kingdom was only as good as its leaders. Keeva had never been afraid to step in and lend a hand. It was something she and her family excelled at.

Now, conflicting emotions whirled where her pride resided. Keeva's plans always worked out. Disappointment was heavy after they hadn't found Epona. Yet, she was glad they'd been able to diffuse what might have been a terrible tragedy.

Falling a few steps behind, Keeva trailed at the back of their group. Naela and Donovan conversed as they approached the trackway that led to royal grounds. The woman of the group skidded to a halt at sight of the castle. "Where are you taking us?"

"I thought that was obvious," Naela replied, leading them to the western entrance. The moon was still high. Outside of the dense wildlands, Keeva could see the frightened look in the woman's eyes. The others kept their heads down while Dain stared straight ahead. "You're all spending the night in the dungeon."

At the gate, Donovan motioned for the guards to open the doors.

"Maybe you'll decide to share why you attacked that fen," Keeva said, her thoughts circling back to the lone dwelling nestled deep in the wildlands.

Dain didn't even look at her when he replied, "I already told you. I was gaining my revenge."

Inside the castle hallway, Keeva lowered her hood and shook her head. "Perhaps a night in the dungeon will help you elaborate."

"I'll take them downstairs," Naela said, turning to Keeva. They stood at a junction in the hall, a set of stairs to the left and a passage leading to the main hall on the right.

Keeva nodded. Donovan, who had an impressed look on his face as he watched Naela lead Dain and his group away, said, "Quite the night. We'll have to report this to Mother and Father in the morning."

"Report what to your mother and father?"

Keeva turned. Tacari stood behind her. He yawned, blinking tiredly before glancing between both of them.

"Tacari," she said, "you're up late."

"I was meeting with your father. He was going over correspondence from Gultero." Exchanging looks with Donovan, Keeva nodded. Another sleepless night for their father wasn't unusual. Anything to keep busy. "Now," Tacari said, his ears twitching in the direction of the stairs where Naela descended, "care to fill me in on why the captain of the guard has six villagers in custody?"

It was dawn by the time Keeva returned to her chamber. Donovan had helped cover for her, explaining that they'd all ventured to the river after discovering villagers were using the land as a dumping ground. This led them to the discovery of the fen on fire.

"You decided to do this in the middle of the night?" Tacari had asked, his dubious gaze flitting between them in the secluded passageway near the royal chambers.

"I was up anyway," Keeva replied. "So, it seems, were you."

"Keeva, it's unwise to travel so deep into the wildlands at night."

"Naela was with me. And Donovan," she added. Her brother leaned against the wall and nodded.

"So both royal children decided to venture, without notice, away from the castle in the dead of night."

"Come now, Tacari," Donovan said, his arms crossed. "You know we're completely capable of handling ourselves. Your defense training has equipped us well."

Ignoring this, Tacari continued. "What if something had happened once you were in the fen?" He eyed Keeva, his dark gaze flickering like the torchlight.

"Naela was with us," she repeated. "We were fine."

"The captain of the guard may be too loyal to her monarchs," he grumbled, cutting his gaze to Donovan, who stood straighter at this remark.

"Tacari, I respect your opinion, but Naela was doing her job. If we hadn't gone out there, the fen could have been lost to fire. It may be the wildlands, but it's close enough to Uterni to warrant protection. Hundreds of fae call it home."

Tacari's nose twitched as he seemed to contemplate this. "As the magistrate, I cannot condone this behavior. You two are the prince and princess of Uterni," he said, emphasizing their titles in a scolding voice, "you cannot be so reckless."

Keeva opened her mouth to protest; he was reprimanding them like when they were children.

He continued before she could speak. "However, as your friend, I am pleased to know you seemed to be in the right place at the right time. Come, we need to tell your father about this."

Their father only half listened to their tale. Keeva recognized his mindset when they'd found him in the study chamber. His sleep tunic was disheveled as he sat behind his desk, several half-eaten turkey legs strewn between goblets of wine and layers of unfurled scrolls.

"Yes. Yes. River cleanup. Very good, sweetheart," he'd said to her, not even looking up. "Good work, both of you."

That had been it. Tacari seemed a little disappointed there was no reprimanding, but the issue wasn't pushed. Now, exhausted and sprawled on her bed, Keeva let the night's events wash over her. She lit her saol, rolling the warm spell-fire between her palms above her chest. Torches on the wall filled her chamber with light, and she shivered as the chill from the night lingered on her shoulders. The complete upheaval of her initial plans wasn't something she was familiar with. She'd had every intention of finding Epona. It had been more difficult than she'd thought to navigate the wildlands.

"Guess I should actually look at a few of those maps next time." She stared into the magenta flames bouncing between her fingers. Her saol flickered hotly as she accepted her failure to find the gatekeeper, thus failing to help her mother. As she watched the flames, though, her thoughts shifted back to the fen. She'd traveled around Uterni often but wasn't familiar with the wildlands the way she was the rocky bluffs and marshy bogs. Now that she'd been in the fen, Keeva couldn't stop thinking about it. It was like when Keeva had first discovered the truth to a minstrel's illusion; all she could see after the discovery was the sleight of hand, the trick maneuver used to make her look the other way.

Knowing the fen existed, knowing there was a woman down there, seemingly all alone, filled her vision.

Her spell-fire split itself in her palms. In her left, she saw flashes of green still trapped in memories of the fen. In the other, a guilty crackle at her inability to fulfill her quest to meet Epona.

Frustrated, Keeva extinguished her saol and rolled over, hugging the pillow beneath her chin. She would have to try again. She needed to find the gatekeeper and speak to her. The image of her mother refusing the apothecary's medicine flashed in her mind. At the same time, the voice of the woman in the fen echoed.

"Stay focused, Keeva," she told herself. But how? She felt everything bubbling to a point in her chest: her mother's health, her responsibilities as princess, the unease left behind by the elf queen, and now, the events of tonight.

She rolled onto her back. She was useless like this. She could feel herself falling closer to the point of being overcome, paralyzed by the seemingly endless list of demands as it sprang up before her. She felt its long legs begin to crush her beneath the weight of responsibility. Her breath came faster. Her chest was too tight.

Glancing at the window, she said, "I've got time before breakfast." Standing, Keeva splashed her face with water, took a long breath, then headed for the armory.

❖

The next morning, Maeve woke after only a few hours of sleep. Last night's incident kept repeating in her mind and continued to do so as she groggily rose and munched on acorn bread. She thought about the princess as she lit the hearth. Maeve heard her asking, "Are you okay?" again and again. No one had asked her that, or anything, in years.

Tugging on her boots, Maeve stood in front of her open doorway to scan the aftermath of Dain's attack. To her left, the pair of birch trees were now scorched pillars, the lower branches of leaves shriveled. Where the tallest fire had been started near the center of the fen was now charred earth. Pieces of basket lay strewn among the smoldering embers, only small fragments left behind. Rowan slithered past, and she noticed the corner of her home where Dain had set his torch. The wood frame of the base where the first boulders rested was blackened, but it looked as if the guard had managed to put it out before real damage could be done.

"What would we have done without them, Rowan?"

He wound loosely around the chopping stump ten paces ahead and hissed.

"Well, I didn't see you doing much to stop them." She smiled, and he flicked his tongue in response. Hands on her hips, she glanced dejectedly at the poles where her trapping catches had hung. All that remained were the burned tree limbs lying in a mangled heap. "Looks like we won't be having rabbit stew for a few days."

Later, she had just returned from the river with the day's water when a basket—carried by the black raven—landed near her door. Glancing up, she caught the bird swooping back up before it dove into the tall branches of an oak. Rowan was already draped over the basket's handle, peering inside. She shooed him off.

"Good, we can make more snares," she said, picking up one grouping of knotted rope, the splintered twine rough in her hand. "Though, a little late," she muttered. "But maybe even more essential now." She moved aside two bundles of bright red apples and a clay jar of flaxseed to find the Caretaker's letter.

Placing the basket at her feet, she took a seat on the chopping stump to read under the dim sunlight.

M—

I've sent more rope. Do keep an eye on your snares; one can never be too careful.

Try not to linger anywhere. Your safety is crucial.

She turned the parchment over, searching for the rest of the note but found none. Frowning, she reread the last part: "Try not to linger anywhere." Was he referring to the day she'd stayed at the river after fetching water? The moments she'd spent watching the nymphs at play? No, she reminded herself, he couldn't possibly know that. The Caretaker lived in the Mountains of Ionad, miles away. He'd told her of his home in detail when these letters first started. Back when she wasn't afraid to ask questions. Before she learned questions often led to answers she didn't care for or sometimes no answers at all.

He was simply being his wary self. Though, Maeve noted, it had been a while since she'd received any stern word of caution from him.

She spent the rest of the day cleaning up her fen and contemplating whether or not to mention Dain in her response. Mulling over the decision with some bites of bread that evening, Maeve stared into the hearth that was burning bright in what was a wonderfully peaceful evening.

"I don't want to worry him," she said to Rowan who was curled in the chair next to her. "He likes to know what's going on. He may already know," she said, recalling Dain and his thugs being escorted away by the princess and her companions. If a member of the royal family had been involved, it was likely news of the incident would spread quickly. "Better he hears it from me first," she decided, wiping crumbs from her fingers and rummaging for her quill. On a stray bit of parchment, she wrote:

Thank you for the rope. It will help assure my snares are primed. Regarding security, I should recount a rather harrowing occurrence.

She went on to describe Dain and his followers, excluding the part where he got close enough to set a torch to her home. Only when she'd finished the letter, setting it aside until she would send it with the raven tomorrow, did Maeve realize her most vivid details enclosed were those pertaining to the princess: her commanding presence, her willingness to help, the sincere tone her voice took on when she'd asked after Maeve. She reasoned such rich recall made sense; royals were impressive individuals, according to her texts. The Caretaker would understand the impression left upon her.

As she lay in bed that night, Maeve closed her eyes and once again replayed her interaction with the princess. She'd only been able to see shadows and flashes of figures, but Maeve imagined her clearly. She was tall and strong and kind. A sensation stirred below her stomach, and Maeve turned on her side, wrapping one arm around herself.

It was probably because she'd had so few conversations in her life that she was holding so tightly to this one. Since her mother had left, she'd only ever spoken with a handful of fae: occasionally with a fairy who lived nearby and once with a pair of gnomes who had gotten lost on their way home. She was always too shy to speak to the nymphs.

The few interactions in her life had, thus far, made her home in on the one with the princess. Though, unlike the others, the princess's voice filled her mind continuously.

A crackle from the hearth scattered her musings. Maeve fell back from the clouds as reality struck her. She'd probably never see the princess again. What need did she have to return? Dain was gone. The situation had been handled.

In place of her dreams crept the gray longing she'd become familiar with of late. "Even if she did return, I couldn't…" Her gaze searched the tattered thatch of the ceiling. "It's only another impossibility." She rolled onto her side, clutching her knees to her chest. Sniffling, she blew out the candle by her bedside, clinging in vain to the improbability of one more unattainable wish.

CHAPTER FIFTEEN

"Y ou look awful." Naela spoke low as she took a seat next to Keeva in the crowded dining hall the next morning.

"Couldn't sleep." Keeva rolled her shoulders and reached skyward in a stretch. She noticed one of the ladies of the court gawk at the defining line in her forearm.

Naela raised a brow but didn't comment on the obvious fact that she'd spent the few hours between their return and breakfast in another training session. She took a drink of pear juice, then said, "Well, I went to speak with Dain at dawn. He didn't give me much. Called the woman he attacked a witch but didn't say what she'd done to provoke him. Kept insisting he was 'gaining his revenge,' which I told him wasn't helping his situation."

"What about the others, did they have any insight?"

"No. I thought the woman would give him up, but she's loyal. They all are." She shrugged. "I'm sure they follow him into trouble all the time, no questions asked."

Keeva yawned, and they ate in silence for a time, the only sounds coming from the court members scattered about the room. The men, women, and fae conversed jovially while a soft tune played from the corner near a fireplace where a blue-skinned nymph plucked a harp.

"When do you want to try again?"

Keeva met Naela's gaze. "Soon." She glanced at where Tacari was talking to Naela's parents at the head of the table. Lowering her voice, she said, "We need to be more prepared. Can you bring me some of the maps you looked at?"

"I can bring them by tonight."

"Good."

"How's your mother this morning?" Naela threw her gaze to the empty, high-backed chair at the end of the long table.

Keeva recalled the image of her mother surrounded by doting staff members when she'd passed by her chamber on her way here. "She's eating, which is good. But it's another day of meetings from her quarters."

Naela nodded. When Keeva remained quiet, she asked, "Where's your mind?"

Keeva stared at the platter of grapes and goat cheese next to her empty plate. She'd been thinking about the fen. The sparring session with a guard hours before had done little to push the mysterious woman from her mind. "I was just thinking about last night," she finally said.

"Bizarre, wasn't it?" Naela leaned back in her seat. "Dain's had several prior offenses, so I'm not surprised by his behavior. Probably thought nobody would find his dirty work way out there."

"Aren't you curious," Keeva asked slowly, playing with the bracelets on her wrist, "about who she is?"

Naela shrugged. "Maybe a former romance of Dain's? He could have been angry she refused him."

"Really?"

"No idea, Keevs. Whoever she is, she clearly wants to be left alone. Who else would live out there? I knew a swamp witch like that once. I tried to do a courtesy check two summers ago. She ran me out of her meadow with a broom."

Chuckling, Keeva sipped from her goblet. Maybe Naela was right; the woman had been incredibly aloof. She wouldn't even open the door. It was probably better to let it be. Still…the fear in the woman's voice was different. There was something else behind it.

"I'm going to organize a group for a river cleanup," Keeva said, an idea forming.

"Now?" Naela's brow knit. She leaned forward. "I thought Epona was our priority?"

"She is, but you saw how disgraceful the river looked. I can't see something like that and ignore it. What kind of princess would I be?"

Naela eyed her but sat back. "All right. But maybe ask Donovan for help on that one." She tugged up her tunic sleeves, revealing several red welts on her elbows and forearms. "The insects out there are a menace."

"Fine," Keeva said, laughing. "See if you can get more from Dain. There's more to his attack then he's letting on.

"I will."

❖

"What do you think?" Maeve held up the half-made basket she was weaving. Her fingers were pricked with splinters from the strips of tree bark she'd gathered and had been braiding together for the last two hours. Rowan was sunbathing under the midmorning sun behind a partly cloudy sky. Spread out on a large boulder, he blinked lazily.

"I think it's rather good," she said, shaking out the cramp beginning to form in her hand. Nearby, one of the burned branches of oak fell with a resounding *whoosh* to the ground. Maeve jumped and stared at the sad image. It was another reminder of what had happened. Dain had left his mark all around the fen: the scorched trees, the burned corner of her home, and in her need to weave a new basket. She'd already repurposed the one from the Caretaker, filling it with a new batch of acorns. It had left the raven cawing when she'd refused to pass it back for his return flight. On the whole, she'd managed to clean up most of the damage Dain had inflicted. Everything was once again in its proper place, the cauldrons righted, the trappings pole rebuilt and hosting a single, scrawny hare, and an extra snare ready and laid out, just in case.

Maeve dropped the basket between her legs and leaned back. She basked in the sunny patch of thick grass where she sat near the chopping stump. She craned her neck, taking in the warmth of the calm day. Rowan gave a soft, content hiss.

"Care to take a turn?" she asked, nodding to her project for the day. He coiled tighter, staring. "You're right, that was unfair. You haven't any thumbs."

He flicked his tongue as she laughed, but her laughter was cut short when a rustling beyond the nearby fairy nest caught her ear. She froze, listening.

A light but determined tread strode less than a quarter mile away, accompanied by the unmistakable sound of somebody fighting their way through the brush. Carefully, Maeve stood. Her eyes found the scattering of broad-faced leaves that covered her new snare. She'd run the rope from the towering oak tree, the one where her bells hung. The hidden loop lay on the ground, waiting for unsuspecting feet.

She swallowed and took several steps backward. Rowan darted closer, his lithe body swimming through the grass. There was a sound like a blade cutting through vines. "Dain." Maeve couldn't risk it. What if he was back to carry out whatever awful act he'd been unable to complete?

Spinning around, she tripped over her basket. She pushed herself up and hurried inside.

A voice called from the eastern edge of the fen, "Wait."

For a second, Maeve faltered. *It couldn't be.* She rushed through the doorway, Rowan diving in behind her. She slammed the door shut, panting as she leaned back against the old wood. Frantically, she searched for something to protect herself. The snares and warning bells didn't seem enough. Quickly, she pulled the curtains over her windows before rushing around the small space of her home. In doing so, she rammed into the corner of her kitchen table, toppling several dishes as a sharp pain ran through her hip.

She grimaced, limping awkwardly to brace herself against the table's edge. She spotted a pestle near the water basin, flaxseed crumbs still stuck to the end. She snatched it up and crouched in front of the door.

Only when her breathing slowed did she realize the hurried breath wasn't her own. She leaned one ear against the wood, listening.

"Hello?"

Maeve shot back. Falling onto her backside, she stared up at the door. Panic shot down her spine when she noticed the wooden block that served as her lock wasn't in place. She met Rowan's gaze from his perch on the bed. He was coiled tight, his head raised, listening, too.

Again, the voice outside spoke. "I…I wanted to know if you were all right…after the other night."

Surely, Maeve was dreaming. She stared at the pestle in her sweaty palm.

"My name is Keeva Glantor."

Glantor. Maeve knew that name. On her knees, she dropped the pestle and scurried to grab the kingdom's text from her bedside table.

With trembling fingers, she found the section on the royal family. It was outdated; "Keeva" wasn't listed.

She closed the book and stared at the door. It took her a moment to remember what the princess, Keeva, had said initially.

"Thank you, but I'm fine."

There was silence for a time. Maeve tracked the princess's footsteps as she seemed to move closer to the window above the bed. "Dain is in the dungeons. He's being questioned about what he did. Or what he tried to do."

Maeve could hear the intrigue in her tone. Not knowing how to respond, she moved to kneel, her gaze bouncing between the window and the door.

"It was a lot, I can imagine. What he did. Is there anything you need? Anything I can do?" Keeva's voice faded momentarily, and Maeve knew she must have turned to observe the fen. "I see you've cleaned up most of it."

"I can handle myself."

"So I see."

Was that a smile in her voice? Maeve wiped the slick perspiration from her forehead. She felt hot, her nerves worked into a knot in her stomach. She adjusted the handkerchief as several strands of hair stuck to the back of her neck. At the same time, she felt a new, pleasant stirring in the back of her mind at this interaction.

"Please, what is your name?" asked Keeva.

Rowan hissed. Maeve matched his wide-eyed look.

"As the princess, I make it my business to know my people."

"This isn't part of Uterni," Maeve said, standing slowly.

"True. But the river near here is. It's your water source, is it not?"

"It is." Rowan hissed again. He was right; she shouldn't have admitted that. What if she was accused of stealing kingdom resources?

"Fae live all over these lands," Keeva continued. "Some are still hesitant to immerse themselves fully in village life."

Again, Maeve could hear the question in her voice. She was trying to figure out who Maeve was. She closed her eyes. She heard her mother's words of warning: "You must never let anybody in. It's too dangerous. You are safer alone."

Biting her lip, she opened her eyes and swept her gaze over the house she'd shared with her mother. She lingered on the hearth, on the loaves of bread stacked on the table. She found the dusty chair, her mother's chair. Her mother, who had kept her safe, who had taught her what she needed to do in order to survive. Her mother, who was gone and had been for years.

She looked at her worn boots. She opened her palms, staring at the callouses from endless chores. She swiped them on her pants, trying to wipe away the pain of being left alone for so long.

Turning, Maeve leaned her right shoulder on the old wood of the door. The pressure opened a valve, the one that kept her longings at bay. She took a deep breath.

"My name," she said slowly, "is Maeve."

Chapter Sixteen

*M*aeve.

Keeva stood outside her humble dwelling in the fen. The tattered, faded red curtain flapped in a quick breeze in the small window to her right. The movement teased her, beckoning her gaze while unwilling to reveal the woman inside.

"Maeve," she said, watching the door, expecting it to open any moment. "Are you certain you're all right? If you would step outside so I can know," she said, squinting at the tiny space near the jamb where the door sat off-kilter. "I would like to see for myself."

Keeva scanned the fen, taking in the incredibly lush lowland with grass that came to her shins. She brushed off some of the damp leaves that stuck to her tunic and pants from her earlier efforts to maneuver through the thick trees and bushes that lined this marshy lowland. She examined the boulders stacked tightly within the walls of Maeve's home. The green from the ground had climbed up nearly the entire height, moss and lichen crawling over layers of gray rocks to claim it as part of the fen. The thatched roof looked sturdy but old. How long had this woman been here?

Maeve's voice interrupted her thoughts. "Thank you for coming. Your people have a kind princess."

Keeva placed her hands on her hips, perplexed by the words and the door remaining closed. She didn't understand why Maeve was being so obstinate about hiding. Nor was she accustomed to her requests being ignored. A distant shout came from the river. Donovan must have noticed she was gone. She'd recruited a small group of guards to begin sorting through the rubbish of the river. Donovan, as she'd expected, had taken on the role as organizer eagerly. They had started to clear debris from the water when she'd slipped away.

Now, knowing she didn't have long before Donovan found her, she asked, "Is somebody in there with you? Why do you keep yourself inside?"

"I'm alone," Maeve replied. Keeva stepped toward the window again. When she did, a low hiss sounded from inside. "Well, Rowan is here."

"Rowan?"

A large silver snake slithered out the window, gliding over the sill and down the wall. It was the same one from the other night.

"Gods." Keeva leapt back. Her saol sprang to life in her right hand, her knuckles recalling the cold scales. The snake coiled in front of the door. It raised its head, its neck a menacing S while it continued to hiss.

"That's Rowan," Maeve explained from inside.

Keeping her eyes on the snake, Keeva asked, "You live with a snake?"

"Yes," the woman said matter-of-factly.

Keeva shook her head. This entire situation was becoming more befuddling by the minute. "Why don't you come out?" Maybe, she thought, there was some sort of curse or spell keeping Maeve from leaving.

"I can't."

Then, Keeva remembered what Naela had said about Dain's questioning. "You know," she said, trying to keep her voice even as the snake's gleaming skin shimmered intimidatingly, "Dain said you were a witch. Did you do something to him? Did a spell backfire?"

"I'm not a witch."

The snake, Rowan, sat posed, ready.

Frustrated, Keeva extinguished her spell-fire and held her hands up, though she knew how absurd it was to believe the snake would interpret this as meaning no harm. To her surprise, though, he lowered his head and quelled his hissing. "Tell me who you are, then."

"I told you my name."

"Why are you here? Why are you alone?" The snake hissed. "Pardon me. Why are you with your…companion snake?" A soft chuckle came from the other side of the door. Keeva smiled. "It's not every day you stumble upon a woman with a guardian as fierce as this." The snake tilted his head. "Perhaps you're a goddess."

Another laugh. Sensing an opening, Keeva stepped closer. The snake, evidently matching Maeve's change of demeanor inside, slithered aside before moving back up the wall and disappearing through the window.

"I'm not a goddess," Maeve finally replied.

"Please," Keeva said, "why don't you open the door?"

"I can't," she repeated.

The resignation in her voice made Keeva pause. She reached out, pressing against the door. Hesitating a moment, she pushed gently but had hardly done so when there was a flurry of movement on the other side of the door, then a sound like Maeve had thrown herself against it.

"Don't."

Keeva pulled back her hand. "I'm sorry. I just...I don't understand."

"I can't open the door."

"Why?"

"It's too dangerous."

"What does that mean?" Keeva pressed her ear closer. She thought she heard Maeve take a deep breath, as if whatever she was to say next took every ounce of her being. Meanwhile, the heavy tread of Donovan's steps drew near.

"I can't open the door for you. I can't open it for anyone."

"Why?"

"Keevs?" Donovan's shout was just on the other side of the trees.

She pressed her palm to the door. "Please. You can tell me."

"I can't open the door because..." Maeve's voice shrank; she must've heard Donovan, too.

"Why?"

"Because I'm a gorgon."

Clamoring through the brush, Donovan called. "Keeva. What are you doing?"

She ignored the question. She didn't meet what she knew was his incredulous gaze. All she could do was stare at the door in disbelief.

Maeve's voice was sad when she said quietly, "It was nice to meet you, Princess."

Chapter Seventeen

Maeve pressed her forehead to the door, listening to the conversation outside.

"Donovan, why aren't you with the group?"

"Why aren't you? I turn around, and you've vanished." The man's voice was slightly deeper than Keeva's. It held a similar cadence, and Maeve noticed how they seemed to know exactly what the other would say. Their dialogue came quick and sharp, like flames sparring on a log.

"I realized we were near the fen," Keeva said. "I was following up."

The man, Donovan, lowered his voice. "Is anyone home?"

Maeve held her breath.

"No," Keeva said. "No one's home."

"Well, then, I've no idea why you're still here. Send a message or something when we get home."

"Right, good idea."

Maeve listened to their retreating steps. She crept onto her bed, grabbing the mirror shard. With one hand, she held the curtain, her back to the open air. Raising the glass, she glimpsed the retreating figures of Keeva and Donovan. Both were incredibly strong-looking, their muscular arms evident beneath the tight material of their tunics. Maeve's gaze lingered on Keeva. She took in her profile when she turned to say something. Keeva's small nose and pointed chin reminded Maeve of a fairy's features. The line of Keeva's jaw drew the gaze to her pink lips. Though she couldn't hear what was said, Maeve was entranced at the movement of her mouth.

Rowan slithered across the back of her calves. Yelping, she dropped the glass. "Rowan!"

He eyed her. Hurriedly resuming her stance, she found that Keeva and Donovan had gone. After sliding down the wall, she fell onto the bed. She glared at Rowan, then frowned at the fact that he had startled her. She couldn't recall the last time that had happened. Keeva's presence had acted as a lure, a siren's song that had drawn her in until her surroundings had melted into a soft mist.

Rowan hissed, then curled around her leg. His cool scales scattered the lingering mist in her mind, dragging her back to the present. The feeling left a hollow pit in her stomach as she recalled a time, long ago, when she'd been shaken from another such moment:

"Eyes on your handiwork. You don't want uneven seams."

"Yes, Mother." Maeve concentrated on the needle and thread she pulled through the coarse brown fabric of the tunic she was mending. She kept her gaze on the needle as it pricked the material, her seven-year-old fingers very aware of its sharp point.

"Very good," her mother said.

Maeve kept her chin down but glanced across the room. Her mother stood on the other side of the kitchen table. Her blond hair hung down her back in a single braid. Her handkerchief kept unruly strands back from her tall forehead as she used their only knife to slice a red apple into thin, nearly translucent strips. Afterward, she poked a single hole into the center of each piece. Then, she ran a long twine through each hole, stringing the apple pieces one by one.

Maeve tugged the thread through its final stitching, her tongue sticking out as she held up the tunic to admire her work.

"Very good, sweetheart," her mother said before hanging the strips of apple across the top of the hearth where it would dry out overnight. The fruit glistened over the flames. Pleased, Maeve kicked out her feet, her toes hardly brushing the floor. "What should we make next?" her mother asked, returning to the table. "Plum or strawberry leathers?"

"Plum! It's my favorite."

"Plum it is." Her mother smiled, turning to scrounge through the clutter that covered their table. Maeve licked her lips, imagining the sweet puree they would bake before the fire. She was rolling up the extra thread she hadn't needed when her mother asked, "Maeve, what's this?" From under a pile of cloth, she pulled out a pair of woven crowns.

Maeve gulped as her mother held one in each hand, facing her. "I...I made them."

"I can see that."

Maeve had forgotten about them. She'd used a combination of river reeds and vines from the fen's border to weave a circle that sat perfectly atop her head. "Do you like them?" she asked meekly.

Her mother's silver gaze seemed to analyze the crowns. "They're lovely. But why are there two? This one won't fit me," she added before smiling, though her gaze was questioning.

Maeve pushed herself back in her chair. "I made one for me and one for...my friend."

Her mother didn't blink. Firelight from the hearth made her fair face glow red-orange, her skin seeming to blaze. "Your...friend?"

Maeve felt small, as if the room had expanded with her mother's fearful gaze. "Yes."

"Who is your friend?" Her mother's eyes flickered to the door, then the windows. Too afraid she'd done something to upset her, Maeve shook her head, shrinking more in her seat. "Maeve." Her mother's voice took on a hard edge. "Who did you make this for?"

"Nobody."

"But you said—"

"My friend. My future friend."

Her mother's hands lowered. Part of the crowns had twisted in her grip. "You haven't met this friend?"

Maeve shook her head. "Not yet."

Her mother's exhale was long and slow. She moved both crowns to her left hand, wiping her forehead with the other. She muttered something Maeve couldn't hear before moving to crouch before her. "Darling, where did you get this idea? This future friend?"

Maeve squirmed in her seat, but her insides eased their unrest at the gentle tone of her mother's voice. "I saw it in a book." At her mother's raised brow, she explained, "It said that when the poor villager married the princess, they both wore crowns. Theirs were made of...of golden rays and silk. I didn't have those things, so I used something different." She stared at her mother, whose eyes seemed to search hers.

"What book told you this story?"

Maeve pointed, leading her mother to a dark corner under the bed.

"Where did you get this?" she asked after finding the book Maeve had hidden. Its waterlogged cover fell open in her grasp as she scanned the first page.

Maeve stammered. "I found it near the river."

Her mother's gaze flew to her. Maeve wasn't allowed to go to the river on her own. It was a rule. One of many that constricted their lives. Now, Maeve could hear the questions. Her mother didn't need to say them. They shouted at her in the silence.

Turning the book over, her mother said, "It's an old tale from the East."

Maeve sat up. She'd clutched her knees to her chest but relaxed the grip she had on her legs. "The East?" She yearned to know more about other places. Anywhere that wasn't the fen she was confined to each day of her life.

"Yes," her mother said. She stood slowly. "I wish you hadn't found this."

Confused, Maeve watched her mother walk to the hearth where the fire burned. She ran a finger down the book's spine. Then, Maeve gasped when her mother threw it into the flames.

"No!"

"I'm sorry." Her mother's eyes gleamed, transfixed on the pages that blackened and curled. Maeve hurried over to see the words she'd escaped into vanish, consumed by smoke and fire. "I know it's difficult to understand," her mother said as they stood watching the book's binding crackle. Maeve cried, tears blurring her vision. "I don't want you to believe in a life that we can never have." Her mother turned and knelt, facing Maeve. "It's unfair. I know." With one finger, she smoothed Maeve's hair, running it down the length of the tresses. "We aren't like everyone else. Friendship. Companionship." She reached for one of the crowns, holding it between them. "We can never have those things."

Maeve was sniveling, her breath choppy as she struggled to control her sobs.

"It's better you understand that now." She grabbed Maeve's shoulders, making her meet her gaze. "It's too dangerous. Relationships with anyone are impossible." Her mother glanced over her shoulder into the flames. A look Maeve didn't understand fell over her face. "You don't want to hurt anybody, do you?"

Maeve shook her head.

Her mother looked at her again, her gaze softening. "And I don't want anyone to hurt you." She pulled Maeve into a hug. "I'm sorry. This is how it's always been. It's how it has to be."

Maeve nodded, returning the hug, even though she didn't understand. She hadn't understood the extent of her mother's words. She hadn't understood the crushing despair that awaited Maeve as she grew older. *In that moment, Maeve could only stand in the safety of her mother's arms, watching the story that could never be succumb to ashes.*

Presently, Maeve dug her palms into her eyes until bursts of light filled her vision. A nearly forgotten idea surged forward: bringing new gorgon life into the world. She hadn't thought about doing such a thing in years. Understanding the loneliness her mother had likely felt that had driven her to create Maeve was unrelenting. Nevertheless, Maeve had sworn she would never subject another gorgon to the life she's had to live.

She squeezed her eyes tighter to chase away the idea of Keeva. Because her mother was right; she couldn't be with anyone. That was how it had always been, and that was how it was supposed to be.

CHAPTER EIGHTEEN

Y ou owe me, Keevs." Donovan shook the final guard's hand, thanking him for his assistance at the river. They had sorted a large section of the discarded goods based on material that could be repurposed versus the items that were truly unsalvageable.

Guards marched into the castle near the main gate. The early evening sky was bright pink with lines of purple framing the first stars overhead.

"Owe you for what?" Keeva asked, her gaze turning to the tall pines marking the start of the wildlands.

"For carrying the river cleanup, to start. It was your idea. 'Princess Keeva cleans up Uterni,'" he said, waving a hand across the sky as if his words were written there. "You neglected to mention you'd be present only in body."

"We did good work, didn't we?" she countered, turning and shoving him along.

"Thanks to the activities supervisor." He lifted his chin, grinning.

"You're insufferable."

"One of us has to be." Inside, they shed their cloaks when a maiden and a page appeared to collect them. "Are you going to write that woman?" asked Donovan.

"What?"

"The woman. The one who wasn't home."

"Oh, right." Keeva rubbed her thumb over her forefingers, remembering the feel of the old wood in Maeve's door. "I should, shouldn't I?"

"Then you can move on," Donovan said. "I can tell you were rattled by it all."

She cut her gaze to him. "I hate to see anyone treated as she was."

He nodded. "Well, if you need help with the quill," he said, clearing his throat presumptuously, "I am well-versed."

She rolled her eyes. "I don't even want to look at what is surely the realm's worst attempt at courting."

"Please, we both know I'm the one gifted with words. Though," he added, his gaze falling, "I haven't found the time of late to write to Etaina."

"Did she finally get tired of you?"

"Hardly. I've just been so busy." He nudged her shoulder. "Chasing you seems to take up most of my time."

"Sounds like an excuse."

From around a corner near the main hall, Naela appeared, out of her guard uniform and in a fresh, forest green tunic that made her eyes shine. "You're back," she said, smiling. Keeva noted the new pattern of her braids and the shiny royal pin at the shoulder of her cloak. "How was it?"

"It went well, thanks to me," Donovan replied. His gaze lingered on Naela, no doubt having also noticed her new look.

Keeva snorted at the ridiculous smiles on both their faces. "Where are you off to?" Keeva asked, picking at the elbow of Naela's tunic.

She swatted her away. "Royal guard banquet."

"That's tonight?" asked Keeva, quickly combing her mind for the week's events.

A flicker of incredulity fell between Naela's brows. "It is. Second new moon of spring, the same day every year."

"Don't mind her," replied Donovan. "She's preoccupied."

Naela moved past them, turning to ask, "I'll see you both in the main hall soon?"

Keeva nodded. "I may be late. I want to talk to Mother."

Naela nodded, then held Donovan's gaze. "See you later?" She smiled.

Keeva waved, then punched Donovan as he watched Naela go.

Upon entering her parent's chamber, Keeva was struck by the stench of henbane caught in the whirlwind of staff circling her mother like flies. She and her mother had exchanged only curt conversation since the last time she'd been in here, but something pulled Keeva to visit. A light had broken through her red anger, guiding her back to this chamber.

"Darling, I thought you'd be on your way to the guard dinner by now." Her mother spoke behind two maidens, one lifting her legs to run a damp rag beneath her knees while another fruitlessly stacked piles of scrolls only for them to be knocked aside by the other woman. A third young maiden replaced the bedpan below.

"Yes," her father echoed from across the room. He stood near his throne, arms out as Tacari helped him into a cavernous, fur-trimmed cloak. "Naela's giving a speech, and they're serving honeyed lamb."

"I'll be there," she replied, moving to the bed. "I wanted to see how things are going."

Her mother eyed her, seemingly wary at her soft tone. Keeva wondered if she could hear the question she'd intended by the careful sentence: "Are you willing to fight?"

"Everything is fine, dear," her mother finally said, dabbing her neck with a damp cloth.

Keeva clenched her jaw and turned to her father, but he avoided her gaze. An argument was futile, and she didn't want them to think she was even more furious at all this than she already was. She closed her eyes, a screen of green leaping to her mind, along with the gentle running of the river. Maeve's voice echoed, and to her surprise, quieted her frustration. "How many gorgons do we have in Uterni?"

"Gorgons?" her father asked, bending to scribble on a scroll as Tacari tried to hand him his crown. "None. Not since my grandfather's time, anyway."

"We would know if there was a gorgon in Uterni," her mother added, sounding amused now that the focus had shifted from her condition.

Keeva frowned, thinking of Maeve. Before she could explain, though, her father added, "They're dangerous creatures. We don't condemn their presence, but if any are out there, they know better than to cross a kingdom of man."

At this, Keeva turned. "Dangerous?"

"I know Tacari told you about the children of Medusa, at least," her mother said, shooting the magistrate a look.

"Of course I did, Your Majesty," Tacari said, giving a sigh at her father's ignorance of his attempts to help him look presentable. He set the crown on the desk and walked toward the other side of the bed. "I vividly recall the day I sat them down and recounted the tale. It was a dreadfully cold winter's day. By the time I was done, young Donovan was quivering in his little boots."

"Oh," Keeva said, laughing. "I remember. But I thought that was merely a story. She's a legend from the South, isn't she?"

Tacari chuckled. "She was more than legend. She was quite real and lived in those wildlands beyond the river." His dark eyes twinkled, one hand reaching up to rub the end of his beard in thought. "It was quite a time for anyone who dared to venture too far out."

Keeva gawked. "She...she turned men to stone."

"With one glance," Tacari added, a sly smile on his face.

Keeva stepped back.

Perhaps interpreting her shock as awe, Tacari continued. "Your great-grandfather told of her capture and demise." He looked at her father, who finally seemed to notice the conversation and nodded approvingly. "Though some say she's still out there," he added wryly. "It's quite the tale but far too long to recount now. Perhaps another time, I'll rekindle the flames of your memory."

"Indeed," her father said, standing and heading for the door. "We've no gorgon in this part of the realm for two generations. I'm certain of it."

Keeva was nearly to the hallway, her mind buzzing and her fingers itching, but not with spell-fire, with the need for a quill.

Her mother tilted her head. "Darling?"

"I forgot. I have something I must do before the banquet. I'll see you soon," she replied, then flew toward her chamber in search of parchment.

Chapter Nineteen

Maeve pulled back the curtain. Sunlight broke through the fen, resting gently on her face. She knelt on the bed, closing her eyes and soaking in the warmth. The glow chased away the lingering gloom Maeve felt about her last and likely final encounter with Keeva.

She returned to her table and quickly skinned the rabbit she'd trapped yesterday. She scraped and cut the last of the meat from the bones when an agitated caw came from outside.

Rowan hissed, coiling tighter around the base of the table's leg. The familiar *thump* of the Caretaker's delivery sounded outside her door, but more caws followed, harsher each time.

"What is going on?" Maeve asked the room, moving to the door to listen. Rustling among the brush near the eastern fen border prompted a deep, rasping call from the raven. This was followed by the most eloquent threat Maeve had ever heard:

"Now, see here. If you don't move along, my saol will be the next thing you see, you wretched, winged pest!"

Maeve tried to stifle a smile, then bit her lip at the unmistakable sound of Keeva's voice. She'd returned. But why?

Another series of caws sounded, then a sound like harsh wind breaking through the overhead branches was followed by a big sigh from Keeva.

Rowan uncoiled, slithering closer to hover with her near the door. Maeve held his gaze, giving a shrug as if to answer the question of what the princess of Uterni was doing here once again.

"You have a delivery," Keeva called. "And if I may, a rather rude carrier pigeon."

Maeve laughed. "That's my caretaker's raven. No one...no one else is ever here. He was probably startled."

"*He* was startled?" Keeva scoffed, then seeming to realize her tone, cleared her throat. "Well, do you, I mean, would you like to collect your items?"

Maeve wanted to pull open the door. She wanted to get a look at Keeva, a real one, but shook her head to rid herself of the fantasy. "What are you doing here?" she asked instead.

"I'm delivering a letter. I wrote one to you after the last time I was here." Footsteps moved from near the door toward the open window. Maeve shot Rowan a look, but they both noted Keeva stopped before being able to look inside. "Now, it seems silly. I wrote to ask about you. It was more to steady my mind, lay out my inquiries, and get my brother off my back."

Maeve leaned against the door. "That tall man with hair like a horse's mane?"

Keeva laughed. "Donovan. Yes."

"He's the prince?"

"Yes."

"And you're...princess of Uterni?"

"I am." Maeve's heart skipped a beat. "And you're a gorgon."

A dull stinging pricked behind Maeve's eyes. "Yes. That's why I live here alone." Rowan hissed. "Well, with Rowan."

"Where's your family?"

"Gorgons are born by magic. I never had a father. My mother left when I was nine."

"Left? Why?"

"I don't know. I think..." Her voice caught. Why was she sharing this? "I don't know. But she told me what I needed to do to stay safe. To keep others safe," she corrected herself.

"Like live by yourself in the wildlands."

"I don't have a choice. I'm dangerous."

It was quiet a moment. The sound of Keeva's boots treaded lightly back toward the door. "It can't have been easy, being here on your own."

The stinging behind her eyes intensified. Maeve knew she was alone, but she'd gotten very good at not thinking about such things. "I have Rowan," she replied, wincing at the catch her voice kept doing. "Sometimes, a nymph or gnome comes by."

"You don't...I mean, they aren't...."

"Hurt by me? No. Fae are immune."

"Why not live with them, then?" Keeva asked. "The fae."

"They don't venture through here for a reason. My great-grandmother...she did terrible things." Maeve sighed, recalling her mother's words. "She appealed to different fae groups, but it didn't bode well to be associated with a gorgon. Not when they were trying to become citizens of Uterni."

"What about the elves?"

Maeve smiled. "My grandmother tried. They're too wary of anyone who isn't an elf."

Keeva snorted. "That sounds right."

A contemplative silence fell between them. Maeve closed her eyes, listening as Keeva's steps returned to the door. Her own shoulder felt tight, taut by a pull, a tug to the woman on the other side. "You live with your family?" It was an obvious question, but Maeve felt at a loss as to what to say.

"There are hundreds of residents within the castle. But, yes, among them are Donovan and my parents."

"The queen and king." Maeve found the history book across the room, recalling names. "King Ragnar Glantor."

Keeva's tone was mildly surprised. "Yes, my father. How—"

"I have old books. My mother taught me to read. I know only of him and his forebears."

"Then, you know not of my mother." Something about Keeva's tone made Maeve turn. She stared at the long grain in the wood. "Queen Asta," Keeva continued. "A great woman and a revered ruler."

The image of a tall, striking woman filled Maeve's mind. She'd heard the sounds of festivals over the years and had imagined the queen and king standing before their people. Still, Keeva's tone held an edge, so Maeve asked, "Is your relationship a good one?"

For a moment, Keeva didn't answer. Maeve heard a sound like Keeva kicking the ground. "She's very sick."

Maeve's shoulders fell. She combed her mind for a response. Recalling a story she'd once read, she hoped this was the proper reply: "Oh. I'm sorry to hear that."

"There's Tacari, too," Keeva said. Maeve frowned, wondering why she pushed the conversation along. Perhaps Maeve had said the wrong thing. "He's like family, like an uncle. He taught Donovan and me our lessons when we were young. Kept us out of trouble as best he could, anyway." She chuckled.

Maeve smiled, imagining what it would have been like to have someone—anyone—to run around with as a child. "That sounds nice," she replied. "Your family, together."

"I suppose." Keeva's steps started again. There was a rustling. "Shall I pass your delivery through the window?"

Maeve's pulse quickened.

"I know you're near the door. I won't…I'll be careful."

Maeve swallowed, then said, "All right." Rowan slowly slithered up the leg of her bed, waiting below the window. When the basket was placed between the curtains, Maeve caught a glimpse of the hands that gripped the basket handle. They looked strong.

Keeva's voice came from the doorway. "See? Careful."

Smiling, Maeve quickly retrieved the basket. "Thank you."

"Who is it from?"

"My caretaker."

"How do you know him?"

"By letter."

A beat of silence. "You've never met him?"

"We write each other. He sends me a basket each moon."

"For how long?"

"For the last seven years or so."

"What's his name?"

Eyeing the jar of honey from the basket she'd placed on the table, Maeve felt suddenly hot under Keeva's questions. "I don't know it."

"You've never asked?"

"I did, once. A long time ago." The memory of old attempts to catch the Caretaker—her fen lined with hidden snares that always remained empty—swam before her. She'd nearly forgotten her early, desperate endeavors for an answer to who he is. "I…" She struggled to gather her thoughts. No one had ever asked so many questions of her. She pressed her hands on the table to steady herself.

"Maeve?"

"I'm sorry. I don't know."

Another silence fell.

"I'm the one who should be sorry," Keeva finally said. "I shouldn't pry. It's your affair, not mine." She gave a soft laugh. "I'm not even within the borders of my kingdom, technically. I've no right to inquire anything of you."

Maeve returned to the door. With one hand on the wood, she said, "I haven't talked this much to anyone in a long time."

Keeva sighed. "I overwhelmed you. Donovan says I can do that. Come on too strong." She snorted. "Naela says that's why I've no luck in romantic pairings."

A flush crept up Maeve's neck, though she wasn't entirely sure why. She pursed her lips and tried to keep her voice even. "Who's Naela?"

"My best friend. She's wonderful, serves as the captain of the royal guard."

Maeve smiled at the way Keeva's voice softened, then frowned at the new spike of something she couldn't name lurching in the pit of her stomach.

Keeva added, "She was here that night when…when those people were here."

"Oh. I remember."

Keeva cleared her throat. "I ought to get back. Tacari is expecting us."

Maeve looked at a piece of folded parchment being pressed beneath the door. Rowan hurried to it, and she heard Keeva stumble back at his sharp hiss.

"This fen features the most opinionated of creatures."

Laughing, Maeve tucked the paper into her pocket.

After a moment, Keeva said, "Well, perhaps we'll speak again some time."

Maeve's eyes widened. Could she have heard correctly? Keeva wanted to return? "I'd like that."

"Good." Keeva's footsteps retreated, then paused. "It was nice talking to you, Maeve."

A feeling like the kindling in the fire leapt to life in her chest and spread through her. As Keeva retreated, Maeve grabbed her shard of glass and scurried to the window. She waited two seconds, then parted the curtain. Within the glass, she caught sight of Keeva, princess of Uterni, disappearing into the brush.

❖

"Keevs, there's a snake in the window."

Keeva turned, a small yelp escaping as she leapt from the bed. At Naela's bark of laughter, she said, "You didn't hear that."

"Sure, Your Highness."

Naela replaced the map they'd been studying—crafting their next moves to find Epona—and carefully moved to the open window. "I think it has something."

Keeva knew it was Rowan but swallowed this declaration. She rather liked keeping her meetings with Maeve to herself. Before Naela could reach out, Keeva beat her to it, untying the green ribbon that carried a scrap of rolled parchment. Unrolling it, she read silently:

Meet me tomorrow at midday? Bring the ribbon.

Keeva smiled. Feeling Naela's eyes on her, she rolled the paper. "A nymph from the wood wants to meet about the cleanup project."

"So they sent a snake?" Naela looked from her to Rowan, who slithered back up the table, over the wall, and out of sight.

"You know nymphs. Unpredictable." She shrugged, tucking the parchment into her sleeve. She held the ribbon, running a finger down its length. The smooth fabric conjured the peaceful air of the fen.

"Mm-hmm." Naela stared. "Well, I'm glad the cleanup is progressing. Donovan and I have our hands full with this elf business. My parents have me training the soldiers in actual attack magic. Your brother is helping to oversee things."

Keeva, lost in thoughts of Maeve, looked up. "Attack magic? Naela, you don't think we'd actually go to war?"

"It's unlikely. The elf queen's quarrel is with Venostes, but it's good to be prepared."

Keeva thought of her mother, frail and hardly able to sit up. What would happen if they were called to battle? She swallowed, cutting a glance at Naela, who returned to the map. She hadn't mentioned her conversation with Sina, how she might have made a deal she wasn't sure she could keep.

"You're right," she said. "What are the odds, truly, of an elf attack against any of the kingdoms?" She pulled up a chair. "Come on. We've got a gatekeeper to find." Keeva forced the uncertainty aside. No news from the east had to be good news. She held on to that and dove into the plan to find Epona.

CHAPTER TWENTY

The sound of footsteps outside caught Maeve's ear. She dropped her needlework and rushed to the door, pressing her cheek to it. "You came."

A smile sounded through Keeva's voice. "I needed to check in on the river cleanup materials."

Maeve's smile fell. "Oh."

"That's my cover story, anyway," Keeva said. "I got your letter." She paused. "It was unexpected."

Maeve took a breath to quell the fluttering in her stomach. She'd thought of nothing but Keeva since the other day. A brazen thought had consumed her, and before she could stop herself, she'd tied the note to Rowan and sent him to the castle. "Did you bring it?"

"The ribbon? Yes." Keeva's footsteps came right up to the other side of the door.

"Will you try something for me?"

"All right."

Maeve stepped back. She wondered at Keeva's quick confidence. "I want…I thought we might try this. Would you walk to the window?"

As Keeva's footsteps moved, Rowan slithered from the top of her bed up to the sill. "Hello, Rowan."

He gave a curious hiss in reply.

Maeve was conscious of her breath when she asked, "Would you tie the ribbon over your eyes?"

A beat of silence. "What are you going to do?"

Maeve licked her lips and stepped closer. "Nothing that could hurt you. I promise. I've been thinking…it would be nice to have a face to go with your voice."

"You want to see me."

"Yes. I'll use my glass." She held it up, despite knowing she was still inside. "It's how I see the world sometimes. As long as I don't look into your eyes, it will be okay."

"Can't I just close them, then?"

Maeve shook her head. "I'd feel more comfortable if you used the ribbon."

Another hiss from Rowan.

"As you wish," Keeva finally said, her voice light. *Was she just as excited?*

A tingle ran through Maeve's fingers when she picked up the glass. Carefully, she crouched on the bed, positioning herself so that her back was to the window. The old man's gray face sprang up, startling her. Maeve shook her head to chase the image away. What had happened that day still frightened her, but her own wants had grown tall and strong. Maeve was smarter now. She would take a risk but a measured one.

After a moment, Keeva called, "Ready."

"It's secure?"

"Yes."

"You're sure?"

"Maeve."

"Sorry." She couldn't help but laugh. "I just…gods, imagine being the one responsible for turning the princess of Uterni to stone."

"Donovan always wanted to be an only child."

Maeve laughed again, then focused on her hand holding the shard to steady it. "All right. I'm opening the curtain." She took a deep breath and lifted the glass.

A jolt, like a sudden, sharp yearning kicked up below Maeve's stomach. She hadn't seen many people in her lifetime. She'd seen pictures in books. She'd seen fae. But she had never seen anyone like Keeva. Her fair skin was smooth over high cheekbones and a pointed chin. Maeve admired her perfect nose before her gaze was drawn to the dagger earring in Keeva's right ear. "Your hair," she managed to say, her throat dry.

Keeva grinned. "You should have seen it last year."

Maeve brought her left hand up, running the pad of her forefinger over the glass where Keeva's curls were reflected. A desperate longing to feel how soft those curls were constricted her chest. "You're so handsome."

Keeva's grin widened.

"I mean...gods. I mean..."

"It's all right. I can take a compliment."

Maeve felt hot. Her gaze fell to the tunic that clung tightly to Keeva's small chest, then to what she imagined to be well-sculpted arms. Slowly, reluctantly, she lowered the glass. Keeva's steps, though, prompted her to raise it and take another look. "Where are you going?"

There was a rustling, then Keeva reappeared, still blindfolded and lazily spinning a thin tree limb. It was one Maeve had used for trapping litter and was nearly as long as Keeva was tall.

Keeva easily twirled it in front of her like a staff as she spoke. "How's your crow?"

Maeve snorted. "You'll insult him." She laughed. "He won't return for a couple of weeks. Just Rowan and me until then."

"When did he show up?"

"Rowan? A year or so after my mother left."

"Before the carrier rook?"

Maeve smiled at Keeva's continued mislabeling of the Caretaker's bird. "Yes, before the raven," she mused, not having thought about such things in a long time. Keeva paused, turning toward the window with a furrowed, curious brow. "It's not her, my caretaker. I thought perhaps it could be, at first. I hoped it was. But the letters...it's not my mother."

Keeva stood still, her thumb rubbing a groove in the wood. Maeve wished she could see her eyes. She wondered what the spark of curiosity would look like in them. She wondered if the irises were green like her tunic or perhaps a bright magenta like her hair.

"You've really never asked him who he is, your caretaker?"

"Not in detail, no."

"Never?"

"He's kind to me. He keeps my supplies ample. He feeds me."

Keeva turned, spinning her makeshift staff again. "You're not curious?"

Maeve shrugged. "My questions always go unanswered." She thought of her mother, of the pages burning, curling in upon themselves as they were consumed in the fire.

"Well, let's change that." Keeva spun, whirling the staff with one hand, cutting it through the air, striking an imaginary target.

Maeve realized her mouth was open when she cleared her throat. "Okay." She felt dazed, and forced her mind to focus, to think of something to say. "Why were you in the wildlands that night?"

Keeva turned again, and Maeve wondered if she could see through the blindfold the way she seemed to study her surroundings. Every move she made was confident. "I was looking for someone."

"Out here?"

She nodded. "Naela and I are searching for Epona."

"Epona." Maeve's attention fell to some of the old texts in the corner. Memories of stories from her mother rushed back.

"Do you know her?"

"I've heard of her. This realm's gatekeeper."

"Yes. I need to speak with her."

A small voice cried out in the back of Maeve's mind: *Let me help you.* "I know fae. Not many. But I...I can ask them where she may be found."

Keeva moved the staff to her opposite hand, leaning against it and giving a broad smile. "Really?"

Maeve felt like she might float away. "I'd be happy to."

Keeva smiled a moment more, then did another emphatic spin and strike. "I know she lingers near fruit groves. Yesterday, Naela read something about an ash tree."

Maeve switched the shard to her other hand, rearranging herself on the bed. "That sounds right. Ash trees are often gateways to the Otherworld."

"I would owe you for helping me." Keeva spun the staff so that its pointed end faced the ground, then stepped forward.

Maeve watched her, still feeling light. She bit her lip. "You could let me return the favor."

Keeva tilted her head. "Return the favor? I think you misheard. *I* would owe *you.*"

Maeve shrugged. "The princess of Uterni couldn't be indebted to a gorgon. You can pay me back by taking your turn."

"My turn?"

"It's your turn to see me." The light feeling engulfed her, and Maeve felt dizzy and happy and something else she couldn't pinpoint. Whatever the feeling was, it drove her to set the shard down, a blaze of confidence surging through her. "Take off the ribbon."

Keeva hesitated. "Are you sure?"

"Yes. Pass it through the window. I'm going to put it on."

Seconds later, Rowan was carrying the ribbon to her. Maeve's heart thundered in her chest. The self-assured feeling that had swept over her moments ago dimmed, but she tried desperately to hold on to it. Gods, what was she doing? Her mind whirled as she lifted the ribbon and tied it so that it rested over her closed eyes. She wouldn't dare open them, but she wanted more of this, more with Keeva. "Come to the window."

"Maeve, I—"

"I promise, it's all right. Consider this your repayment," she said, surprised at the slyness in her own voice, then at the catch of Keeva's breath.

Maeve reached out and found the windowsill, the curtains still parted. She lifted her chin, felt a breeze. A finch sang in the northeast corner. The fairy nests buzzed softly. Then, a cool hand came to rest atop her own. She gasped.

"It's just me," Keeva said gently.

Maeve swallowed. A piney scent caught on the air, and she took a deep breath. *Gods, she even smells handsome.* She clenched her jaw as Keeva's fingers ran up to her wrist. She could feel the callouses at the top of Keeva's palms. When it was quiet still, Maeve's stomach fell. "Keeva?" Suddenly, the thought that she hadn't cut her hair in ages consumed her mind. Did she still have bread crumbs on her chin? Gods, what if—

"I'm sorry," Keeva said. "I was just admiring the gorgon in the fen." Maeve felt her face warm. "It's nice to see you."

Maeve smiled. Before she could respond, the same cool palm left her wrist. An empty feeling wrapped around her hand but was washed away when Keeva cupped her face. Maeve stiffened, and Keeva's hand retreated.

"I'm sorry."

"No," Maeve replied, her own hand shooting forward, somehow finding Keeva's wrist. "I'm sorry. I've never...there's never been anyone. I don't..." she mumbled, feeling foolish. "Gods, I mean..."

"It's new," Keeva said, resting her hand a moment more on Maeve's wrist, then pulling back her hands. "I understand, Maeve. I told you that I can come on too strong."

Maeve wanted to tear the ribbon from her eyes. She wanted to call out as Keeva's footsteps started backward. She wanted to feel Keeva's hands on her again. Rowan slithered up her calf, breaking her stream of thoughts. "Will you—"

"Be back?" Keeva's voice held what Maeve imagined as her signature grin. "There's a very pretty gorgon who may be able to help me find Epona. I think it's safe to say I'll return."

Maeve's smile stretched so wide, her face hurt. "I'll send word to you when I learn more."

"I look forward to another visit from Rowan."

Maeve laughed and waved. Somehow, she didn't know how, but she was positive that the princess of Uterni waved back before she disappeared beyond the border of the fen.

Chapter Twenty-one

N ice shot."

Keeva wiped the sweat from her brow and turned. Donovan stood in the armory doorway. She tossed him half a smile before yanking the arrow from its mark half an inch from the bull's-eye. "Thanks. Haven't seen you today. Mother and Father keeping you busy?"

He strode toward the row of spears. "Always. Though," he added, a contemplative look crossing his face, "I rather like the distraction. The mood around here has been so grim."

Keeva returned to her spot across the room and reset her arrows. The lichen used to dye the fletching green reminded her of Maeve's fen. She wondered what Maeve was doing now.

"Of course, the staff is wondering where you've been lately. You seem just as busy."

Keeva blinked. "What?"

Donovan spun the spear, eyeing her. "River cleanup keeping you occupied?"

"Actually, yes." She lined up her next arrow. Torchlight flickered over the edges of swords resting along the far wall. She weighed her next words. "I may have gotten a lead on things." She took a breath, held it, and let the arrow fly. It sunk just above the center of the target.

"You mean..." He replaced the spear, crossing his arms.

"A way to help Mother."

His face fell, and the look in his eyes made Keeva's stomach sink. "Donovan, don't you want her here with us?"

"Keevs, of course I do, but—"

She quickly aligned another shot, the tightness of her grip slinking into her voice. "But what?"

"Some things aren't meant to be fought."

For a moment, she stood still. She closed her eyes. Jaw clenched, she quietly replied, "You're wrong," and let the arrow go.

Donovan started again. "Keeva, please—"

"Keevs, there you are." Naela hurried into the room.

Thank the gods. Another argument was the last thing she wanted right now. In an attempt to lighten the mood, she joked, "Did I leave a trail of bread crumbs behind me today?"

"I wish you had. Nobody can seem to find you anymore. Tacari cornered me yesterday, concerned you'd taken a secret ship to Venostes."

She snorted to hide a grimace. "None of their remedies have worked, anyway." She thought again of Maeve and was eager to visit the fen. She was to return when Maeve sent word with Rowan, word that she had found a way to Epona. It had been three days, and no word yet.

Naela exchanged looks with Donovan. "Well, I'm glad to see you're finding time to practice." She shifted her stance, adjusting the wrist guard, then fiddling with the end of her braids. Keeva spent longer than necessary fetching her arrows as Donovan cleared his throat. The air was heavy with tension. A small amount of guilt kept Keeva's gaze on her bow. She'd found a new partner in the hunt for Epona in Maeve. The last few days had found her near the river, near the fen, more often than not. Closing her eyes, Keeva conjured Maeve. She imagined her wide-set face, smooth skin, and the adorable bump near the top of her nose. Maeve's blond hair seemed to fight against her worn handkerchief. She hadn't told anyone about her. She knew Naela would help her still, but Keeva wanted to keep Maeve to herself. She was a haven from this tension, these pitying eyes.

"How are the young guards?" Keeva finally asked, replacing the bow in a nearby stand.

"Not where I'd like them to be, but they're getting there," Naela said. "They find it difficult to take our practice sessions seriously."

"Do you blame them?" Donovan said. "Nearly two centuries of peace has us complacent."

Naela shook her head. "It's still good to be prepared. They'll get there." Keeva nodded, catching the reassuring smile Donovan gave

Naela. "We'd better get back to it," she said, and Keeva realized she was talking to Donovan.

"We?" asked Keeva.

"I wrangled your brother into helping me demonstrate some of the drills."

"Oh, right." Keeva frowned, a little surprised Naela hadn't asked her. She was more proficient in attack magic, after all. She tried to meet Naela's gaze but found her avoiding it. "Well, have fun. Hopefully, we don't go to war before Donovan can learn how to properly throw a spear."

"Har, har," he said, turning to go but not before giving Keeva one more wary look over his shoulder.

"By the way," Naela said, "your parents are looking for you."

Keeva replaced the quiver of arrows. "Thank you." Naela smiled and started to go. "Hey," she called, "keep my brother in check."

"Always," she replied, seeming to hesitate a moment. Keeva wondered if she wanted to say something else, something about Epona. Or ask where Keeva had been for the last few days. Instead, she only nodded and followed Donovan down the hall.

Chapter Twenty-two

K eeva hurried through the flora lining the fen, ignoring the river nymph eyeing her from behind a towering willow until Maeve's home came into view. Through the open curtains, even at this distance, Keeva could see her sitting at her kitchen table peeling apples. She smiled and called out.

A startled, "Princess!" was followed by Maeve nearly falling backward before ducking out of sight. Keeva wondered if that had been a blush flying to Maeve's face before she'd vanished, the curtain closing a second later. When Keeva approached the door, Maeve called, "I thought you'd be later."

"I couldn't wait." A series of thumps sounded inside, then what might have been a mild curse preceded an annoyed hiss from Rowan. Keeva sidestepped the snare she knew Maeve had placed near the chopping stump. At all of the ruckus, Keeva frowned. "I'm sorry to have startled you. I was eager to get here." At Maeve's silence, she added, "You said you have news of Epona?"

The goings-on inside seeming to have settled, and Maeve answered. "Yes. There is an ash tree near a plumb grove. The nymphs, they know where it is."

A surge of excitement nearly lifted Keeva off the ground. Finally, she thought. Finally, she had the key to helping her mother. "That's wonderful. When can we go?"

"I...I won't be going. I don't see how I can."

Keeva was thrilled until Maeve's words slowly sank in. "Oh. I suppose it would be difficult to navigate blindfolded."

"I would only slow you down."

Something in Maeve's voice gave her pause. She stepped closer, placing her palm on the door, a gesture she'd done enough times, she could recall the pattern of the grain within the wood. "How far have you gone? Beyond this fen, I mean."

A sad laugh. "It's not safe to wander far."

Keeva shook her head. People hardly ventured into the wildlands. Surely, Maeve could explore from time to time. Her trepidation was understandable, but Keeva didn't fully understand her fear.

"They can accompany you, though, if you like," Maeve was saying. "The nymphs."

"That's perfect, yes. Should I meet them back here tonight?"

"At the river, when the moon is high."

"I'll be there." She turned, her elation at what tonight might bring threatening to carry her away with the breeze, but she paused. "Thank you." Then, she remembered what Maeve had been doing when she'd arrived. "I noticed the basket of apples. Is there anything in this fen that isn't green?"

Maeve chuckled. "Some elderberries but not a lot, now that I think about it."

Keeva smiled, enjoying being the one to make her laugh. "I could help if you like."

Maeve was quiet.

"Toss me a spare knife and some of those apples. I'll sit right here." She plopped down, her back against the door. Rowan, who had come down from the window, slithered over her ankles approvingly. "Tell me what you're going to make."

Keeva listened to Maeve's recipe for a sweet apple bread that left her mouth watering. "You'd be a fine addition to the castle's cooking staff," she mused, her knife starting in on another apple. "They're good, mind you, but there's never any variety."

"What's your favorite dish?"

"Venison with radishes and a cold goblet of mead to wash it down."

"I've never had any of that."

Keeva stopped mid-peel, turning to talk over her shoulder. "Not even radishes?"

"They don't grow in this soil."

"Well, I'll have to bring you some. That is, if your caretaker doesn't mind the change."

"I'm sure he'd allow a root vegetable."

"Good."

They talked until the sun was dipping behind the western trees. Keeva admired her handiwork and set the knife beside a cloth filled with peeled apples. "Well, I ought to get back." She squinted toward the edge of the fen. The shadows seemed darker, and they reminded her of the sense of doom waiting at the castle. A large part of her didn't want to leave. "My family already thinks I've run off to another kingdom."

After Maeve's soft chuckle, Keeva carefully placed the bundle of fruit in the window before returning to the door. Stretching, she heard a rustling inside, then Maeve's voice. "Will you take some fruit leathers with you? I…I fear I've made too many for myself. You could share them with your tall brother or the guard captain."

Keeva grinned. "All right." Her mouth opened when Maeve said firmly, "Turn around."

"What?"

"I…I'm going to open the door. Turn around, please."

Maeve's command surprised her, and she bit her lip to fight the other feeling it stirred within her. Keeva did as she was told and focused on the line of trees. The door creaked open.

"I'm coming out."

A quick reply fell from Keeva's now dry throat. It was followed by a peculiar yearning as Maeve's footsteps drew closer, her shadow falling beside Keeva's. She smiled, imagining Maeve's pink lips pursed in concentration. Biting her lip, she recalled the way Maeve's tunic neck sat wide on her broad shoulders, revealing smooth skin yearning to be kissed. A whiff of berries caught on the breeze, and Keeva wondered if it was from the open door or if Maeve always smelled sweet.

"Open your hand."

Keeva moved her right hand behind her. Expecting a cloth or pouch, she was startled when Maeve's fingertips found her own. She smiled, relishing the sensation of Maeve's skin against hers. She swore she heard Maeve's breath quicken before her hand, sadly, retreated. Keeva closed her eyes, overwhelmed with the desire to turn, to look over her shoulder. A leather pouch fell into her empty palm.

"Good luck tonight," Maeve said, her breath a gentle wind near Keeva's ear. It sent a shiver down her back as Maeve stepped away and closed the door behind her.

Keeva didn't dare turn, though she desperately wanted to. She yearned to burst through the door and discover the color of Maeve's eyes. She craved the knowledge of her face; did her cheeks dimple when she smiled? She wasn't sure. She wanted more. She wanted, ultimately, the impossible.

That night, Maeve lay in bed, light from the crescent moon streaming between the curtains. She'd allowed herself the faintest glimpse of the world tonight, a night she knew Keeva would be out in.

She held up her right hand, the moonlight playing across her fingertips. She could still feel Keeva's hand, could feel her skin, toughened but still soft in places. Such a small moment, yet Maeve was consumed by it. Perhaps because it had been so long since anyone had been near her, so long since she'd had any form of touch. Maybe she was merely lonely. Whatever the reason, the longing in her chest seeped into her arms, searching for that touch, wanting more.

Maeve dreamt of the day her hopes for companionship had been thrown into the fire. In her dream, she stood beside her mother, watching the pages of her book meet the hungry hearth. This time, though, Maeve grabbed for the pages, shocked when the flames that curled their edges did nothing to her. She hugged the book close to her chest and smiled. Her desires lay intact, safe in her arms.

❖

Keeva pinned her cloak, put out the torch in her room, then carefully opened the chamber door. The hallway seemed deserted until a pair of guards walked past as she stepped out. They eyed her boots and cloak but saluted her.

"As you were," she said, and they continued their patrol toward her parents' chambers. Keeva could hardly walk past their quarters without choking on the stench of henbane and dried blood. "Soon, Mother," she whispered.

At Donovan's chamber, she hesitated. Naela's voice sounded within. Surprised, Keeva leaned closer. She considered the spell her brother had taught her, one they had used to eavesdrop on their parents as children but didn't need to conjure her spell-fire to hear that the talk inside was all business. Naela was explaining the training drills they'd incorporate in tomorrow's exercises. Good for Naela, she thought with a smile. Somebody who can get Donovan to listen to someone other than himself.

She was nearly to the eastern gate when a familiar *clop* was followed by Tacari's voice: "Where are you off to at this hour?"

Grimacing, she took a breath and put on a smile before turning. "Tacari, you're up late."

He stood below the torchlight, his bushy brows raised at her deflection. "You know I don't keep regular hours." He used his staff to poke the pin holding her cloak in place at her shoulder. "Fancying a trip to the village?"

Keeva nodded. "Visiting a public house."

"Make a new friend? What's this one's name?"

"You wouldn't know her," she replied with a casual shrug, hoping her tone matched. "She's not from Uterni. Only passing through." She stepped forward. "I'd rather not keep her waiting."

He smiled. "I'll go with you."

Nearly at the gate, she spun around. "What?"

"As your escort. Besides, I could use an outing in the village."

"Tacari, that's not necessary."

"When was the last time we got a drink together?" He gave a hearty laugh. "It will be fun. And I'd love to meet your latest paramour."

Frustration slinked across her spine as she frantically tried to think of a way out of this. Seeming to read her face, though, his smile fell. "You're not going to the village, are you?"

She straightened, lifting her chin. "No."

He frowned, passing his staff to his other hand. With that motion, the kindly uncle facade transformed into the businesslike magistrate. "Keeva, where are you going?"

"It doesn't matter. All that matters is that I've found the key to helping her."

His frown deepened. "There are creatures out there, Keeva, creatures eager to sink their teeth into a member of the royal family."

She scoffed. "Are you speaking ill against your own kind?"

"Just because I'm fae doesn't mean I agree with every one of them. Most of us, yes, want to live our lives in peace. But some"—he stepped closer—"relish chaos. Not unlike humans. A member of the royal family making deals with a fae—"

"I haven't made a deal with anyone," she replied hotly, her spell-fire springing to life at her fingertips. She flashed back to Queen Sina and their meeting weeks ago beneath torchlight not unlike this, but she pushed the memory away. "Now please, step aside."

Tacari seemed to study her. He shook his head. "Princess, I urge you to think wisely here. Your mother is ill. These things happen, but that doesn't mean—"

"These things happen? What is a kingdom without its queen?" She felt hot, angry, and worked to quiet her voice. "She's too young. We need her. It's not her time."

"That's not for you to decide."

She unclenched her fist, her saol dissipating, and she pulled herself up. "Please, let me pass."

"Keeva, you're being reckless."

"I'm nothing if not in control," she fired back. Shadows seemed to spring from the corners, darkening her mind. She couldn't stand this. Nobody supported her here. Fuming, she said through gritted teeth, "Magistrate, as your princess, I command you to step aside."

His eyes widened. She'd never used her status as a means to get what she wanted. But she didn't have time for lectures. Her mother didn't have time. Finally, the shock seemed to retreat behind his eyes, and he bowed and stepped aside. She hurried past him, unable to look back. There was no time to dwell on guilt. She had a gatekeeper to meet.

Chapter Twenty-three

The river nymph met Keeva as promised. She was petite in stature, her cornflower-blue skin sleek as she led the way. Keeva was briefly dazzled by the fierce mane of hair that seemed to fall like water behind her back. They walked in silence under the night sky, venturing deeper into the wildlands. Only once did the nymph toss a flirtatious look her way. Keeva gave her a tight smile but pointed ahead. This was business. As they wound through endless birch trees and high grasses, Keeva noted every gnome hill, each fairy nest, every marker. When the nymph turned south, deeper through a grove of plum trees, Keeva understood why she and Naela hadn't found this place. It was as if the night drew its blanket closer upon this section of the realm. Keeva conjured her saol as the moonlight seemed to retreat behind the clouds.

She was halted by the nymph's shimmering hand. Through the brush, a small clearing appeared. It played host to one of the largest ash trees Keeva had ever seen. Its trunk was broader than three men. She couldn't see through the thick boughs and elms to find its highest point, as if only the gods were worthy of the tallest branches.

The nymph turned to go. Keeva said, "You're leaving?"

A grin played beneath sapphire eyes. She pointed behind Keeva.

The darkened bark of the trunk began to shift. Its muddy color brightened as the wood continued to shift and swirl. Blue fire lit within the trunk, a sudden wind meeting it, twisting the bright cobalt into the shape of a door.

Nearby, two figures broke the dark seal of the clearing's edge. An old man, hunched and pale with sallow cheeks, shuffled forward. A step behind him walked the gatekeeper.

From behind a series of plum trees, Keeva whispered, "Epona."

The fiery gate expanded, now tall enough to match the man's height as he stood before it. Keeva dimmed her spell-fire, bringing it into her palm.

Epona was taller than Keeva expected, similar in height to the elf queen. Her long face and dimpled chin reminded Keeva of the elves, though the lines of her nose and cheeks curved softly in comparison. She seemed ageless like them, her dark brown skin smooth. She wore fine garb, her cloak like those worn by the gods in the castle tapestries, a bold magenta that fell over a pearl-white, knee-length tunic. Her leather sandal straps wound in an intricate pattern around her ankles and tied just below her knees. Her dark hair, following the pattern of her sandals, was spun into a braid. Marigold chrysanthemums dotted the thick strands.

"No horse," Keeva whispered, recalling Naela's story and wondering at the way tales were embellished. Not even the gatekeeper was immune to lavish details.

Without hesitating, the man stepped through the door. Keeva covered her face at the flash of blue that sprang out across the clearing, engulfing him. When she looked again, the man was gone.

Once the light faded, Epona brushed back her cloak, a mildly pleased look on her face. She moved to follow the man when Keeva called, "Wait!"

Epona turned, a smile greeting Keeva as she hurried forward. "Princess Glantor, to what do I owe the pleasure?"

Keeva pulled up, taken aback. She glanced back to find the nymph gone, and her throat went dry. Behind Epona, the gate shrank slightly, its elements still silently competing for space in endless eddies. She swallowed and cleared her throat. "I've come to make a request."

Epona's smile widened. Her eyes, a soft indigo, shined inquisitively. "A royal request? I do suppose there's a first time for everything. After three centuries, I should have expected it." Her voice lowered, and she tilted back her head, looking skyward. She laughed as if the sky had sent her a response. She squared with Keeva, who caught the glint of her gold necklace. Epona placed her hands on her hips, opening her robe wider. Keeva spotted a small golden key at the end of the necklace. Only when Epona stepped forward did Keeva meet her gaze.

"I've come on behalf of my mother, Queen Asta Glantor. She's very ill. She's been very ill for several years. Nothing helps, and her health is deteriorating quickly."

Keeva wasn't sure what she expected, but Epona's eyes shone, and her lips were turned down in a sympathetic frown.

The show of genuine pity made the words lose their place on Keeva's tongue. They came out stilted and slow. "A kingdom needs its leader," she managed to say. "She...my father...we all need her."

"Spoken like a loving daughter."

"Then you understand why I'm here."

Epona's brows knit. "I'm afraid the reason is yet unclear."

"You cannot take my mother into the Otherworld."

The confused line between her brows smoothed as she gave a sad smile.

"Uterni needs its queen. Please, you have to let her stay."

Epona seemed to study her. She threw a glance at her gate, then licked her lips before saying, "Your Highness, not even I decide when a member of man is called to the Otherworld. The gods control that fate."

"You escort the departed to their final journey. You control who walks through that gate," Keeva replied, gesturing to the great ash.

"Yes, but—"

"You can keep Uterni's queen in her right place." She winced at the break in her voice. "You don't have to take her from us."

"I told you, it's not up to me."

"It is, though. Don't you see?" Keeva's voice was high, and she spoke quickly, her breath short and uneven. "You don't have to escort her. If you don't take her, she can stay. She'll have to stay here with me." She took a breath to steady herself. "With us."

Epona's shoulders rose and fell. She shot another look at the gate, then at the sky. Desperation sprouted within Keeva's chest. It made the muscles in her arms sing with tightness. She clenched her jaw, now hating the pitying look reaching out from the gatekeeper's gaze.

"I'm sorry, Your Highness, truly." Epona took a step closer. Behind her, the tree spit licks of blue fire, its light blazing, halting the gatekeeper in her tracks. She grimaced as if feeling a tug from her great gate. "I fear your request is impossible. I truly am sorry." She turned, and Keeva leapt forward, grabbing her arm and holding her in place.

"No. You can't...this isn't right! It's not her time."

SAM LEDEL

Epona looked from Keeva's tight grip to her face. Again, Keeva felt genuine sorrow from the gatekeeper's gaze before she threw another worried look toward her fiery gate. "I'm sorry. Now, I must go."

Keeva didn't let go. Tears marred her vision. She couldn't be denied. This was it; this was how she would save her mother, how she would keep her in this realm where she belonged. This was the key.

Her gaze slid to the necklace. Epona's eyes followed. The friendly tone she'd taken on thus far came out clipped and wary. "Do not lose yourself to this, Princess. It would not be wise."

Keeva stared at the glinting key. She was fast. She could snatch it and run before Epona could blink.

"Princess."

Finally, Keeva refocused. The gate was expanding again, this time to match Epona's height. She couldn't be sure, but the ropes of fire seemed to lash out, reaching for their gatekeeper to return. At the same time, a flash of warning ran behind Epona's eyes. Keeva reluctantly released her arm and stepped back.

Epona lifted her chin, her face somber. "Go safely, Princess." She walked through the gate. Another flash of light flared. Keeva shielded her face until darkness once again consumed the clearing.

The stars continued their indifferent trek across the heavens as she stared at the ash tree. How could Epona not understand? Why couldn't anybody see how devasting it would be for her mother to be gone? Frustration boiled at her fingertips. The boldness of her saol burned in her hand and behind her eyes as she forced tears away.

Then, with a snarl, she hurled her spell-fire at the great ash. Magenta light burst into sparks, simmering to a sad end against the indifferent bark.

Chapter Twenty-four

M aeve."

The cry of her name startled Maeve from sleep. It came again, distant and desperate. For a moment, she saw herself huddled beside her mother, eyes and ears slammed tightly shut, willing the sad stranger out of their fen.

"Maeve, are you there?"

This voice was no stranger, though, and chased away the memory. "Keeva?" Rowan stirred but remained unwilling to show himself from beneath a potato sack near the low fire. Quickly, Maeve lit a candle and hurried to the door as Keeva knocked.

"Are you there?"

"Keeva, it's late. What are you…" She remembered the gatekeeper. "Did you find her? Epona?"

A sound like Keeva slumping against the door was followed by a dejected, "Yes."

Maeve's chest tightened at the broken sound. She wished there wasn't a barrier between them; the longing to help Keeva overran any cautionary thoughts she might have had. She hurried to the cauldron, partially to give herself something else to focus on, and heated water over the fire she stoked back to life. "I'll put on some tea. Chamomile does wonders."

A series of sniffles came from Keeva's side of the door. "All right."

As the water boiled, Maeve listened to Keeva recount her rejection from the gatekeeper. "I can't believe she wouldn't hear you. You're the princess."

"I suppose she's technically not under the kingdom's jurisdiction." A thoughtful silence was followed by, "Honestly, she seemed almost as afraid of her gate as I was."

Maeve chewed her lip. "She's not quite a god. She probably answers to them." Realizing she was getting lost in thoughts of the godly hierarchy, she added, "Still, I'm surprised. You deserve to be heard."

The other side of the door was quiet for a time. Maeve readied two mugs. Her heart rate quickened as she poured the water over the leaves. She was ready to pass the mug through the window but nearly dropped it when Keeva said, "Can I stay here? I don't want to be alone."

Her palms sweaty, Maeve shot Rowan a look as he peeked out from beneath his potato sack, curious now. To her surprise, he only gave an indifferent flicker of his tongue. She couldn't believe her own words as she said, "You could come in if you like."

The scraping of boots sounded outside the front door. Maeve set the mug down, imagining Keeva standing, an equally surprised look on her face. "Are you sure?"

Maeve found the ribbon under her pillow. "You'll have to wear this. You mustn't take it off. Not even for a moment. Do you understand?" she asked, again taken aback by her own authoritativeness.

"Are you giving the princess of Uterni orders?"

Maeve felt hot at Keeva's stern but playful tone. "It seems I am."

"As you wish, then."

Maeve passed the ribbon through the window; the sound of blood rushing in her ears was nearly deafening. She felt dizzy. Someone was about to enter her home, her sacred space. And not just any someone: the princess of Uterni.

Keeva called that she was ready, and Maeve stood at the door. Carefully, she lifted the lock, then held the handle to pull it open. Briefly, her mother's voice called her, urging her to be safe. The Caretaker's dark writing etched itself into the walls, beckoning her to seclusion. She shook her head, clearing it of their voices. Keeva wasn't reckless. They were being safe. The desire to be there for Keeva outran the loud warnings in Maeve's head, replacing them with the need to be close.

The door opened, and for the first time, Maeve got a good look at the princess under soft moonlight.

"Hi," Keeva said, smiling beneath the blindfold.

"Hi." Maeve took her hand, a feeling like a flower blooming to life in her chest when she did. Maeve smiled and led her inside.

❖

"You're right, the tea does help." Keeva took another satisfying sip.

"I told you it would."

Though she couldn't see it, Keeva knew Maeve was smiling. "If I drink any more, though, I'll be up half the night. Small bladder." Despite being blindfolded, she found she had a good sense of where things were. Perhaps thanks to her innate spatial awareness combined with the way Maeve had insisted on a detailed description of her surroundings. There had only been one stumble, causing Maeve to emit the most adorable yelp before Keeva caught herself and managed to recover with what she hoped was a charming smile.

Maeve chuckled from across the table where they sat opposite each other. "Very well." She was quiet a moment. "Thank you for listening to me earlier. I didn't realize how much I liked talking."

Keeva pushed the cup around. "I like listening to you." She took a sip quickly, aware of contentment swirling in her lungs. "You're a good storyteller."

"You think so? Rowan never gives an inch on whether or not I make sense."

Giving a laugh, Keeva said, "Tough critic. You're better than some of the bards in the castle." She flashed a smile at Maeve's silence. "I hope I didn't make you blush."

"That does keep happening to me lately," Maeve replied.

Happiness dispersed the lingering despair from Epona's clearing. Keeva turned at the sound of an owl. "I forgot how late it is."

"Will your family be worried?"

She snorted, dipping her chin. A flare of guilt shot through her when she recalled her last conversation with Tacari. "They'll be fine."

Maeve was quiet again. The air seemed to swirl with questions, but Keeva was grateful when Maeve only said, "I'll set up a blanket for you."

"Thank you." She tracked Maeve's movements throughout the small home. When Maeve seemed to linger near the hearth, Keeva stood. "I'd like to give you something."

A soft hiss sounded below the table. Rowan had slithered over there a minute ago, and Keeva swore she could feel his beady eye on her now. "I mean no harm," she said, raising her hands. "I just want to extend my thanks." The guilt of disappearing from the castle again rose high, and she ached for an outlet, for someone who didn't know her bad habits.

Maeve whispered something, presumably to Rowan. When she still didn't move, Keeva cleared her throat. "Would you come closer?"

"All right."

Keeva kept a smile on her face, though a ripple of nerves raced below her ribs. She followed Maeve's footsteps, turning so they stood facing one another. Keeva stepped closer, grabbing for Maeve's hand, but she startled back. "It's all right." Keeva could hear Maeve's breathing. Or was that her own breath betraying her? "May I...may I hug you?"

This time, Maeve's voice was barely audible. "You may."

Keeva wanted more. She wanted to lean closer. She wanted to find Maeve's lips and pull them to her own. She wanted to disappear into Maeve, someone who listened, someone who didn't judge her. Somehow, she managed to only reach out. She pulled Maeve's right hand behind her, bringing them closer. She yearned to reach up and push back the handkerchief in Maeve's hair, to run her fingers through the soft tresses. She placed Maeve's hand on her own lower back, and a heavy heat filled the breath of space between them.

Keeva ran her hands up Maeve's arms, her fingers grazing the coarse material of her tunic until she found her shoulders. The ends of Maeve's hair tickled her knuckles. When Maeve wrapped her other arm around her, Keeva closed the remaining space, pulling her into a hug.

At first, Maeve's body was still against hers. She could feel Maeve's heart pounding and smiled over her shoulder. "It's okay." Slowly, Maeve relaxed. She even shuffled closer, surprising Keeva and squeezing her tighter. They stood like that for a long time.

Relishing the feel of her body against Maeve's—her hands fighting the urge to run over those glorious hips—Keeva said, "I'm glad we met."

Against her cheek, Maeve's face lifted in a smile. "Me too."

Keeva held on, ready for just one night away from the gloom that waited back at the castle. A night to regroup. A night free of judgment. A night to feel loved.

She needed a plan. She needed to act. But for now, she needed this. She needed Maeve.

❖

Cold slithered across Keeva's skin. She jolted awake, flinging her arm out as Rowan continued across the side of her chair. Only when she glared at his skeptical gaze did it hit her.

The blindfold.

It lay below her chin, the knot that had loosened in the night resting low on the back of her neck. She started to lift it, then hesitated, listening. She stared at the earthen floor of Maeve's home in the dawn light. A faint creak came from the hearth, followed by a sharp crackle of dying embers. Morning jays sang outside. Fairy nests buzzed, and a fly hummed in the upper corner of the room. There was no sound, she discovered, from the bed where Maeve slept, save for the steady rise and fall of her breathing.

I shouldn't. It's too risky. Gods knew that she loved a challenge.

She stood and leaned against the kitchen table in front of her. Her palms pressed into the wood. In her peripheral, she saw the outline of Maeve's figure. She faced the wall, her back to Keeva.

Keeva turned, her movements silent. Her gaze fell fully onto Maeve. She lay under a single, tattered blanket. Her hair was golden in the early morning light.

Closer now, Keeva watched Maeve's shoulder rise and fall before her gaze slid to Maeve's hip, then her legs, which bent gently at the knee. The image of herself wrapped in Maeve's arms came suddenly, and Keeva blinked, startled by her own vision and the peaceful feeling that accompanied it.

A low groan from Maeve cut through the reverie. Keeva sighed. She wanted to stay, to sit in the quiet with Maeve. From beyond the fen, the castle seemed to call her, its incessant bustle tugging her back to reality. Reluctantly, she untied the ribbon. She reminded herself she didn't have time for this, whatever this was. She needed to help Uterni's queen keep her throne.

After one more glance at Maeve, Keeva slipped outside.

Chapter Twenty-five

Y ou look like something the bogwitch spat out," Donovan muttered as Keeva shoved goat cheese and bites of pear into her mouth. She washed it down with a goblet of cider, then quickly poured another.

"Do something new to your hair?" she countered before using her free finger to poke at the thin braid that ran from his temple into his ponytail. A matching one was on the other side.

He swatted her away before pulling her to stand. The main hall was beginning to brew with members of the court. She started for the main passageway, ready to veer left toward her chambers and a nice bath. Keeva felt exhausted and famished after having returned only a few minutes ago.

Donovan nabbed her cloak, pulling her with him. She squirmed out of his firm grasp. "Where are we going?"

"Mother and Father's chambers. We've a letter from Queen Sina."

She coughed, crumbs catching in her throat. "What about?"

He shot her a look before waving cordially to passing guards. From the side of his mouth, he said, "You'll see."

Tacari emerged from the door of their parents' chamber. Keeva didn't miss the way he studied her as if searching for the young girl he'd helped raise. She wondered how unrecognizable she must have been last night. The idea made her tremble, and she pushed the thought away. She lifted her chin, shoved aside her guilt, and moved into the room, Donovan tugging on her arm.

Expecting more clamor and chaos behind the chamber door, the quiet hit Keeva like a wall. Her father sat at the foot of their mother's bed. She was propped up, her forehead lined with sweat. New shadows sat deep beneath her tired eyes. Leech marks lined her inner forearms, red and glaring, when she raised her hand. Keeva's gaze was finally drawn to the piece of parchment filled with blue ink.

"Good. You're here." Her voice was weak but her demeanor lively. "Your father and I need a word."

Donovan shoved Keeva forward, then turned to go.

"With both of you," their father added.

They exchanged glances.

Donovan frowned. *This is your fault.*

Keeva elbowed him. *My fault? I have no idea what's going on!*

"Keeva, we received this notice from the elf queen this morning. We sent word, but Tacari said you were out with the sun, working on the river cleanup."

She'd been ready to explain not being in her chambers this morning, but her mouth promptly closed. Tacari had covered for her? Even after the way she'd treated him?

"Never mind that," their father said. "You're here now. This is serious, Keeva. We have a very important question."

She nodded. Her mind ran fast with possibilities of what they were going to say: *what are you doing disappearing all the time? What are you thinking, mingling with a gorgon? Why have you abandoned us?* "What is it?" she finally managed to ask.

Her mother took a slow, rattling breath. "Sina is ready for war. She's adamant this man from Venostes—whoever he is—will help keep her clans safe. She is ready to help take on this darkness he claims exists in the southern kingdom. A darkness that will spread across the realm." She paused, her dark-rimmed eyes holding Keeva's gaze. "She is planning an attack and"—she read from the parchment—"is 'pleased to know Uterni stands with us in this fight.'"

Normally, Keeva thrived under scrutiny. She adored holding a captivated gaze. But as her family's attention bored into her from all sides, the urge to crawl beneath the nearest chair consumed her.

Her father shifted, the bed creaking as he faced her. "Your brother told us the two of you had hoped to speak to Sina last time she was here."

Keeva caught Donovan's gaze. He dipped his chin.

Traitor.

"We discussed the idea, yes," she answered. "We didn't like the way the meeting ended."

Both her parents shook their heads. Her mother took another strenuous breath, then coughed. "Not every meeting goes the way we hope. That doesn't mean you can call your own without our knowledge."

"I didn't." She looked again to Donovan, but he kept his gaze low. "I only spoke with her briefly near her chambers before she retired for the night."

More coughs erupted, and their mother turned to stifle them with a cloth. Red peppered her lips when she lowered it. "Keeva, what did you say to her?"

"I didn't say anything. I mean…I didn't…I just…"

"Did you promise an alliance?"

The words stuck in her throat. Panic confined her neck and chest. War was never really an option, she reminded herself. It couldn't be. "I thought I was doing the right thing."

Her mother's gaze widened and flew to their father. Stunned silence rang loud like a gong. Finally, her mother said, "We must draft a response. We must do it immediately before—" More coughs. This time, they didn't stop. Keeva hurried forward with Donovan.

"Mother?"

Their father stood, rushing to her side. "Asta, sweetheart?"

Her mother's breath shortened. Blood gathered between her teeth, dropping onto her hand as she tried to silence her coughs.

"Fetch the herbalist," their father bellowed. "Where's Tacari?"

"Mother. I'm sorry, I didn't mean to…"

But her mother's eyes fluttered closed before Keeva could finish, and she fell back on the pillow, unconscious.

Chapter Twenty-six

For Maeve, it was like Keeva had coaxed a stopper from its bottle. The next day, she couldn't seem to stop talking to any passing creature. She spent two hours getting to know the fairy family who had resided at the fen's edge for years. A rather perturbed looking gnome, having wandered in accidentally, sat through her latest recipe for gooseberry pie. She couldn't believe what she'd been missing by isolating herself. Even within her small world, there was so much life.

When the *thump* of the Caretaker's package sounded outside that evening, she wiped the acorn dough from her fingers. "Think we'll get more raspberries, Rowan?"

He flicked his tongue and followed her outside. Crouching, she pulled back the cloth and frowned at the single jar of flaxseed next to a small honeycomb.

"That's odd." She found the scroll and brought everything inside. Across the clearing, the raven cawed.

She set the basket down, and sat beside the fire to read.

M—

You must be more careful. Think of what your mother might say. Do not forget who you are: a creature who possesses terrible power, undoing souls in a glance.

You know better.

She cast the parchment aside in a huff. "What does he know?" she said, glaring at Rowan, who wound around the clay jar atop the table.

She crossed her arms, turning her angry gaze to the window and the raven beyond. "Nosy bird."

Maeve fumed over a cup of tea, her thoughts bubbling with frustration. She was being careful. She just…enjoyed Keeva's company. What was so wrong about that? The Caretaker's words drifted out of the steam: *do not forget who you are.*

She knew exactly who she was. She knew the risk. The longing wrapped around her limbs, a constant reminder of the years spent alone. She pictured Keeva, heard her voice, felt her body close.

The raven cawed again from the trees. Maeve closed her eyes. *Think of what your mother might say.*

She knew how her mother would feel. She had taught Maeve to be careful, to fear everything and everyone. She'd instilled so great a dread about the outside world, Maeve never went far. It was safer that way.

But was it better?

A tiny part of Maeve wondered if her mother had ever felt the pang of longing. Had she known what it was like to find someone, to want to be closer to them, despite everything?

Maeve took another drink. "How dare he bring her into this?" She slammed the cup down. "He didn't know her." She stood, an unfamiliar sensation building in her hands, in her chest. It squirmed and twisted until a chisel took shape. Its sharp point took in her frustration, burning bright as it began to chip away at the chains her life had been shackled with. To her surprise, the lightness was welcoming. Warm.

She tore the letter in a flurry and tossed it into the fire.

The third maiden in an hour scampered out of her parents' chamber, and Keeva's stomach roiled at the bloody rags piled in the bedpan. Through the narrow windows across the hall, a cold wind wove over the tapestries. Torchlight flickered in the bleak afternoon—the sky gray and angry—when Tacari stepped into the hall where Keeva stood.

His watery eyes seemed to study her. He looked at the chamber door, then back. "You could go in."

She shook her head. Keeva had been standing there since midday, unable to bring herself to face the grim truth waiting within. "Donovan says she's not eating," she finally said, sadness and frustration tightening her chest. She wrung her hands to alleviate some of the pressure building in her body.

"She's weak."

Keeva nodded but kept her gaze on the door. "Father?"

"He's with her now, but he leaves tomorrow for the Elf Lands."

"Elf Lands? That's a long journey. We've never gone east. Queen Sina—"

"Is ready to attack our southern neighbors." His gaze hardened, and Keeva shrank under it. "These are desperate times."

She licked her lips, and her fingers itched for a spear, a bow, something to throw. Tears burned as she replayed Epona's rejection. Too much was happening, and Keeva couldn't help but feel responsible.

"Keeva," said Tacari, reaching out to rest one hand on her shoulder, "I remember a time, years ago, when you, Naela, and Donovan were playing in these halls. The two of them had disappeared, hidden away in a corner somewhere, and you came running up to me, utterly furious at the fact that you couldn't find them."

She couldn't hold his gaze and crossed her arms. The dark corner, too far for the torchlight to reach, was where she focused. "Tacari, is now really the time?"

He ignored her and continued, his voice patient and light. "I told you it was merely a game, but you wouldn't hear it." A smile lifted his bearded chin. Keeva finally looked up. "You spent all night searching, even missing dinner, adamant you had to find them. Of course, by that time, they had moved on, enjoying a sweet bread in the main hall, the game forgotten."

Keeva stepped back, finding a wall to lean against. She tightened her grip around herself, meeting Tacari's gaze. Her entire life, he had always found a way to use his words as a balm. He had consoled her when she'd come in second in the archery contest when she was ten. He'd encouraged her in riding lessons, even more so in her studies. He was always there, always ready to support her.

But she wasn't that little girl from his story. This wasn't a game of hide and seek. This was her mother's life. She'd been rude to him last time they'd spoken, but he hadn't been on her side. He hadn't supported her then. And now, the only person in the castle who understood her was dying. "Tacari," she finally said as another maiden rushed from the room toward the kitchen, "she needs help."

"We're all doing what we can."

"No." She straightened and started past him but turned. "We're not. We're watching her die. I won't be a part of it. I won't stand here and wait for the end to come." Her life had been a comfortable cycle for so long, idyllic in every sense. She knew that. She knew how lucky she was. But the image of her family together in the main hall, her mother's seat vacant, dragged a dagger across her heart. She and Donovan knew a lot, but she didn't feel ready to take on the mantle of responsibility that would follow her mother's passing. More than that, she didn't feel ready to handle this life without her.

"Keeva."

She shook her head. "No. I'm done listening to you."

His gaze turned startled.

Regret shook near her ribs, but she didn't flinch. "If nobody here will help me, that's fine. I'll go to somebody who will."

His hurt expression withered to confusion. Keeva rubbed her hands together, about to explain, then decided against it. She shoved past him and headed toward her chamber.

The startled maiden who had been rearranging the bearskins gave a hasty bow. Keeva found her cloak, longing to see Maeve. She turned for the door but was stopped by Naela.

"Who stole your saol?" Naela placed a hand on her hip, her face unimpressed by Keeva's urgent manner.

"I've got to get to the river," she said quickly, attempting to sidestep into the hall.

"I was there this morning with Donovan. The tree nymphs seem to have things under control with the cleanup." When Naela didn't move, Keeva pretended to adjust the water basin on the table. "Unless, of course, you're not actually going to the river."

Keeva knew Naela was giving her a chance to tell her the truth. The words wouldn't come.

Naela sighed. "Donovan says you've been seeing a gorgon in the fen."

Keeva stepped back. "What? He has no idea what he's talking about." She huffed and looked away. Feeling defensive, she straightened and said, "You've been spending an awful lot of time with my brother."

Naela's mouth fell open, and she stepped into the room. They both shot the maiden a look, and she fled into the hallway. Naela closed the door. "He's helping me and my parents with guard exercises. He's helped a lot, actually. He's really good at teaching, believe it or not."

Keeva rolled her eyes. "I'm sure he's taught you a lot."

Naela raised a brow, and the smallest tingle of yellow spell-fire lit her fingertips. Keeva swallowed, surprised at the rare show of emotion. Not knowing what to do, she grimaced and stared at her boots. After what seemed like ages standing silently, Naela said slowly, "Keeva, I know you're upset about your mother's health, but that was uncalled for."

Closing her eyes, Keeva took a breath. She pictured Maeve and the tranquility of the fen. "I'm sorry. I just...nobody is doing anything about it."

Naela nodded, and she seemed to absorb the words. "This gorgon...she helps you?"

Keeva considered the question. Maeve had helped arrange the meeting with Epona, but she had also been there when that didn't work out. She'd listened with unbiased ears and let Keeva vent her frustrations. Keeva imagined holding Maeve and being held in return. She smiled. "In more ways than one."

A glint of surprise crossed Naela's face, but she smiled. "Your secret is safe with me, Keevs."

"And Donovan?"

Laughing, Naela said, "I'll make sure he doesn't talk, and I'll try to keep him from rummaging through your scrolls. But Keevs," she added, frowning, "I don't understand how you can make that work."

Pursing her lips, Keeva shrugged, glad the room felt light again. "We just have to be creative."

Naela looked intrigued. "Oh? Well, you'll have to share details another time." She reached out, giving Keeva's arm a shove. "I just wanted to check in. My best friend is harder to catch these days than a trout from the river."

"I know. I'm sorry, again, for what I said."

Naela squeezed her hand. "You're forgiven. But this means I get an extra round of arrows next time we have a go at the targets."

Keeva laughed. "That's fair." Throwing an arm around Naela's shoulder, Keeva led them into the hall. "Thank you." She leaned to the side, pressing her head to Naela's temple, grateful. "I actually have some more to fill you in on. Come on."

At the dining hall table, Naela whispered, "What makes you think things will be different this time when you see Epona?"

Keeva threw a glance to the court members hurrying past. She picked up a jam-coated knife, letting the candlelight glint off its edge.

Looking alarmed at the blade, Naela said, "You're going to threaten the gatekeeper of the Otherworld?"

"I'm just going to remind her who I am. Who we are. She'll realize she can't take Uterni's queen."

Naela pursed her lips, a worried expression in her eyes as she seemed to search Keeva's gaze. She glanced at her plate, then nodded. "When you go this time, I'll be with you."

"Naela, you don't have to."

"Keevs, we started this together. You may have fallen for a gorgon, but I'm still your best friend. I'm with you."

Keeva didn't know what to say. She dipped her chin, her tongue thick with emotion. Reaching out, she squeezed Naela's arm. "Thank you."

In the hall, Keeva inhaled deeply. For the first time in days, she felt hopeful. She let that hope fill her up and carry her outside toward the river. Toward Maeve.

Chapter Twenty-seven

Maeve hummed as she finished the latest letter to the Caretaker. She'd opened the curtains, letting the bright sunlight stream in. Rowan seemed to appreciate this as he lay strewn out across her mother's chair in a square of light.

It was Keeva, she knew, who had emboldened her to pick up a quill and write. It was the rekindled curiosity that asked the questions she'd long ago buried. Ink spilled across the parchment in a fury, hardly able to contain her zeal to learn about the past. If the Caretaker was going to insist she be cautious, she reasoned, he owed her answers.

That night, she was startled awake by the raven's call piercing the night air. Nearly falling out of bed, she apologized after stepping on Rowan on her way to the door. For a moment, she listened. A soft thump against the wood followed another caw. A rolled scroll sat outside her door.

Lighting a candle and throwing a log on the fire, Maeve sat at the table. Rowan gave a disgruntled hiss as he slithered up to join her.

She hesitated, her fingers frozen over the twine. The Caretaker had never sent a response so quickly and never in the middle of the night. She glanced around at the firelight throwing shadows, and she caught shifting images in the darkness. Memories of her mother danced around the room, then were consumed by the harrowing silence that seemed to fill this space since she'd left. A tall figure followed, walking through the room like a spirit, then looming just beyond the fen.

Fear dampened her forehead, and she swiped at the gathering perspiration. She wished Keeva was here as she took a deep breath. "Well, Rowan, here we go."

I found your correspondence quite confusing. What sort of questions are these? Do I know of a white, ghoulish spirit that lurks near gooseberry shrubs? Could that same spirit have something to do with your mother's vanishing?

Ridiculous. You'll remember, I've little knowledge of your fen from my home in Ionad. I know you're smarter than to believe that your mother was taken. Yes, she was a gorgon, but sometimes, people leave.

Do not wander far. There may not be a spirit, but there are those who would want to see a gorgon harmed. Trust me.

I do hope the rope I sent last moon has been put to good use in keeping your snares secure. Think of the hunters, of the terrible humans living in the bogs and cliffs they call a kingdom. They would rid the wildlands of you in a heartbeat. Nothing is worth the risk.

The still air settled heavy around her. A single line glared among the slanted script.

Sometimes, people leave.

Could her mother have left her of her own free will? Could she have believed that abandoning her young daughter was the best thing for both of them? After what her own mother and grandmother had done?

"It doesn't make sense." Maeve's temples ached, and she leaned forward, her head resting against her open palm. Tugging the candle closer, she reread the note. He hadn't answered any of her questions. She looked out the window, peering into the dark night. She imagined the raven in its perch. A dark thought crossed her mind: sending Rowan out after him. It had to be the raven, always watching her with its beady eye, ruining this for her. The Caretaker was worried about the humans, but the ones she'd met were kind.

Memories of Dain sprang to the front of her mind. "I guess they aren't *all* kind." Still, Keeva and her companions were sweet and good-hearted. She knew it. Keeva was thoughtful and brave and liked Maeve despite her being a gorgon. The shadows swirled closer, and unease gathered in her gut. It followed Maeve to bed as she tossed and turned through a sleepless night.

❖

"Naela, you're doing it again."

She sighed. "I can't help it, Keevs. I've never met a gorgon before, let alone a gorgon my best friend is in love with."

Keeva—who'd been smiling at Naela's persistent, upbeat humming—felt like she'd been plunged in the river at winter. Even through the pale light of their collective saols, she found Naela's surprised face as she said, "I'm not." Then, disoriented and glancing at Donovan behind them, she added, "I mean...it hasn't been that long."

"Love sneaks up on us," Donovan added, moving ahead to navigate a series of thick, low-lying elms. They'd crossed the shallow part of the river and were near the edge of Maeve's fen. Keeva scoffed for good measure, though her heart rate sped up.

"Remind me what changed your mind to join us?" she asked, grateful when Naela's amused gaze turned to him.

"Someone needs to be able to tell Tacari and our parents what happened to you when this plan completely dissolves, and Epona pulls you into the Otherworld."

"Come now," said Naela, giving Donovan a shove. Then, to Keeva said, "Ignore him. No one is being pulled into any other realm tonight. This is a meeting, nothing else," she added, looking pointedly at Keeva.

She nodded, though tension licked at her heels, and her saol brightened in turn.

Donovan glanced over his shoulder, one brow quirked. "Right. A meeting, nothing else."

"But first, let's meet this gorgon," Naela said, practically giddy as she pushed Keeva ahead.

After a short knock on the door, Maeve called from inside.

"It's me," Keeva replied. Donovan cleared his throat. She rolled her eyes. "There's some people who would like to meet you."

At Maeve's silence, Keeva motioned for the others to step closer. Naela looked from her to the closed door. "I'm Naela, captain of the Uterni guard. It's nice to meet you."

"It's nice to meet you, too. I'm Maeve."

"I've heard a lot about you."

"You have?"

Keeva elbowed Naela as Donovan answered, "Keeva talks about you when she thinks we're not listening. And I'm—"

"Prince Glantor. It's an honor."

"It's an honor," he echoed, smirking and bumping Naela's shoulder. "Hear that?"

"Don't hurt yourself," she jabbed, and Keeva didn't miss the playful smile between them.

"You're going to see Epona again?" Maeve asked.

Keeva followed her voice, now at the window. "Strength in numbers," she said. "As much as I hate to admit it, my brother is the more eloquent one. He'll help persuade the gatekeeper and show her we can't lose our mother."

"By the way," Naela said, "I thought you'd like to know Dain is still in custody. He refuses to talk." She gave a reluctant look to Keeva. "We can only keep him another moon. Maybe by then, he'll change his mind."

"Thank you for telling me." After a beat of silence, Maeve said, "You had better start out, the moon will be high soon."

Keeva nodded. Naela and Donovan started for the trees after complimenting Maeve on the fruit leathers. Keeva started to follow but hesitated. Moving closer to the door, she said, "Maeve."

"I know. Hold on."

Moments later, the door opened slowly. Keeva smiled at Maeve's ability to read her thoughts, her wants, as she found her standing with the ribbon over her eyes. "How did you know I wanted to see you?"

Maeve's smile widened. "Gorgon intuition."

Keeva glanced at the others before hurrying inside. She pulled Maeve into a hug, soaking in the feeling of their bodies close. Her chin rested easily on Maeve's shoulder, and she breathed deeply. When she opened her eyes, she was surprised at the sudden sensation of Maeve's lips on her neck.

The kiss was light, almost timid, and Maeve quickly nuzzled back into her. "Go safely, Keeva."

"I will."

❖

"Over here." Keeva held up a hand to halt the others. She pointed to the giant twisting ash in the clearing.

Naela asked, "Now what?"

"Now," Keeva replied, dimming her saol, the others following suit, "we wait."

In the darkness, they lingered quietly near a cluster of birch trees. Naela retied the leather laces on her wrist guards. The air overhead was heavy, rain clouds gathering, and the scent of damp pine sat among the shadows.

A rabbit stirred in the brush. Keeva found Donovan's gaze on her. She could read his concern in the tightness of his jaw.

You didn't have to come.

Of course I did. Tacari knows you're planning something.

He can guess.

Donovan threw a glance at the clearing over her shoulder. *Don't be rash, Keevs. This is the gatekeeper you're dealing with.*

I'm well aware. She stared back at him. His green eyes held hers a moment more, then fell to his boots.

Keeva took a deep breath. She hated that he didn't have faith in her. It had started to feel like no one did. Everyone seemed perfectly fine with her mother dying. Everyone but Maeve.

I won't let it happen.

Naela's hushed voice broke the stillness. "Look."

On the opposite side of the clearing, Epona led a young woman toward the tree. Like before, the trunk shifted, fearsome light twisting to form a doorway.

Keeva motioned for them to follow. They didn't light their saols as they treaded carefully through the tall grass. The young woman walked through the gate, and they shielded their faces from the blazing light.

When Epona followed, Keeva motioned them forward. She had to squint, the light from the gate was so blinding. Naela rested a hand on her shoulder for guidance, and Donovan had done the same in turn.

She was inches from the gate now. As far as she knew, no one had ever done what she was about to do. Keeva shuddered at the idea. The gate light shivered. She reached out, surprised at the lack of heat or cold from the flames.

"Keeva, I think it's closing," Naela said behind her.

She called over her shoulder, "Ready?"

"Ready," they answered in unison.

After a final look back at the clearing, Keeva stepped through the gate.

❖

Rowan coiled around Maeve's arm as she sat in her mother's chair. A strange, terrible feeling had sprouted in her stomach since Keeva had gone.

"They'll be all right," she said, her unfocused gaze stuck on the same spot it had been on for the last few minutes.

Her mind, typically calm like the narrow creek where the river turned south, swam with worry and to her surprise, memories. Memories of her mother holding her, reading to her, showing her how to bake. Forgotten laughter crackled from the fire's simmering logs. Maeve pulled one knee close in the darkened room. A deep ache to have her mother here again wrapped around her, followed swiftly by the Caretaker's words:

Sometimes, people leave.

"She couldn't have." Maeve wiped at tears. She thought of Keeva, and the unease in her stomach wriggled. What if she ran into trouble? What if, after her dealings with Epona, Keeva had no more reason to visit? Maeve hoped that what she felt between them was as real as it seemed. The way Keeva touched her, held her…it had to be, right? Rowan hissed at the sharp crack from the fire. The burned pages of her book drifted through the smoke.

It's safer. You have to be alone.

Sleep would be useless tonight. Turning to rest her cheek on her knee, Maeve sighed as she realized she didn't want to be alone. Not anymore.

CHAPTER TWENTY-EIGHT

D onovan gasped first.

"Gods," Naela said, her voice hushed. Even Keeva's mouth fell open at the cavernous passageway they found themselves in after passing through the gate. Huddled close, they spun as the door shrank and dimmed at their backs. Keeva was certain none of them breathed as they watched their only way out disappear.

Naela's breath came steadily over her left shoulder. Donovan's swallow was audible over her right. Keeva took a deep breath to quiet her nerves as they took everything in. Ten paces ahead, the young woman walked, seemingly in a trance as Epona kept a gentle hand on her back, guiding her toward a similar door one-hundred yards away. At least, Keeva thought that was the distance. The opposite side of the great room, like the surrounding walls and even the floor, seemed to be constantly shrinking and expanding.

"It's like it's alive," said Donovan.

Keeva nodded. It was like they were inside a great beast, trapped within its chest. Each surface seemed to reestablish itself every few seconds, leaving her disoriented. She had expected the smell of sulfur or dead earth, but a pleasant mix of moss and marigold blossoms filled the air.

Naela spoke Keeva's thoughts. "It's another world." Their awestruck silence was the only reply.

What might have once been trees were now like gnarled and twisted ribbons of water. Saols burned in bright colors where leaves should have sprouted. The path between them and Epona resembled ice. Keeva took a wary step to test it. Solid earth appeared between a sheet of frost-colored fog. Dim light emitted where she stepped before vanishing again.

Light, water, and fire, it all danced and swam in hushed dizzying waves around them. If this was the gateway, Keeva could only dream of what lay beyond.

Silently, they walked in unison, filed tightly and careful to follow Epona's path. Whistling wind and creaking bark echoed in eerie, distant calls. At the same time, Keeva was hit with the sensation that they were being watched. But as she scanned the dazzling surroundings, the glowing rocks, the vines of water, she found no one. There were, however, several dark passageways dotting the shifting walls. Tunnels? Keeva could only guess.

She led them toward the eastern wall where they stepped behind a water and rock formation as tall as Donovan. They watched the young woman pause before the next great door. This time, a lock formed. Epona removed her necklace, pressing the key into it.

Quickly, Keeva and the others hurried forward. Once the young woman disappeared through the doorway, Keeva called, "Epona!"

The gatekeeper turned. A look of surprise graced her face before she smiled. "Your Highness." She nodded to Donovan and Naela. "Prince Glantor. Captain. This is unexpected."

"We've come to speak to you about Queen Asta," Keeva announced as Donovan and Naela flanked her. Behind Epona, the door continued to whirl and whip great licks of fire, as if impatient and hungry for its keeper's return.

Epona sighed, replacing the key around her neck and throwing a glance at the door. "I'm afraid your visit will be unsuccessful. As I said before, not even I control when it's time for someone to cross over."

Donovan stepped forward, and Keeva recognized the charming smile and genial tone he often took when speaking to merchants. "Gatekeeper, my sister's plea is heartfelt and not just one of a loving daughter unwilling to part with her mother."

Keeva frowned and shot him a look, grimacing at Naela's surprised expression.

"Queen Asta is a revered and respected leader. What is a kingdom without its monarch?"

"Monarchs pass on, do they not?"

"Of course," he continued.

Keeva shifted, glancing over her shoulder. The feeling that someone else was there, someone watching them, grew.

"Our mother is young," Donovan said. "Surely, you can let her remain another year." Keeva elbowed him. "Two years. Please, as the future rulers of Uterni, we ask you for this kindness."

Epona had been still as she listened, her dark eyes narrow but gleaming. Perhaps Donovan coming along had been a good idea after all; maybe his powers of persuasion had worked. Even Naela threw her an encouraging smile.

But Keeva's hope faded as Epona turned away. "I'm sorry. It cannot be done. There is an order to things. Those souls whose time it is must pass through the gate. If they don't..." She paused, pulling her cloak tighter as a shudder overtook her. At her next words, Keeva's dismay twisted into anger. "I suggest you go to your mother," she said. "Go to her now. Spend what time you have left with her. Be well."

The fires around them turned red, rising up to fill the vast chamber. Keeva heard Donovan reply, accepting this defeat, but she started forward, the red blaze blinding her. Naela called her name, but Keeva pushed on. "No." Her saol burned at her fingertips. "Not like this."

"Keeva!"

Ignoring Naela's shouts, Keeva's aim was steady as she let her spell-fire fly. It hit Epona's arm, making her stumble long enough for Keeva to reach her. She yanked Epona's cloak, turning her so they were face-to-face. The wall's red flames filled Keeva's vision. It was all she could see as Epona, wearing a frightened look, said, "Your Highness, don't."

She couldn't stop. She reached for the key at the end of the necklace.

Donovan's hand was on her shoulder, but she held her ground and pulled, hard.

The chain broke. Epona screamed as if the ruptured metal had split something open inside her. She buckled and doubled over, the piercing sound filling the chasm. Keeva shrank away, the key in hand. Epona seemed to grow taller, and the door's flames turned into gnarled black hands, the wrath of Dagda reaching out to pull Keeva down.

"Keeva." Donovan pulled her away just before the door burst into white flames. The walls shook. The floor trembled. "We have to go."

Naela echoed him. "The walls are collapsing!"

Streaking ribbons of water shot from every angle with spindly fingers. Naela pushed Keeva aside before they could tear at her cloak.

Donovan shouted, "Where do we go?"

"This way," Naela said, and Donovan yanked Keeva behind him. She felt numb and cold. Epona was stuck to the earth as she yelled, reaching out for Keeva and the key. The floor sprang up, encasing Epona's legs, immobilizing and trapping her between worlds.

What did I do? Keeva hardly had time to think about the consequences before she realized they might have been trapped, too.

They ran. The air they cut through was dense now, multicolored smoke marring their path and vision. The walls splintered in great bursts of bark. Keeva looked back once more. Epona writhed and wailed as the earth climbed to her waist; her arms were outstretched, searching. Keeva gripped the key and looked away.

Donovan swerved just in time to avoid a stalactite that shot up from the ground, nearly knocking him back. Naela leapt over the gaping hole it left behind. All around them, the earth seemed to be revolting, shooting skyward in tempestuous geysers. "We're not going to make it," she shouted over the crashing of more boulders.

Through the debris, Keeva caught a worried look between Donovan and Naela. She gripped the key tighter, refusing to be responsible for what could be a complete disaster: half the royal family and the captain of the guard trapped forever between their world and the next. Tacari would kill her.

Darting between spouts of fire, they dodged ribbons of steam that seemed eager to wrap around their ankles and shoved through wind ready to throw them sideways. Epona's shrieks echoed, but from a small tunnel just ahead, a voice called, "This way!"

Donovan looked at her. *I don't think we have a choice.*

We don't.

They headed for the entrance. A small blue light bobbed, revealing a man in the shadows. "Follow me," he said.

Keeva pulled ahead, following him into the dark. Fifty yards into a winding passageway, the quaking lessened, the threat of collapse seemingly gone. Keeva held the key tighter. She couldn't meet Naela's gaze nor Donovan's as they worked to catch their breath. This hadn't been the way this was supposed to go. None of this was supposed to happen. But, she thought with a wary look sideways, hadn't she been ready to do what everyone else was unwilling to even try?

She shoved the grating panic in her mind aside. The man who'd led them here stood against the opposite wall a few feet ahead. His saol bobbed at his feet, lighting muddy boots with specks of what looked like blood.

"Who are you?" Naela asked, one hand on her dagger. "Why did you help us?"

His voice was clear and bright and had a well-spoken cadence. "I'm not supposed to be here. Much like you."

Keeva squinted. He was only a little taller than her, fitted with a tunic featuring puffy sleeves and a belt, though any weapon it might have held was now gone. "Who are you?"

After a moment, the man's saol flew to his hand, and he stepped forward. They all gasped as the light exposed a deep gash in his side. Despite the wound, his pale face seemed bright, hazel eyes glinting beneath buoyant brown hair. "My name is Brennus Diarmaid, prince of Venostes. I was murdered, and now I need your help."

CHAPTER TWENTY-NINE

M aeve gave up on sleep. Thoughts of Keeva whirled in fervent spirals in her mind. The moon dipped toward the western edge of her fen, and for a time, she lay munching on acorn bread. She imagined Keeva, Donovan, and Naela meeting with the gatekeeper. She imagined a grand conference before a great door. Eloquent words streamed between them.

Warmth nestled near her heart at the idea that she had been helpful in arranging such a meeting. While a small part of her still felt off, she reasoned she was only worried because she cared. The idea that she'd been a part of someone else's plan to help the kingdom frightened away her worry. Being helpful to someone else, someone she liked, was something she had never experienced. She quite liked it.

That thought filled her, and she quickly found the old belt hanging on the wall. She ran her fingers down the worn threads. Uterni's colors seemed more vivid as she put it on, like they felt as bright as she did. Rowan uncoiled and slithered between her feet as she slipped on her boots. In the mirror, she smiled at her reflection.

Is this what it felt like to belong?

"Come on, Rowan," she said, adjusting the sleeves on her tunic. She headed for the door. "Let's be bold."

Together, they headed for the river. Maeve hesitated near the gooseberry shrubs. Her mother's figure appeared in the midnight shadows, methodically picking each ripened fruit. The basket at her hip was nearly full when her mother paused. For a moment, Maeve thought she'd fallen into a memory as her mother's eyes found hers.

An icy feeling pricked her shoulders. Rowan gathered himself at her feet, but as quickly as it happened, her mother's gaze shifted, looking past her, wide and frightened. A tall figure, white as snow in deepest winter, flew from the nearby thicket.

Her mother screamed. The basket fell.

Maeve rushed forward. "Mother!"

Her sharp cry tore through the vision. The figure, her mother, they both vanished, scattered under thorny roots. Maeve swallowed, looking around, but she was alone. "It wasn't real," she whispered, sweat trickling down her back. She repeated herself, and Rowan gave a wary hiss. "The moonlight is playing tricks," she said. After a minute to gather herself, she pressed on.

At the river, Maeve stood back from the bank. She adjusted the belt low on her wide hips. Across the water and through the trees, the distant, dim torchlight of the castle shone.

Goods lay in neat piles thirty yards north along the river, Keeva's cleanup efforts coming to fruition. A pair of water nymphs sprang out from a boulder-laden patch of foam, then disappeared, shimmering into the murky bank.

Rowan coiled at Maeve's heels, uneasy at their venture to this border so late at night. She ignored him, though. Her gaze drifted instead to the layers of bog, the intricate wooden tracks upon them, beckoning her to a kingdom she could be a part of, a hope that grew more vibrant each second, bright as the starlight.

She found a shallow passage in the water. The opposite bank was mere yards away. She took a deep breath, then stepped in.

The raven's call froze her mid step. Its cry sounded deep and low; she cowered, clamping her hands over her ears as it squawked louder.

She didn't understand. The raven was here? Frantically, she searched the night sky, the dark trees, for the Caretaker's bird. Smaller creatures fled in the nearby brush. Rowan hissed as another wail cut through the night. Then, she saw it.

Overhead, obsidian wings opened wide. The raven soared over the highest treetop from the west. It stood out even against the charcoal sky, great wings marring the starlight. Maeve's courage shrank as the raven cried again, then dove.

Rowan hissed and bumped her ankle, but Maeve was stuck, frozen by the sight of the bird careening toward her at a startling pace. She ducked at the last second, the air whipping past her ear as the raven peeled by. *What is happening?*

She tried to run, but the river bottom was slick, and she stumbled. The raven circled back overhead, cutting across her path and giving another warning screech. Frantic, Maeve steadied herself. The village homes seemed so close. The castle, the kingdom, lay just out of her reach. A heavy longing pitted her gut before she checked the sky. Frustration roiled in her chest. Again, she stepped forward. This time, the raven dove, and she just had time to shield her face as his claws tore across her skin.

Clutching her forearm, she found three thin lines of blood. Her breath heaving, Maeve cursed the raven and retreated.

Rowan was coiled, his head raised in a menacing S when the raven circled again. Maeve found the path back to her fen after scampering up the bank. The raven dove. She fell, ready for claws that would sink into her legs, but its cry was stifled in a flash of silver scales.

Turning over on the grass, she found the raven thrashing between Rowan's jaws. Its wings spread wide, forcing his mouth open. It broke free quickly and tumbled onto the bank. Rowan lunged, but the raven took flight. It gave a final cry, then disappeared beyond the tree line.

Maeve fell onto her back, breathless. She reached out. Rowan slithered closer, running over her hand. "Thank you." He flicked his tongue, then seemed to scan her injury. She held it up. "Only a flesh wound. I'll be all right."

She sat up, pulling her knees to her chest. Why had the raven attacked like that? She scanned the river. "It was like he didn't want me to cross."

Rowan hissed low, slithering around her in a protective circle before heading for the fen. Maeve stared forlornly across the water. She had been so close. So close to feeling like she was part of something, somewhere. Like she had people who knew her, who wanted her to belong.

Standing, she adjusted the belt. It was damp and dirty from when she'd fallen. Only for a moment, she let herself be sad. She let the truth of things settle, let herself feel the sinking isolation. Then, she pulled back her shoulders, her fingers eager for a quill as she headed home.

❖

Donovan spoke first. "Prince Diarmaid, you're…"

"Dead." He said it almost incredulously, reaching to feel his wound. Bile rose in Keeva's throat at the hard black blood. "And please, call me Brennus."

"What happened to you?" asked Naela.

He shook his head. "An ambush. The elves attacked us."

All three of them exchanged glances. Keeva shot Donovan a frightened look. *Father.*

I know. He was too late.

Keeva shook her head. Overwhelming worry consumed her. Her father hadn't arrived in time to speak with Queen Sina and stop the elves from attacking Venostes. What had happened to him, then? Epona's key lay heavy in her hand.

"How long have you been here?" Donovan asked.

"I'm not sure." A crease fell between his brows. "Time moves differently here. If it moves at all. Days. A few weeks or a few moons." He shook his head. "I wish I knew." His gaze met theirs. "What I do know is that out there"—he pointed toward the depths of the passageway they'd yet to walk—"there is no time. Unrest is uprooting my homeland."

Donovan twitched at her side. Had Queen Sina been right?

"My sister needs help."

Naela shifted. "Your sister?" She looked past him. "Is she…"

"No. She's alive. But gods only know for how much longer. She was taken. She's strong. And she's fighting. I can feel it." He made a fist and brought it to rest over his heart. "She was always the stubborn one between us."

Naela's voice was cautious when she asked, "Why haven't you crossed through the gate?"

Donovan lifted his chin in support, specks of spell-fire glowing on his fingers.

Brennus glanced at the soft golden light, his eyes sad. "I should have crossed over, but it didn't feel right. There was a pull from out there." Again, he motioned to the dark. "After Epona came for me, it was like I was in a trance. I was headed for that great gate, the one you saw. But then, the voices started. My family's cries. My sister's voice, Aurelia speaking to me. I could hear their desperation. Their pleas for help. They're in trouble. My entire kingdom is." His shoulders rose and fell, though no breath escaped him. "I fled into the shadows and found this tunnel. I'm not sure why she didn't follow. To think, the gatekeeper could show sympathy."

Keeva bit her bottom lip, recalling the sad, regretful look in Epona's eyes when she had turned away Keeva's desperate plea.

"Whatever the reason," Brennus was saying, "I'm not supposed to be here. I can feel it." He raised his hand, and only then did Keeva notice the opaqueness of his skin. She could see through it, the rock evident behind him. "That's why there's no time. I need to cross over but only once Aurelia has been helped."

"If she's been kidnapped, how do you know where she is? Where are we supposed to go to help her were we to even do so?" Keeva asked. She felt the others step closer, their suspicions clear in their shuffling feet.

A small smile lifted his pale face. "I don't recommend death, but it does give one a strange glimpse into out there." He pointed into the dark, then gestured to his temple. "I can't see everything, but I get flashes." He closed his eyes. "Aurelia on horseback, then dragged through the wildlands. But I've also seen better moments. She's found others on her journey, and they're heading west. The Mountains of Ionad loom near."

Donovan crossed his arms. "Ionad? That's at least a two days' journey to its heart." Keeva, meanwhile, felt the spark of an idea. "What do you expect us to do?"

"The dark force is after the woman she travels with. They can't defeat him alone. Not in Ionad."

Keeva ran a finger along the edge of the key, nodding to herself as Naela asked, "Why should we believe any of this? You could be a clever spirit, a conjuring of Epona's magic."

He gave a small laugh. "Follow me."

Again, they exchanged glances as Brennus turned, heading farther into the tunnel's depths. They lit their saols and followed. It didn't take long before the passageway widened, and an archway appeared, the dark woods in view just beyond.

"That will get you back to where you came from. You're right," he said, facing Naela. "You have no reason to believe me." Brennus bowed his head. "I won't cross over until I know Aurelia has made it through the mountains. I'm her brother," he added with a shrug, "I abandoned her once. I can't do that again."

Though it could hardly be possible, Keeva could still hear Epona's agonizing wails. She pocketed the key, unable to bear its weight. The idea that had kindled to life at the prince's request took full shape. *This was something good.* Something good to chase away the dark shadow of what she'd just done.

"Fine," she said, stepping past him. The others followed, exchanging looks, and they stood with their backs to the archway. Cool night wind tugged at their tunics. "We'll help you."

Brennus's gaze widened. "You will?"

"Yes. We'll help your sister. Whatever this dark force is, it hasn't met a member of Uterni yet." She pulled herself up, placing her hands on her hips.

"Keevs," Donovan started, but she cut him off.

"You have our word, Prince Diarmaid. We'll leave as soon as possible."

"Thank you." A contented smile lingered as he stepped back, the black shadows consuming him until he was gone.

Keeva avoided the others' gazes as she hurried out the tunnel. Sure enough, they were back in the wildlands. Their wildlands. Only a mile from Maeve's fen. Epona's key seemed to burn inside her cloak. Keeva ignored the angry singe and pressed on.

Chapter Thirty

To Keeva's surprise, Naela and Donovan didn't say a word once they found their way back to the castle. All words seemed pointless inside the dark halls. They were spent from their trek through the woods. Naela and Donovan asked what she'd been thinking, why she'd taken the key, and how she could have made a promise to a dead prince.

She didn't have an answer to any of their questions. Not any new words, anyway. Stealing Epona's key had been a knee-jerk reaction. Her lowly desperation had grown greedy hands and overran her mind. Helping Brennus was a way to cover up the new feeling in her stomach, an irksome guilt she couldn't shake.

Alone in her chambers, she used twine she'd meant for one of her spears and made a necklace of her own. Standing before a foggy piece of glass, she tucked the key beneath her tunic.

Dawn light crept through her window. She leaned against the table, collecting herself. She wanted to go to Maeve and tell her what had happened. She shook the sinewy strings of memory, the sticky, unshakable sounds of Epona's screams, from the corners of her mind.

"No key, no passing over," she said, then repeated those words again and again. She closed her eyes. The mantra still on her lips, she crossed the room and found the turbulent waves out over the cliffside. She took a long, slow breath. She had to look ahead.

Later that morning, she pressed her ear to her parents' chamber door. Quiet. Gently, she stepped into the room.

The air was thick and hot. A blazing fire roared opposite the great bed to her left. There, Tacari stood, pressing a rag to her mother's head. She lay pale and motionless among the bearskins.

"I'd ask where you've been, but gods know how much truth would sprout from your words," Tacari said, his voice low. At the bedside, Keeva found her mother asleep. The candlelight grazed her sunken cheeks. Her frame seemed frighteningly slight, and a faint, thready pulse beat in her wrist when Keeva clasped her hand.

"I took care of things, Mother," Keeva said, watching her chest rise and fall. "Things will be okay," she added, looking up. Tacari set the rag aside.

"Keeva—"

She squeezed her mother's hand. "I have news," she said, cutting him off. "Venostes is under siege. The elves attacked them."

Tacari straightened, finding his staff against the nearby wall. "What? When?"

"A moon ago, maybe less." She licked her lips, uncertain how to explain the fact that she had learned this from a recently deceased prince.

"Your father left one moon ago."

"I know. Do you think…do you think he was too late in getting there?"

Tacari moved a piece of hair from her mother's forehead. Keeva felt a strange sense of nostalgia, recalling all the times he had done that to her when she was young and ill. "That would be the best scenario."

"We could send more guards east to follow and make sure he's all right."

He nodded. "That would be wise."

They both stood quietly, watching her mother, her eyes fluttering in her sleep. Their last conversation crept out from the corners of the room. She bit her cheek, an apology ready on her tongue. Instead, she said, "Send for me when she wakes, please. I'll prepare and send the guard party for Father. Then, Donovan and I are headed to Ionad."

"Ionad?"

The key beneath her tunic felt hot, making her skin itch. "We have royal business there. I need…" She swallowed. *I need to do something good. Something right.* "I need to go there."

"Your kingdom needs you here. Needs its leaders." He pulled himself up to his full height. "Keeva, your mother is sick. Your father is gone. You plan to send the guards away, and you and your brother are taking a vacation?"

Her gaze widened. "It's not like that, Tacari." Heat crept up her neck. He did have a point. The village had been talking. Those who had family outside the castle had brought in the local gossip. People knew the queen wasn't well. The king had left to much fanfare, and the kingdom anticipated his return. To add to that, Dain had been collecting a following, leading to more unrest in the village.

Keeva clenched her jaw. "Leaders take action, Tacari. This requires all of us." Her tone softened. "As a leader, I must delegate at times. Uterni is in good hands until we're back."

He stopped and turned in the doorway. His mouth was open in mild surprise. She smiled, and he returned it. "As you wish, Your Majesty."

When he was gone, Keeva walked around the bed and crawled in to lie beside her mother. She rested her head on her shoulder. "I won't let you go." Tears slid silently down her nose. "Please don't go. Please."

Desperate hope seeped into her lungs. She wanted to be right. She wanted to be in control. But now, after everything? She felt like all of it was wrong.

❖

Maeve laid an extra snare after breakfast. The raven had returned. His distant croak reminded her he was watching. *Maybe this will make him happy.*

Rowan had been testy all morning, reluctantly taking a mouse she'd caught for him. "Don't be mad at me." She tossed another log onto the fire despite the warm air outside, summer on the horizon.

"Maeve, are you home?"

She grinned. "Keeva." Then, louder, "I'm home." She found the ribbon. "Just a moment."

The ribbon secure, she opened the door. Keeva fell onto her, collapsing in a hug. Maeve let out a surprised *oh* at the show of vulnerability. "Are you okay?" she asked, letting Keeva lay her weight upon her. She held her steady, her arms wrapped around Keeva's waist.

"I missed you."

Maeve smiled. "I missed you, too."

Keeva surprised her by cupping her face. She pulled back slightly as she sensed Keeva leaning close. Keeva's lips found hers. She stiffened at first, shocked at the soft smooth feel of their lips together.

Her hands fumbled up to Keeva's shoulders. Keeva's lips opened, and Maeve pulled back to catch her breath.

"I'm sorry," Keeva said.

Maeve took a breath, aching to look into her eyes. "Don't be sorry." She found Keeva's face and put her palms on warm, soft cheeks.

Before another kiss, though, Keeva grabbed her wrist. "Maeve." Her voice was concerned. "Who did this to you?"

Maeve lowered her arm, running her hand over the fresh marks left from last night. "My caretaker's raven. I was trying to cross the river, but he wouldn't let me pass."

"Wouldn't let you?"

"That's what it seemed like." She sensed Keeva's unspoken question. "You're wondering why I was at the river." Keeva found her hand, and she smiled when Keeva placed a kiss on her knuckles. "I was thinking about you and imagining your meeting with Epona." Keeva shifted, her grip tightening. "I guess I wanted to walk through the village. I felt like I was helping you." She shrugged. "I wanted to be like everyone else."

"That raven and I are going to have words one day. It shouldn't have attacked you." She hesitated. "Do you think your caretaker gave it orders to do so?"

Instinctually, Maeve was ready to defend him. *He's overprotective. He wants to keep me safe.* She opened her mouth to say all of these things, but something stopped her. This was different. Those old mantras were replaced with a new thought: *he wants to control me.*

The idea shook her. Trembling, she reached for Keeva, finding her other hand. "I don't know. It doesn't matter now. Tell me everything about last night." She smiled, eager to change the subject.

To her surprise, Keeva didn't respond immediately. Maeve led them to her bed, careful to find the edge before pulling Keeva to sit beside her. They faced one another, hands still clasped.

"Well," Keeva said, clearing her throat, "we did speak to Epona."

"That's wonderful. Did she see things differently this time?"

"Not quite."

"She didn't show pity?"

Keeva's laugh was small and sad. "I think she did, actually, but she still insisted there was nothing she could do."

"Oh." Maeve wasn't sure what to say. Thoughts of her own mother disappearing rang in her mind. She sympathized with Keeva and could only imagine how agonizing it must be to watch a parent suffer as the queen had.

Keeva shifted on the bed, bringing their hands into her lap. "Maeve."

"Yes?"

Donovan's voice made both of them jump. "Keeva!"

"Donovan?" She didn't move.

His shout was angry. "Keeva, I know you're in there."

Maeve asked, "Is everything all right?"

Keeva spoke quietly, her words rushing out like the river in summer. "Maeve, I should tell you something."

"All right."

"Our meeting with Epona... I..." She stood, and Maeve reached for her.

Donovan pounded on the door. "Keeva, you can't hide from this."

Maeve again tried to find her but couldn't. "What is he talking about?"

"What do you mean?" Keeva shouted back, but Maeve caught the falter in her voice. "Is Mother all right?"

"No. You know she isn't. And the village...something is wrong. I don't understand it, but Naela thinks it's because of what you did."

A crackle sprang from the fire. Maeve jumped and felt cold.

Finally, Keeva spoke, low and dejected. "I'll be right there."

The same sick, squirming feeling from when their group had first set out stuck in Maeve's stomach. "Keeva?"

"Maeve," she said quietly, "I did something."

"To Epona?"

Donovan barked through the door, "She stole the gatekeeper's key."

After the wave of shock subsided, Maeve had to force her eyes to stay closed. "You...what?"

"I had to. She left me no choice."

Maeve's legs felt heavy, yet she trembled. Keeva, princess of Uterni, had stolen from the gatekeeper? "Why?" she managed to ask, finding the table and leaning against it.

Keeva hurried forward, finding Maeve's wrist. Her grip was strong, and Maeve sensed deep guilt in her. "Maeve, you have to understand. My mother...she's the only one who saw me for so long. She understands me. She can't go, not now."

Sympathy morphed into something else at her words. "Keeva," Maeve said carefully, "I know it's difficult. Believe me. My mother left, and it was terrible."

"Maeve, your mother isn't queen."

The air seemed to fly from the room. Maeve stepped back, dropping her hands. "Are you saying my mother being gone isn't the same?" Her voice rose, and she heard Rowan stir nearby. "Are you saying the life I've spent without her wasn't difficult? That I couldn't possibly know what it's like to lose a mother?"

"No, Maeve, I didn't mean that." Keeva drew near, but Maeve pushed her hand aside.

"I said I would help you meet Epona. You made me believe you only wanted to talk to her." She shook her head. "I didn't want to be part of something like this."

"Maeve…"

"Keeva." Donovan pounded again at the door. "There's no time."

They were quiet. Maeve let Rowan slither between her legs. She knew he was preparing to lunge. She only had to say his name. "You better go," she said finally.

"Please, Maeve—"

But she turned her back. The gesture sent Rowan forward. A loud hiss was followed by Keeva's startled steps backward. Maeve bit her lip to keep it from quivering. When the door closed, Maeve tore off the ribbon. She felt sick, like a thousand coals had been set afire beneath her skin. Letting out a cry, she turned and threw the ribbon into the fire.

CHAPTER THIRTY-ONE

D onovan, slow down."
Her brother flew back to the village, not caring as she grew breathless running to catch up over the wooden trackways, down through rows of homes, and toward the seaside. Keeva skidded on the sloping trackway down a steep turn, throwing out her arms for balance. Ahead of them lay the market, but they cut right. Here lay the last and oldest row of homes, ancient and moss-covered, where fishermen often spent their last days. A crowd had gathered around the front door of one.

"Your Highnesses." A woman with long gray hair and lines like dry riverbeds etched deep in her sallow cheeks ran out to meet them. "Please, he's in here."

The crowd parted, still murmuring as Keeva followed Donovan into the fisherman's home. She recognized the old man from village events. He always did show magic with a local gnome to entertain the children.

Donovan shook his arm and spoke gently. "Mitre, how are you?"

The old man's dark eyes were wide as he turned, searching. His face was smoother than the woman's, but time was evident in gnarled knuckles and scars scattered across his arms. He lay on a cot near the fire, skin ashy gray, and deep shadows beneath his eyes. A rag lay over his neck, kept in place with his left hand.

"Prince Glantor. It's an honor. I don't mean to cause such a fuss."

"Nonsense, Mitre. We only wish to understand what happened."

Keeva also wanted to understand. She frowned and turned to the old woman, whom she believed to be Mitre's wife. Fear sat in her eyes as Donovan helped Mitre sit up. His wife kept her distance, standing behind a small table. Bony fingers clutched a gods' token that hung around her neck.

"I was down in the rocks, like I do each day. My spear caught between some boulders in the water. I went to get it, but the tide came in. Lost my footing. I slipped and…" Mitre searched the ceiling. "And I fell."

Donovan nodded, and Keeva stepped closer. Mitre hesitated, then removed the rag from his neck.

Keeva gasped, and Donovan stepped back. The woman spoke in a hushed voice behind them. "The gods are angry with us. We did nothing to deserve this."

Keeva gaped at the hole in Mitre's neck. A perforation the size of a spearhead ran from below his ear halfway down his neck. Keeva's stomach turned at the sight of vocal cords.

"There was so much blood," Mitre said, his eyes fearful. "I tried to stop it, but I grew faint, and everythin' went black."

"How did you get back here?" asked Donovan.

"Some of the other fishermen found me. Said I floated back with the current." He coughed, a dry swallow audible. "Said I was dead."

Donovan blinked, then turned to meet Keeva's gaze.

"But you're…" She licked her lips, feeling hot under the firelight. "You're still here."

"Was the strangest thing. Everythin' was black and cold." Seeming to notice her frightened gaze locked on his neck, he covered the wound. "I waited for Epona, but she never came. Then, I woke up here."

"He should have crossed over," the old woman said. "I love my husband," she added, looking from Keeva to Donovan. "But this isn't right."

Keeva understood the fear in her eyes. Mitre shouldn't be here. A wound like that was fatal. He should have crossed over. But he couldn't.

"Stay inside," Donovan was saying as he stood to go. "We'll do everything we can to make this right. I promise."

Like a guilty wolf pup, Keeva plodded behind her brother. Along the trackway, she worked up the will to mutter, "Donovan, I didn't mean for this to happen."

"Well, it's happening."

She pulled her cloak tighter, willing herself to stand taller as she said, "You don't have to go with me." He shot her a look. "To Ionad. I'm leaving at dawn tomorrow. I can go alone." She took a shaky breath. "I did this."

His mouth was a tight line. The end of his ponytail flicked angrily behind him. "You should visit Mother. I've got to go see another villager. A young girl…" He shook his head. "I'll see you in the morning."

He turned brusquely down the eastern trackway. Keeva slowed, scanning the village homes. This wasn't supposed to happen. She'd only wanted to keep her mother here. The wind kicked up. The air cleared her mind for a moment. She stepped outside of herself and saw what she'd done. Saw how selfish she was being, how like a small child she was acting. A daughter unwilling to face the realities of this realm. Unwilling to let the natural order of things come to pass.

The key around her neck seemed to sink into her skin. Epona's cries echoed. She couldn't have done all of that for nothing. Keeva pulled her cloak tighter and headed for the castle.

"Mother." Keeva sat alongside her mother's hip on the edge of the bed. She'd sat for nearly an hour there after dinner, dismissing the chamber maidens. Tacari had come by to administer more henbane. He'd helped drop water onto her mother's lips from a rag, scattered droplets falling onto her dry skin.

"No word from your father," Tacari had said, not meeting Keeva's gaze. "Naela and her parents left at dawn this morning."

She'd nodded. Everything was piling up around her; she felt trapped, stifled by a stone wall built by her own hand. She'd spent hours in the armory earlier in the day, but not even the satisfaction of hitting things could diminish the awful feeling she'd been saddled with. Her father was unaccounted for. Maeve was angry. Donovan would hardly speak to her. And her mother…

Keeva was rubbing the fine material of her mother's tunic at her shoulder when her eyes fluttered open.

"Keeva, sweetheart." A wan smile sat beneath her foggy eyes. "How do you feel?"

"The pain is less."

"That's good." Epona's key tugged beneath her tunic.

The hopeful look in her mother's eyes was short-lived. She winced and curled herself tight, and her limbs stiffened.

"Mother?"

"It's only pain, darling."

The tight smile didn't assuage Keeva's dismay. "I'll send for Tacari."

"No." She sputtered through a series of coughs. "No, sweetheart. I'll be all right." Slowly, she turned onto her back. Keeva helped situate her among the bearskins. After a long sigh, her mother said, "There is something I should tell you, Keeva."

Keeva wondered if she knew about the necklace, about what she'd done.

"You should know this. I thought you did, but I need to say it." Her voice was raspy as her watery gaze landed on her. "I love you, darling."

Her breath hitched, and Keeva bit her cheek to hold back the emotion surging in her chest.

"We don't say it enough. Your father and I. But I love you with every part of me."

Keeva swallowed, willing herself not to cry. "I love you, too."

"Your father and brother...they take up so much space in this realm. You know that. People see them. They listen to them."

In her mother's gaze, Keeva saw what she was trying to say. She saw the understanding of what she'd felt for years. The reason why she worked so hard to win each competition, to be strong, to stand out... to be seen.

Her mother reached up, and Keeva dipped her chin. "I see you, Keeva. I always have." She ran her fingers through Keeva's hair. "You never needed this. You never needed to work yourself to the marrow. You never needed to win for me to pay attention." Her voice broke. "You are just as seen as your brother. Do you hear me?" Keeva leaned back to meet her gaze. "I see you. I have always seen you, and I always will."

A great pressure built inside her lungs. Two competing bodies pressed against the walls of her heart. One verged on tears and yearned to hug her mother, yearned to cry and weep and let herself feel the truth of this moment. It urged her to do what the voice in the back of her mind shouted, to return the key and make things right. But the other side—the side she knew well lately—pushed back and pushed hard. Its red eyes glared, its guilt-ridden arms clenched tight around her, pulling on the key. It wouldn't let her let go. "Hold on, Mother," she said. "I can't do this without you. I won't let you go." She sniffled, swiping at her nose. "I can't."

Her mother fell back against the bearskins, knees to her chest. For a moment, Keeva watched her fall into a fitful sleep.

In the armory, Keeva found her favorite spear. Polishing the black onyx stone, she pushed aside every emotion, forced it back behind her parents' chamber door, and prepared for the journey to Ionad.

Chapter Thirty-two

Maeve leaned against the chopping stump amid the damp, early morning air. Through the steam drifting up from her wooden mug, she scanned the edge of her fen. Dark thoughts had festered in her mind all night. She'd tried to force them out, shove them to the pools of green along the border of her home.

The darkest thought of all sat heavy within the shadowy elms: *was my mother right? Is it too dangerous out there?*

Maeve blinked, the sounds around her distant and dim. Keeva had lied to her. Hadn't she? She'd used Maeve to get to the gatekeeper under the guise of talking to her. But now...Maeve knew something was wrong. She could feel it. The realm's balance had skewed. Ghoulish screams seemed to echo between the trees at night. Her own thoughts shrieked in confusion and chaos. She didn't know what to think. She'd trusted Keeva, and that trust had been broken.

Rowan slithered by. He gave an agitated hiss at the dew-covered grass. She watched him, the black pattern on his scales reminding her of the raven. Her gaze flew to the trees. She could feel him watching. She could feel his talons on her skin, tearing her flesh. For what? To keep her here?

Maybe it was better that she stayed in her fen. Maybe everyone was right. Maybe she was better alone.

"Maeve." Keeva's voice startled the quiet air from over her right shoulder. "Maeve, please, we need to talk."

Maeve kept her eyes forward. A strange defiance steeled her. She was unwilling to close her eyes. A taste of danger seemed right in her fitful state. "I don't know if I want to talk to you."

Keeva's footsteps drew nearer. Maeve imagined her only a few paces behind, her bright hair shining amid the dark dawn. Her sculpted arms reached out. Her face was drawn in a serious frown.

When she took another step, Maeve tilted her head in warning. "I wouldn't come any closer."

The silence seemed to stretch between them. "Maeve, I didn't mean to cause all this. Epona…she wouldn't hear me. I felt like I had no choice."

Maeve listened, carefully placing her mug at her side.

"I'm sorry for what I said before, about your mother. I shouldn't have said that."

"You're right."

"I just…my mother has always known who I am. She's known I don't speak the way Donovan does. I can't command a room like my father or gracefully hold court like she does. I'm too direct. I'm too loud. Too different." Her voice softened. "I'm too much."

Maeve's gaze found a distant birch tree.

"My mother accepted me the way that I was. I thought I'd have more time to learn. More time to change. More time before…" She took a long breath. "I need more time."

Maeve pulled her knees to her chest. "I understand," she said. "If I could have had more time with my mother…one more year, one more week, a day." She cleared her throat. "I understand."

Keeva took a step, but Rowan shot out from a nearby tree in her direction. "Maeve?"

She closed her eyes. She understood Keeva's pain. Still, she wasn't ready to forgive her. She'd taken a risk letting Keeva close. And what had Keeva done with that? Maeve could hear the sincerity in her words now, but it wasn't enough. Her mind spun with dread. In the frenzy, old pain surfaced. "I hurt someone once. I was eight." Curious silence told her Keeva was listening. "An old man wearing your kingdom's colors. He was at the river. It happened so fast." She opened her eyes, unable to relive it again. "I hurt people."

"Maeve." Keeva stepped closer.

It was all too much. "You better go."

Another hiss from Rowan prompted Keeva's steps. At the edge of the fen, Maeve heard her pause. The air seemed to scream with worry from where Keeva stood. Maeve could feel it. She wanted to go to her, to forgive her, but she couldn't. Not yet.

Once Keeva was gone, Maeve went inside. She moved stiffly, feeling stuck in a strange dreamscape. She made more bread. She sat by the fire. She lay in bed. By midday, she was exhausted. Staring out the window, she thought she heard the raven. Or was the caw only in her mind? She had expected another letter. The last note she had written to the Caretaker was different from the others. She hadn't held back. A surge like the ocean's waves had thrown the deeply buried questions onto the page through her quill. She needed to know. Somehow, she knew he had answers. Her rations had become minimal. His words were terse.

She recalled the time a troll had passed by the river one spring. A wolf and her pups were drinking. The troll had thrown pebbles at the pups, barking laughter at their frightened cries. The mother had approached him. The troll had only laughed more at her bared teeth and raised hackles. He'd found a fallen branch, poked her. Teased her. Maeve had watched the mother's lips curl, a low snarl that began in her gut and finished on the sweaty flesh of the troll's neck.

Part of her wondered if she had poked the wolf.

Maeve stood before the mirror and searched her reflection. Who was she now? What had happened to the quiet gorgon in the fen? What had happened to her routine, her simple life?

A light played behind her shoulder in the mirror. Her mother stood there, smiling. Maeve smiled back. The dizzying whirl this spring had brought seemed to spin around the room, but Maeve held tight to the point of focus. Something inside her told her she was close to the truth. All of this was leading somewhere, somehow. For the first time, answers lay just beyond the walls of her home, just beyond the trees.

She only had to wait.

❖

Keeva thought about Maeve the entire trek to Ionad. She and Donovan took the shortest route, but it was still a two-day journey. They camped in a shallow cave overnight, munching on fruit leathers and dried tree-dweller meat swiped from the kitchen. The tall black peaks loomed as they traversed steep cliffsides and scrambled over rock fragments into the belly of the mountains.

"I think I hear something." Donovan's voice broke through her drifting mind.

They'd been quiet thus far. She stopped and listened. A voice echoed from somewhere nearby. They sped up, hurrying around a dark, nearly lifeless stretch of terrain.

Shooting her brother a glance as he walked beside her, Keeva said, "What are we going to say?"

"What do you mean?

"We can't just walk up to the princess of Venostes and say, 'Hello, your dead brother told us you'd be here.'"

"Why not?"

"Donovan, that sounds insane."

"Well, this situation is insane. We need a plan."

"Why don't we act like we're here for another reason?"

"What reason is that?"

"I haven't thought of it yet."

"Well, think quickly," he said, slowing and crouching behind a boulder. "Look."

Down the path stood a young man, maybe a couple of years younger than them, with hair even brighter than her own. His fiery locks blew in the unforgiving wind, and his dirt-smudged, freckled face was pinched as he and a slender elf worked to help a tall, semiconscious man bearing a nasty gash in his forehead. The height difference between the three seemed to make it difficult for them to prop the man's arms around their shoulders.

"Come on," Donovan said, and they hurried out. To the trio, he asked, "Can we help?"

The man jumped, dropping the other man's arm, which fell with a thud at his side as he slumped. He fixed them with frightened hazel eyes. He looked like he'd been out here for moons. His tunic and pants were filthy, and hungry shadows sat beneath his eyes. The elf swiftly set the man against the rock and pulled an arrow from his quiver, aiming it at Donovan's chest. The freckled man managed to pull himself up. Keeva imagined he was trying to be intimidating as he conjured his saol and stepped forward, but he looked small against the dark rock. "What d'ya want?"

Keeva held up a hand as Donovan did the same, eyeing the elf. "We don't want to hurt you. We're here to help."

The young man glanced between them. "We need to get my friend back to his cave. There was an ambush. The pooka went after them."

"Them? There are others?"

He dimmed his saol and nodded, his stance still defensive. "My friend Jastyn and Her Highness, Princess Aurelia."

Keeva shot Donovan a look. "Please, where did they go?"

He pointed north. "That way, I think. We came to help Vreis." The man's eyes were filled with tears. "He didn't deserve to get caught in the middle of this."

His words hit Keeva hard. She thought of Maeve. The key tugged again beneath her tunic. "We'll help them," she said.

The young man and the elf exchanged looks. Seemingly reluctantly, the elf sheathed his arrow. An accepting silence filled the air.

"Clean that wound once you get him back home," Donovan said. He seemed like he wanted to follow and assist but held himself back. "You'll be okay?"

The man nodded. "It doesn't want us. It wants Jastyn."

"It?" Keeva asked. "The dark force?"

The elf took a step forward, his brow furrowed. The young man's face shifted, his gaze startled. "How did you—"

"There's no time," she said, cutting him off. "Go safely…" She paused, waiting.

"Coran." He pointed to his chest. "This is Rigo," he added. The elf raised a brow but gave a small nod.

"Coran, Rigo," she said. "We'll find your friends."

Donovan grimaced, then stepped forward when Coran squatted and tried to tug Vreis's arm over himself but stumbled. "I can help walk him back, if you like."

Coran looked wary and eyed Donovan, then her. But he nodded, his arms hanging tiredly at his sides. "It's just a quarter mile."

Donovan easily swooped under Vreis's arm and propped him upright, much closer to Rigo's height than Coran. "Lead the way," he said, and Coran scurried ahead. To Keeva, he called over his shoulder. "Go. I'll catch up."

She nodded and started down the northern path.

Ionad wasn't a hospitable place. Keeva wondered why Coran and his friends were traveling through here. She continued along the path, spear in hand. What was she going to do when she found the others? What was this dark force? She had no idea what to expect. All she knew was that if the elf queen feared it, she would need to be careful. Tacari's warning voice ran in her mind. *"A kingdom needs its leaders."*

She shook her head. She was trying to keep its leader on her throne. A small new voice asked, "What kind of a ruler does Uterni need? Is a bedridden monarch, barely able to hold herself up, in such pain she can't stand, the leader the kingdom deserves?"

She's my mother. I can't be left with Donovan and Father. Who will see me then?

An image of Maeve formed before her. She walked along the nearby path, the ribbon tied neatly over her eyes, but her steps landing easily, as if she could see the mountain.

Maeve saw her. Or she had before Keeva had messed everything up.

A series of shouts echoed ahead of her. Keeva slowed. A series of crevasses lay ahead, meeting in a ledge thirty feet above. As she scanned the best path to scale it, footsteps sounded behind her, and Donovan appeared.

"Safe and sound," he said, and she pointed to the rock wall, then to where the shouts were coming from. He nodded.

Keeva swiftly strapped her spear to her back using the ends of her cloak. Together, they scaled the wall. Childhood years spent scrambling up the Uterni seaside cliffs proved useful, and they were over the edge quickly.

Donovan was right behind her. On the other side of the ledge, she situated her spear next to her, and they crouched, staying low behind a boulder. Despite that, she felt exposed among the open air of the empty stretch along the dip in the mountain's peak. It wouldn't matter, Keeva realized, because what was happening in the clearing below was clearly not about them.

"By the gods," Donovan said, and Keeva swallowed past her dry throat, unprepared for what they saw.

High in the air, a massive, screeching pooka hovered. Its wings beat the sky, spirals of dirt and rock kicking up from the force. In its long claws, Keeva spotted what they were looking for.

"The princess." Keeva motioned, and Donovan moved closer. It had to be the her. She looked just like Brennus. Only her eyes—wide, frightened, but determined—were a beautiful sky blue. Her tunic was torn and bloody around her shoulders where the pooka's massive claws had wrapped beneath her arms. She thrashed, scratching and clawing and fighting with every ounce of energy she possessed.

Donovan started forward, but Keeva held him back. "Look." She pointed toward the dusty earth where pockets of simmering spell-fire died out among the rocks and shrubs.

Her brother stiffened. "The dark force."

Not far from a black horse with fearsome, red eyes, the hooded figure seemed startlingly human. Though his rotted arms and mottled flesh made Keeva's stomach roil. He had another young woman firm in his spindly grasp. It had to be Jastyn. She was thrashing, too, though Keeva could see her energy and life leaving her with each passing moment.

"We have to help her, too," she said.

Donovan grimaced, his gaze flying around, analyzing the chaos before them.

Keeva's body sang, her spear tight in her hand. She bit her lip, eager to begin. Eager to remember what it felt like to do good.

Her brother nodded, then smiled. "Divide and conquer?"

"You know it."

A silent count between them. Then, they leapt over the edge.

Spell-fire tore from their hands toward their targets. Keeva timed hers with the young woman's attempt to kick the dark force. Her magenta light hit him at the same time as the young woman's feet, but it wasn't enough. She slid down the rock wall, running down into the clearing, but not before tossing Donovan her spear. He readied it, aimed, then hurled it down. It landed with a satisfying thud beneath the dark force's hood, and he released Jastyn.

Overhead, golden lights flew toward the pooka. Keeva grinned as her brother's sais, encompassed with spell-fire, hit their target. Aurelia screamed as she fell. Keeva heard Jastyn yell, too. She positioned herself just right, and Aurelia fell easily into her arms.

"Are you all right?" she asked, setting the princess down carefully.

"I'm...I'm okay," Aurelia responded.

Keeva imagined she was in shock; her eyes were so wide, and fear poured out from them. Satisfied the princess would be okay for a minute, Keeva leapt sideways. The familiar taste of victory sat smooth on her tongue, and she wanted more. Finding Donovan's sais lodged into the pooka, she jumped atop it and twisted the daggers for good measure. The defeated scream from the creature told her he was down, and she yanked the weapons free. A swift kick to its leg had her practically sauntering away. She threw another saol at it as a victory lap.

Her breathing was hard, and she turned to assess the clearing. Jastyn and Aurelia had found their way to the clearing's edge, out of harm's way. Donovan was unsuccessfully wrestling her spear away from the dark force. He struggled a moment more before he was finally able to dislodge it. He grinned at her, but he dropped it when he tripped on a rock.

"Look out," she called, and Donovan flattened himself against the earth as she fired a saol. Recovered, he fired his gold saol, and together, they wrapped around the dark force like vines. To her surprise, Aurelia appeared at her side. Keeva looked to Donovan. He nodded, and Aurelia returned the gesture before firing her saol into theirs, the colors twisting in a blazing tangle around the dark force.

The horse that had stood nearby ran toward them, seeking its rider. The dark force gave a howl, then fell onto the beast's back. They rode skyward, then disappeared in a clap of thunder and dark clouds.

As the sky cleared, Keeva and Donovan found the others. They had handled things quite well, she thought. They had saved the princess and her companion, not to mention Coran and Vreis. Keeva felt an inkling of pride. They hadn't let anything slip about the fact that they'd met Aurelia's brother at the gate of the Otherworld or that they even knew who they were. That was, until she came back to earth and realized Donovan was talking.

He mentioned Vreis, and an awkward silence followed. "I mean to say, they're fine. That tall fellow and your freckled friend." He grinned stupidly, then said, "The Mountains of Ionad don't normally host such an offering of activity."

From there, Keeva felt like she was under a spell where she couldn't stop talking. It spread to Donovan, and they ended up in a rapid-fire conversation until Jastyn interrupted. She hoped they bought her excuse about using Ionad as a training ground. *Maybe they'll believe that we're guards.*

When the princess asked if they were both members of the royal guard, they cried in unison, "Yes!"

Gods, we sound ridiculous.

We can't stop now.

When Jastyn and Aurelia explained that the dark force had infiltrated their kingdom, and their prince was gone, Keeva could only hope their reactions were sincere. They couldn't know Brennus hadn't passed over. Aurelia and Jastyn looked utterly exhausted, and whatever drove them west was not Keeva's business. News that Aurelia's brother wouldn't cross over was the last thing they needed by the looks of them.

While helping them back to their cave, Keeva couldn't help but watch the way Jastyn fell into Aurelia or the way the princess held on to her like she never wanted to let her go. They might have rebuffed her assumption that they were together, but it was clear they were in love. Keeva's heart ached. She knew she'd been falling for Maeve, but now Maeve was upset with her. Knowing she was the cause of her upset drove Keeva mad and left her feeling even worse about things.

"You nearly gave us away at the end there," Keeva said under her breath, looking back to make sure Aurelia hadn't followed them once they'd said good-bye.

"I forgot we were supposed to be guards," he muttered, shrugging. "I think we did wonderfully. Nothing odd about us at all."

She laughed and shoved him, happy when he grinned. The tension between them had eased during the fight with the dark force. Keeva decided to take this as an opportunity to talk. "Donovan, I know you think I made the wrong choice."

He looked at her but didn't say anything.

"I know you think I never make the right decision."

"You certainly didn't taking the gatekeeper's key."

She leaned back, taking in the darkening sky. "I just...I don't know if I can explain it."

"Try."

"You know you're bigger. You're bigger in everything. More people listen to you. More people want to be with you." His brow furrowed. "Etaina. Every other lady of the court. Naela." She tossed him a look. He opened his mouth, then only sat on a boulder, a knowing look in his eyes as she continued. "Father has always favored you. You'll rule before me. You'll be heard before me. You'll be who the people trust. You already are." She took a long breath. "I didn't even know that fisherman's name."

"Keevs, the people like you."

"They tolerate me. The princess who's not afraid of any challenge, except facing the truth. Mother saw me. When you were out in the village, when Father was traveling, when Tacari was handling responsibilities I missed, Mother saw me. She knew why I started changing my hair. She knew why I ran to the armory. She saw me trying to lose myself in anyone who would pay attention."

"We all see you trying, Keevs." He paused, staring out over the cliff's edge back toward Uterni. "Do you know why I wrote to Etaina?"

The subject change caught her off guard. She joined him on the boulder, then asked, "You have a thing for flighty foreigners?"

He snorted but kept his gaze on the horizon. "I could talk to her about whatever I wanted. She didn't know me the way everyone in Uterni does. The way Naela does," he added, throwing her a knowing look. "Each exchange was a moment of reprieve from the castle, my responsibilities, Mother..." He trailed off, grabbing a pebble and tossing it over the side of the mountain.

Keeva watched him, surprised at the confession. "Is that why you keep Naela at arm's length? I've seen the way you look at her lately."

"She's too close to home."

"But she's wonderful. She's Naela."

"I know." He smiled. "I've always known that."

She nodded. She'd had no idea he was doing the same thing, only his distractions took different form. And like always, he hid it better. After a while, she said, "I just...I don't want to fall behind. Donovan, I don't know if I can."

"Keevs, coming in second doesn't mean you lost."

"Doesn't it?"

"Take it from someone who has come second to you in every archery competition for the last seven years." He grabbed her arm, making her face him. "Winning is wonderful. Getting the outcome you want, yeah, it's pretty perfect. We don't live in a perfect world, though, Keeva. The people want a leader who is great. But they also want someone who is vulnerable, who is willing to talk to them, who knows when it's time to make the hard decision."

She let his words sink in. She replayed the last several years. She was never on the grounds, except for a tournament. The castle had been a shield, a distraction. She was always pining after a court member or a maiden or a member of the stable team. She was always practicing for the next competition. In between her studies, she was in her chamber, trying to find the right color, the right look, the right way to be.

How many nights had she avoided her parents' chamber because of what lay inside? How many nights had she spent ignoring the truth instead of enjoying the time she had?

She'd never even tried to know what it was like to be out there, to be seen for anything besides Uterni's winning princess.

She had given up before even beginning.

The knowing grew warm inside her. It pricked behind her eyes, and she slowly met her brother's gaze. "I'm a selfish person, Donovan."

He smiled softly, his own eyes watery as he hugged her. "We're all a little selfish, Keevs," he said over her shoulder. "You've been thinking with your heart, which I've always admired about you. Your heart isn't wrong. It's just not right this time."

She started to reply, but only a choked sob came out. She leaned forward, her forearms on her knees for a moment before she couldn't stop the cries. It poured out of her, the dam bursting. Donovan leaned close and wrapped an arm around her. She cried, the buildup of years flying away, out of her reach, her attempt to keep this truth inside no longer possible.

"We need to get back," she said, sniffling. Donovan helped her stand, and they started toward home.

CHAPTER THIRTY-THREE

The next night, Maeve had a terrible dream. She stood in the river, Uterni's village just beyond. At first, the water was calm, drifting lazily past her ankles. Above, the air was clear and bright. But when she tried to move forward, the river blackened. Jade feathers fell from the sky. She tried to scream, but a harsh caw was all that escaped her lips. Frightened, she tried to move, tried to run back to her fen. But the river's water churned harder. It spun her in a ceaseless maelstrom. Beside her, the feathers took shape. They glared, bright and white, and a man stood before her. His dark eyes bore into her. A menacing sneer twisted his narrow face. He reached for her throat. Before his hands could find her, she woke up.

Her screams startled Rowan. He hissed and bolted beneath her table, wrapping around one of its legs. She tried to slow her breathing. Sweat lined her forehead. A sinking feeling pitted itself in her stomach. Sitting up, she searched the empty night. The tree branches moved listlessly in a light wind. Everything was calm. Inside, Maeve's heart thundered.

Keeva and Donovan returned late. She collapsed into bed, utterly exhausted but content. She'd done it. She'd kept a promise to Venostes's prince and helped his sister. Sleep came quick that night as a sense of pride wrapped around her like a warm blanket.

"Wake up, Keeva."

Grumbling, she turned over to find Tacari tossing a clean tunic onto her bed. "What's going on?"

"It's your mother."

Keeva bolted upright. "Tacari…is she…"

"Dress yourself and come to her chambers. I've got to fetch Donovan." Without meeting her gaze, he left. Keeva threw on her tunic, and tugging her boots on in the hallway, she started for her parents' chamber. It was early; torchlight fought against the waning twilight in the hallway. Naela appeared from her chamber three rooms away, still in her sleep tunic.

"Naela," Keeva said, skidding to a halt and pulling her into a hug. "You're back. Does this mean you found my father?"

Naela gave a surprised laugh at Keeva's display of emotion. She stepped back. "We did. The elves wouldn't let him into their kingdom. Sina had already ordered the attack on Venostes." Her voice fell. "He was too late. Sina knew he was there to state Uterni's neutrality. We'll have to tread carefully now." She shook her head, the smile returning. "But we're back. And so are you. How was it?"

Keeva knew she was asking about Ionad. "Good. Really good." She smiled. "Tell you about it later? It's my mother." Her gaze drifted over Naela's shoulder.

She nodded. "Of course." Pulling her into another hug, she said, "I'm glad you're back."

After promising to meet her in the main hall for dinner later, Keeva ran to her parents' chamber. Inside, she found Tacari, Donovan, and her father on the other side of her mother's bed. She smiled at the welcome sight. "Father, welcome back."

He looked tired and still wore his sleep tunic. "Thank you. And thanks to the royal guards. I'm afraid I was in a rather sticky situation in the east. But I'm here now. That's what matters." He reached out, taking her mother's hand.

Keeva stood opposite them. To her surprise, her mother sat up, and a healthy pink flush filled her cheeks. The stench of henbane lingered, but it was less. A steaming cup of ginger tea sat on the bedside table.

"Mother, you look…"

"She looks well," Donovan said, his eyes gleaming with surprise and disbelief.

"I feel well, my darlings." She patted Donovan's hand resting on her leg. "I feel the best I have in ages."

"The pain," Tacari asked, "is it…"

"It's odd," she said. "I had a terrible night. Fitful, aching. It was as if my bones were in a spiteful war with my muscles, like my body was gnawing itself to pieces."

"Gods," Keeva said, trying to take in everything. The sight of her mother sitting up, talking to them, felt too good to be true.

"But when I woke, it was like everything lifted. I feel like myself again."

Keeva smiled. Donovan wiped a tear, and their father muttered relieved words into their mother's ear. She held his face, her own a mask of serene calm Keeva hadn't seen in a long time.

Tacari asked the question on their minds. "How?"

Wiping her eyes, their mother looked at each of them. "I don't know. I'm not sure why this is happening, but I want to enjoy it." She beamed. "I want to enjoy this day with you. All of you." She reached toward Keeva, whose chest felt ready to burst. Had she done it? Had she managed to find the secret to keeping her mother here? The key tugged again beneath her tunic, but she ignored it. Epona couldn't touch them now. They were safe.

"Well," Tacari said, emotion thick in his voice as he started for the chamber door. "This calls for a feast. I'll notify the kitchen. The royal family shall dine like the days of old." He turned, one hand near the top of his staff as he smiled at them. "It is good to see you like this, Your Majesty."

She smiled. "Thank you, Tacari."

By midday, Keeva wasn't sure what to feel. It was as if she'd fallen back in time, like a spell had been cast and each room, each member of the castle was transformed. All was as it had been before her mother had fallen ill. Fires roared, lutes and lyres filled the corners of the main hall with music, and at the head of the great table, their mother and father sat side by side. Her mother needed help walking from room to room and seemed relieved when she was finally seated. Still, Keeva could hardly eat, she was so elated with the vision. But it was real: her mother was well enough to be up, to be among the people who loved her. Keeva's heart swelled.

Next to Donovan during dessert, she whispered, "I did it."

He motioned to Naela, whom he'd been talking to, and leaned closer. His smile fell, but she saw it linger in the corners of his downturned mouth. "It is something."

She grinned. "She's better, Donovan."

He eyed her over his goblet. *And what about Mitre, and the other villagers who have suffered terrible fates? What of them?*

Maybe they're better, too.

They're not, Keevs. They're stuck. They shouldn't be here.

She frowned, her mother's laughter drawing both of their gazes. *She's not stuck.*

He shook his head. "Let's just enjoy this, shall we?"

Her mood soured. She moved to sit beside her parents. Epona's words came to mind, and Keeva focused on them to ease the guilt that lingered from Donovan's reminder. *Enjoy the time you have.* That was what she intended to do.

That night, after a lively recounting of their adventure to Ionad with Naela near the fire, Keeva said good night to her parents. Her mother walked back to their chamber on their father's arm. The image exhumed a happiness in Keeva that had been buried beneath nights in the armory and endless healing potions shipped from other kingdoms. Her mother was all right again. In turn, *she* felt right again.

As she prepared for bed, her thoughts drifted to the fen. A day spent with her mother, family, and friends was a jarring comparison to the way Maeve lived. She pictured Maeve alone in her home. She'd been alone for so long. Keeva's neck itched with something akin to guilt. She knew it wasn't her fault Maeve's mother was gone, but now, here was her own mother, well again. It didn't seem fair.

The last conversation she'd had with Maeve came back to her. Earlier in the evening, she'd spoken with Tacari. Their words were brief, but she'd needed help. He'd located fragments of death records from the year she'd asked after, the year Maeve had been eight years old. Something hadn't sat right with her about Maeve's story. She was a gorgon, but she struggled to believe such a young gorgon could have ended the old man's life so quickly. Reluctantly, she'd told Tacari about her. He'd seemed dubious but willing to indulge her far-flung hope.

As she washed her hands, Maeve's face swam before her. "I have been selfish," she said to her empty chamber. She had been wrong to keep the truth from the woman she was falling for. Her own needs had clouded her vision; they'd drawn a jagged line between her and Maeve. Keeva shook her head at her irritating ability to sabotage something that was new and good. Something she felt blossoming into love between her and the gorgon in the fen.

She had just grabbed a quill and parchment and hopped into bed when Rowan slithered through her window. A note was tied around him. She leapt up and snatched it. He did a circle around her room as if investigating. "No rats here, I'm afraid," she told him.

He gave a hiss, then slithered back the way he came.

Maeve's handwriting greeted her from the torn parchment:

Something is wrong. I'm afraid. Can I see you tomorrow?

A sense of relief washed over her. Maeve wanted to see her again. A flutter spiked in her chest, and she took the parchment back to bed with her. Outside, a gust of wind kicked up from the cliffs, and her wooden shutters clacked against the wall. The sound seemed to kickstart her mind as she registered the fear in Maeve's words.

What was she afraid of? She looked to the window, then her door. She could go now. But the wind picked up more, and the memories of today widened and grew tall, building a shield to the outside world. She wanted to stay warm inside the reality of the day. A day filled with laughter and light and her mother's brightness walking the castle halls once again.

Besides, Maeve said tomorrow. She'd go first thing. Happy with the prospect of the new day, Keeva drifted off to pleasant dreams.

CHAPTER THIRTY-FOUR

Y ou came."

"Of course." A soft thud told Maeve that Keeva had leaned against the door. "What's going on, Maeve? What are you afraid of?"

Maeve turned so that she leaned against the inside of the door, imagining her back pressed to Keeva's. She'd written the note in haste; last night, her entire body had been fraught with worry and fear. Each noise from the fen, normally a welcome, familiar song, had set her on edge. She wasn't sure if she could even explain what she was feeling now.

"Maeve?"

"I think I'm going mad."

"What do you mean?"

She licked her lips, her words coming out slow as she tried to articulate her thoughts. "I keep hearing him, the raven." She stared blankly around the room, her eyes fixing briefly on the candlelight, the fire, then on Rowan watching her curiously from beneath the table.

Keeva replied, "I don't hear anything now."

"Not now. Last night and when I first woke this morning."

"Could it have been a dream? Dreams linger and feel as if they've followed us into this realm."

"Maybe." Maeve hesitated before adding, "I've also seen... things."

Keeva's footsteps shifted. Maeve imagined her turning to face the door. "What kind of things?"

"My mother."

It was quiet. Maeve fidgeted, anxious at having shared such information. She wrung her hands. *Gods, I do sound mad.*

To her relief, though, Keeva's voice was gentle when she replied, "How often has that happened?"

"I've always seen her. Since she left, I mean. At first, I thought she had returned but that she was too afraid to come near. Over time, I realized those visions were only memories. Old images replaying. Out of spite or sorrow, I'm not sure. But now"—she tried to keep her voice even—"now it's like a warning. Like each time I see her, she's trying to tell me something. Something bad is coming, Keeva. I just know it. I can feel it."

Another beat of silence. "Maeve," Keeva finally said. "Can I come in?"

Maeve wrapped her arms around herself. She stepped toward the hearth. "It's not safe. I—" She tossed a look to the fire. "I threw the ribbon away. It's gone."

Keeva took a deep breath, then slowly exhaled. "Rightfully so. I was awful." A faint rustling sound came through the door, like she was fidgeting with her belt. "A chamber maiden gave me a new one a week ago. I held on to it just in case." She hesitated. "In case you were willing to talk to me again."

Maeve couldn't help but smile, even if she wasn't sure what to feel. She was supposed to be angry. She was supposed to be upset at what had felt like a betrayal. But the longer Keeva stood outside her door, the more she wanted to pull it open and hold her close, hold Keeva in her arms and never let her go. She wanted to keep her near until this awful sense of foreboding left her in peace.

"You'll have to sit near the fire," she decided to say. "Rowan is still rather annoyed with you."

Keeva's smile was clear in her voice. "It's a deal."

Inside, Keeva did as she was asked. The camel brown ribbon sat fixed over her eyes while she sat stiffly by the fire. Maeve stood on the other side of her table. She reasoned the more distance there was between them, the stronger her resolve would remain.

"I want to apologize," Keeva said after a minute of only the fire crackling. Early morning light streamed in through the window to Maeve's right.

"Didn't you already do that?"

"I didn't do it enough." Keeva rubbed her thumb against her fingertips, one foot bouncing lightly against the floor. "Please, I'd like to explain myself."

Maeve grabbed a slice of acorn bread from the table and tore a piece. She rubbed the crumbling dough between her fingers, anxious but eager to hear what Keeva had to say. "All right."

Keeva's shoulders rose and fell before she said, "I'm so sorry, Maeve. I had asked you for help with Epona, but I didn't reveal the whole truth about why I wanted to see her. Granted, at the time, I wasn't even sure what I was going to do. I didn't know I'd act the way I did. Regardless," she said, lifting her chin and smiling, "Maeve, you're the only person..." Her smile turned knowing. "You're the only one I have been able to talk to about my mother. I confided in you and you in me. I should have honored that with the truth." Carefully, she tugged the key out from the neck of her tunic.

Maeve stiffened. "Is that..."

"Epona's key." She nodded.

"You still have it."

"It's working, Maeve. My mother, she's well again. Yesterday, it felt like it did before. She was her old self. We spent the day together. All of us. It was surreal and magical and—"

"Like it used to be."

Keeva's mouth stayed open, but her next words seemed to catch in the space between them. Maeve wondered if Keeva realized what she'd said. She frowned at the idea that how things used to be was an unreachable possibility. How, deep in the cavernous recesses of her heart, Maeve knew life with her own mother might never return. Keeva's chin dipped, and she fingered the knee of her pants. "There's more."

Maeve sensed her unwillingness to share whatever was coming next. "Please, Keeva. The whole truth this time."

Keeva's lips pursed before she slowly nodded. "There are some in the village who aren't the way they should be. People, members of my kingdom, who have suffered fatal injuries and should have crossed over but haven't."

"Haven't?"

"Can't," Keeva corrected, her jaw clenching. "They can't cross over."

"Because you have the key?"

Keeva played with the end of the necklace. "Perhaps."

"Keeva, don't you think those people deserve to move on?"

She sat quietly. Her lips fell in a frown, and she slipped the key back beneath her tunic. "I'll figure it out."

Maeve stepped around the table, now only a foot away. "Epona… she can't open the gate without her key. She can't help those souls cross over into the Otherworld."

"I know. But Maeve—"

A jarring caw cut off Keeva's reply. Maeve jumped. Rowan slithered around her feet in a protective figure eight. Her heart raced as she asked. "Keeva, did you—"

"Yes. I heard that." She stood, her body in a defensive stance. Despite herself, Maeve moved closer, reaching for Keeva and finding her hand. "It's all right, Maeve."

A familiar voice cut through the fen.

Keeva stepped in front of her, putting herself between Maeve and the door. "Donovan?"

A different voice, this one older, followed. "Your Highness!"

Maeve heard the confusion in Keeva's voice. "Tacari?"

"Ta-what?"

"Tacari," she said over her shoulder. "He's the magistrate." Swiftly, Keeva hurried to the door. Maeve stood still, afraid to take a step. The caw echoed in her mind, harsh and taunting. The pink lines on her forearm seemed to burn as Keeva called, "What are you doing here?"

Rowan slithered anxiously beside her.

Donovan was at the door now. "Keeva, you must hurry." Tacari's labored breaths sputtered between Donovan's words. "It's Mother."

Keeva stiffened. She reached for Epona's key around her neck. "No. She can't."

"Your Highness," Tacari called urgently, "it's time."

"No." Maeve stepped back at Keeva's raised voice. "No, she can't. I have the key. It's not possible."

Maeve said softly, "Keeva."

"No," she barked again. "You're wrong. You're all wrong."

Donovan sounded exasperated when he called, "Keeva, stop. Stop this and come home."

Keeva leaned against the door, her forehead pressed to the wood. Maeve couldn't move for a moment. She wasn't sure what to say. Slowly, she managed to inch her way closer. She grasped Keeva's shoulders, smiling at the way she relaxed into Maeve's touch. "Keeva."

Her voice was broken when she said, "I fixed it. I thought I fixed it."

Maeve pressed closer. "It's all right, Keeva. You should go with them."

After a moment, Maeve felt her give in, felt her accept the truth on the other side of the door. Her body relaxed. "Very well," she said. She reached up and found Maeve's hand. Then, she turned and, surprising Maeve, cupped her face. "I'm sorry."

"It's okay," she said, the tears surprising her. She kissed Keeva, hoping to pour the love and support into her lips. She kissed her harder, deeper, hoping Keeva understood she wasn't alone in this. Neither of them was alone.

Pulling back, Keeva sniffled, then pulled open the door. "Step back," she said to the others. Maeve did so, too, averting her gaze.

But when the door opened, the raven's cry cracked open the morning sky.

Tacari gave a strangled shout.

Donovan cried out. "Away, beast!"

"The raven," Maeve called. "He's back."

A determined look fell over Keeva's face. "We'll handle him," she said, then flew outside.

"Wait," Maeve called after her, lunging forward. Dread rang in her mind. Frantically, she closed the door and found the shard of glass. Scrambling atop her bed, she pulled back the curtain. Her heart sank.

Donovan waved off the raven, but it swooped upward, then dove at a menacing speed. His spell-fire missed, and he rolled sideways before the raven's claws could sink into his shoulder. Keeva had shed the ribbon. Maeve watched it fall, indifferent, into the tall grass just outside her door as Keeva's spell-fire flew, too, but the raven soared higher, flying a wide circle above the tree line. Maeve yelped when a tall man, his beard like a satyr, appeared in the window.

"Stay inside," he told her.

Her hand trembling, she kept her gaze on the glass. "You're hurt."

A two-inch, talon-sized gash ran down his bearded cheek. "I'll be fine." His dark, curious gaze held hers. Behind him, Donovan and

Keeva stood back-to-back in the center of the fen, searching the sky, saols ready in their palms. "My dear, look at me."

"But—"

"I'm fae. It's all right." Maeve swallowed but did as she was told, turning to meet his gaze. He smiled kindly. "I'm Tacari. I'm sorry we have to meet under these circumstances."

Confused, Maeve asked, "You…you know about me?"

"Princess Glantor thinks she's a chestful of secrets. But she wears her heart on her sleeve. She also asked me to find this." More spell-fire burst behind him, and he ducked as gold and magenta smoke filled the fen. He passed a small scroll through the window as the raven dove again, narrowly missing Keeva.

"What's this?"

"The truth," he said, ducking again. "Or so Keeva believes."

Maeve nodded. "Please, come in. It's not safe. The raven…he's dangerous."

Tacari opened his mouth to respond, but Keeva's shout came first. "Tacari, look out!"

Maeve cried out as the raven peeled toward him. She watched in horror as his talons sank into Tacari's neck. "No!"

He screamed, and her stomach sank at the awful gargling sound that burst from his throat. Blood pooled around the raven's talons as it reared back and bored its sharp beak through Tacari's other cheek.

"Get off him!" Spell-fire burst at the window.

Maeve ducked as the raven screeched and flew away but not before dragging his talons through Tacari's neck. She felt sick. Frantically, she found the glass. Rowan slithered in hectic circles inside, moving back and forth in front of the door, hissing angrily. Gods, what was she supposed to do?

The raven cawed again. Outside, Keeva and Donovan shot more spell-fire. Shaking, Maeve crawled across the room. Tacari's pained moans were at the doorway. Still trembling, she inched open the door.

"Tacari," she said, her stomach churning at the blood pouring between his fingers where he tried in vain to press against the wound. The hole in his cheek was berry red, blood trickling into his beard. A walking staff lay listlessly nearby. "Here." Keeping her gaze fixed on him, she grabbed beneath his arms. Somehow, she wasn't sure how, she managed to pull him inside and close the door. She wanted to find

Keeva, she wanted to help, but Tacari was bleeding. She knew he was bleeding too much.

Maeve found a rag near the hearth. "Press this to your neck." His breathing was already haggard, his face pale. He gasped, and she helped him hold the rag over the wound. "I'm so sorry," she said. The Caretaker's words echoed. *You're too dangerous.*

She fought back tears. Gods, he was right. After everything, he had been right. She shifted Tacari so he leaned against the stone wall of the hearth. His legs lay awkwardly out before him. Fetching water, she glanced over her shoulder. Her throat went dry when his eyes turned glassy. "Tacari?"

His gaze held hers, the light within it dimming.

The raven's cries continued outside, mocking her between the spell-fire. Keeva shouted, "Donovan, look out!"

Maeve dropped some water on Tacari's trembling lips. She leaned an ear to his mouth. His breath still came, though it was weak and labored. "I'll be right back," she told him. Quickly, she tied the rag around his neck to dissuade more bleeding. She had to go. She had to help. But how? What could she do? Her powers were useless against a raven. She considered trying to lure him into a snare, but that would take too long. She could let Rowan out, sick him on the ungrateful bird.

But when she went to the window and peered into the glass, she knew Rowan wouldn't stand a chance. The raven flew over the fen right toward her door. Its beak parted, and she braced for another caw, another terrible sound, but instead, a man's voice filled the fen.

"You're too dangerous, Maeve."

She nearly dropped the glass but for the surge of fear and dread that tied her hand to where she watched the raven's wings widen. Its body stretched, growing tall. Below, Keeva hurried to Donovan. They crouched near the chopping stump. The raven's feathers turned slick and seemed to melt into one another, elongating as its talons shifted. They stretched downward as the raven moved to land. Then, so quickly Maeve wasn't sure it could be real, the raven was transformed. In her fen stood a man. Maeve's heart thundered in her chest as there was no question as to who he was.

"Caretaker."

He was tall, his knobby legs wrapped in black, animal hide pants, a black cloak tied around his neck that fell over bony shoulders. His narrow face was pinched in what Maeve could only describe as hate. Dark eyes narrowed at her home over a long, sloping nose. His stringy black hair fell to his shoulders. The Caretaker's skin shone in sharp contrast to the rest of him; it was white as snow.

His voice was high and scratched like claws against tree bark. "Maeve. Enough of this."

She sat stunned, staring into the glass. Keeva and Donovan had shuffled toward the edge of the fen, seeming to assess him. Maeve had imagined the Caretaker hundreds of times. Every possibility, she thought, had been conjured over the years, an endless sea of faces. But each of those faces had been kind. They'd been warm and caring and holding out a helping hand to her with each passing year. Each incarnation had been worried for her. They'd kept her safe. Kept her fed.

Kept me trapped.

The thought hit her hard, as if the great willow tree nearby had fallen through the roof of her home, shaking her out of a lifelong trance. Outside, the Caretaker raised his chin, a wicked grin on his face as if he'd read her mind.

"Why are you doing this?" she called.

"I gave you everything you could have ever needed, Maeve. I gave you everything you needed to be careful." He shook his head. "I gave you everything, and you didn't listen." He walked slowly, his black boots treading carefully, unhurried, toward her.

Keeva sprang forward.

"No, don't!" Maeve shouted, but Keeva had already let her spell-fire go. It hit his shoulder in a blaze of magenta sparks, eliciting a high, piercing cry. When Donovan lunged for him, they both seemed startled by his strength. The Caretaker stumbled under Donovan's size at first, but black spell-fire sprang from his hands. Donovan cried out as it burned into his shoulders. The Caretaker lifted him, and Donovan's eyes were wide as he was tossed across the fen like a wet rag.

"Stop hurting them," Maeve cried.

"I'm not," he said, straightening and swinging his gaze back to her. "This is your fault, Maeve. It's all your fault."

A sharp stabbing hit her as his dark eyes held hers. Their gazes locked, Maeve saw it. She saw the visions of her mother, the terrified look in her eyes, the flash of white before her mother screamed.

"You…" she started, fearful of the words as they tumbled out. "You're the one who took her."

He grinned. "Your mother deserved the end that came to her. She wouldn't listen." He gave a mocking pout. "Like mother, like daughter, I'm afraid."

Maeve's stomach churned as his words tore through her chest. She felt as if the bed was giving out beneath her. She wanted to scream, wanted to shout, but she couldn't before Keeva leapt onto his back, one of Maeve's snares thrown around his neck. He cried out as she wrestled him to the ground. Keeva's face was fearsome as she conjured spell-fire and dug her fiery fingers into his chest. To Maeve's satisfaction, he gave a strangled cry.

Behind her, Tacari tried to say something. He was pointing toward the door. When Maeve looked back at the glass, she was certain her heart was being crushed in her chest. "Keeva!"

The Caretaker had managed to pull Keeva down, throwing her hard onto the ground at his feet. Donovan had recovered, though he seemed dazed as he stumbled forward to help. The Caretaker sent more spell-fire into his chest, and Donovan was laid out on his back once again. Keeva gathered herself and ran for her brother. Maeve's caretaker muttered beneath his breath. The ground shook. The stretch of green grass broke open. Gnarled roots shot skyward. The Caretaker spoke louder, his arms tracing shapes in the air, then directing them at the twins. The roots followed his orders, and Maeve watched them fly toward Keeva and Donovan as they tried to find shelter toward the fen's edge. Roots wrapped hungrily around their ankles, slinking up their calves as they searched the ground for something to hold on to, but the roots twisted and wove higher around them, dragging them to a nearby ash tree.

"Keeva!" Maeve shouted tearfully. "Stop it!"

The Caretaker ignored her as he muttered a final spell. The roots encased Donovan, whose strong frame was no match for the snares. Keeva, too, struggled against the vines and roots. Then, within a matter of seconds, they both were trapped, pinned and writhing in pain against the tree.

"Stop," Maeve shouted again, tears blurring her vision in the glass. "Stop hurting them!"

The Caretaker seemed to analyze Keeva and Donovan a moment more, a curious but satisfied look on his face. He brushed his hands as if to clean them, flicking his cloak behind him. "I told you. None of this is my doing. This is all your fault." He gestured to the ash tree, to the serrated lines of earth left behind by the upturned roots.

"Why are you doing this?"

He bent and swiped at the top of the chopping stump, clearing it of debris. Then, he sat, one knee crossed over the other, his arms folded neatly in his lap. "Come out, and I'll explain."

She felt dizzy. This couldn't be happening. She looked again at Tacari. His eyes fluttered. The blood seemed to have stopped, but a pool of it lay beneath him. Rowan was on her bed, curled and giving a continuous, fearful hiss.

Keeva's muffled cry was like a dagger in her chest. "Maeve!"

"Very well," she called. "Just leave them alone."

In the glass, the Caretaker's smile stretched wider. "Lovely. I'll wait here." She started to move when he added, "And Maeve, leave the glass."

A cold drenched her body. "But…"

"Leave the glass," he repeated.

Shaking, she set it carefully down. What was he doing? What had she done to deserve this? Her throat was dry as she stared at the shard near her pillow. Her lifeline to the outside world, to the world of man, was severed. Maeve took a shaky breath. At the door, her hands felt heavy. Her legs were like boulders. She closed her eyes, then called, "Keeva, Donovan, close your eyes."

A strangled cry came from them, as if the roots had tightened, climbing higher around their necks.

"I'm waiting," the Caretaker said.

"Fine," she replied, surprised at the heat in her own voice. "I'm coming." Taking a slow, deep breath, she opened the door and stepped outside.

CHAPTER THIRTY-FIVE

Helpless. That was how Keeva felt.
Donovan.
Keevs.
Can you move?
He wriggled, his great frame struggling against the roots. He groaned and cried out as they only seemed to dig deeper into him.
My sais.
Where?
My boot. But I can't—He cried again as the roots tightened over his chest.
Her mind spun. They needed to move. They needed to help Maeve. They needed to go to the castle, to their mother.
Donovan, was she...
His tear-filled gaze gave her the answer.
Epona's key singed her chest as Maeve's door creaked open.
Keeva forced herself to turn and face Donovan. "Close your eyes." His green gaze met hers a moment more before he did so. Keeva wanted to look. She wanted to see Maeve face her caretaker. But she knew it was too dangerous. Reluctantly, slowly, she closed her eyes. The fen disappeared as she listened, throwing up a prayer to the gods that they would make it out of here before it was too late.

"Why are you doing this?" Maeve asked again. She stood just in front of her door. From her periphery, she could see Keeva and Donovan trapped against the tree. It was as if the roots and vines had formed a giant nest, entangling them against the wide trunk. The Caretaker studied her, his beady eyes seemingly amused.

"I suppose I haven't been completely honest with you." He tilted his head, the gesture so like the raven. "Let me go back to the beginning."

She stood, listening.

"I knew your great-grandmother. Medusa, as the rest of the realm called her. I adored her. No," he said, a wistful smile lifting his sallow cheeks. At this distance, he looked old, though Maeve couldn't be sure how old. "That's not the right word. I did adore her, but I did so much more than that. I loved her."

Maeve frowned. Her mother had never mentioned any man. The stories of her grandmother and great-grandmother always featured them alone, forced to live in isolation in order to survive. "My great-grandmother was excommunicated," she said, repeating her mother's story. "She...she killed men."

"I am pleased to hear that is the story that persists. All these years...gods, it feels good to know my words won out."

"Your words?"

"You see, I loved your great-grandmother. I loved her so much. I courted her. Pursued her. I gave her everything she could have wanted." His face changed then, the friendly mask falling to reveal a sinister glare. In it, Maeve felt as if he wasn't looking at her but through her, beyond the fen and into the strands of time. "She refused me. She said she loved another. Well"—he shrugged—"I couldn't have that. Not after everything I had done for her. He was easy enough to kill, her paramour. And making it look like her hand, well, that was even easier."

Maeve's mouth fell open. "You...you drove her away?"

He nodded, still seeming to look through her. "You could say that. After losing her pitiful suitor and obtaining the fear and hate of the kingdom for his murder, her mind was weak. She created your grandmother, as you know, then disappeared into the wildlands. I suppose she couldn't live without that foolish man." He pointed toward the river. "She died just over there, near those gooseberry shrubs your mother loved so."

The pieces of what he said slowly fell into place. "You killed her."

He continued as if he didn't hear. "Your grandmother was even more intoxicating. But stubbornness seems to run in the family. She was easier to handle. Your mother, on the other hand…" He clucked his tongue, and fury raged beneath Maeve's skin. "She was a woman to contend with. I tried and tried and tried to win her over, but she insisted she needed to stay with you. To keep you safe." He scoffed. "I only ever wanted to care for her and for you." He stood then, reaching into his cloak. Maeve wanted to run. She wanted to scream until every inch of the Caretaker was nothing more than rubble left from the chasms of pain ready to burst from her throat.

He held a brown handkerchief delicately, passing it between his hands.

The ground fell out beneath Maeve, the marshy land swallowing her whole. "That's my mother's."

"She put up a fight, I do give her credit for that. But the gorgon women seem to have something against me. I can't imagine what." Maeve was repulsed at the sincerity dripping from his voice. "She cried out for you, Maeve, in her final moments."

She wasn't sure how she kept from vomiting. Her insides shook, and her chest heaved. She felt hot, like she'd fallen over smoldering coals as the Caretaker reached out, standing before her. He ran a bony finger down her cheek. "That's why, Maeve, I tried to keep you safe. You're too dangerous to men. You can't see us for what we are. Men like me, we only want to care for you. We only wish to love you." She flinched. He lowered his hand. "It's better this way."

She wanted to shout. All these years, all this time, she'd thought he was kind. She'd thought he was helping her. She'd thought her mother was still out there somewhere. "You didn't want to keep me safe," she finally said. "You wanted to keep me for yourself. Just like my mother and my grandmother. All because…" She struggled to understand. "Because they refused you?"

His eyes burned darker, and he slapped the handkerchief to his thigh, shouting, "I loved them! I loved them, and they wouldn't let me!" Spit flew from his mouth.

Maeve turned her cheek, her resolve returning at his pitiful reply. "That was so long ago," she said, pulling her shoulders back. "How are you still here?"

Keeva spat from the tree. "Sold his soul."

The Caretaker snarled.

"Is she right?"

He gave a shrug. "Dagda is always ready to make a deal. I promised to secure the realm against its gorgon threat. In turn, he promised me longevity." He stretched out his lanky arms. "So long as I keep the gorgon women hidden away, a pariah to the rest of the realm, I'm safe."

Maeve scoffed, a new sense of power surging through her.

The Caretaker seemed to sense this, his posture shifting, his smile falling. He lifted the handkerchief, tight in his fist, just below her chin. "Here's my offer, Maeve. Go back inside. Go back inside, and forget any of this happened. Forget this minor squabble. Forget your little hopes and dreams of a life beyond the river." He pointed to the ash tree. "Forget your precious princess." His voice dropped to a whisper as he leaned next to her ear. His breath smelled rotten against her cheek. "Forget her, Maeve. Forget all of it."

Trembling, it took her a moment to realize her fists were balled at her sides. It astounded her how quickly her feelings toward this man could change. How, for nearly a decade, he'd acted as a beacon of goodwill, a giving soul ensuring she was fed and cared for. His truth had shown itself now. Why?

Her gaze slid to Keeva, still struggling, still fighting against the vines. Her feelings for Keeva had brought out his truth and given her strength. Keeva had helped her realize another way of life was possible. Had the same thing happened for her mother? Her grandmother? If so, the Caretaker had extinguished those dreams, doused them in a flood. He'd made sure the gorgon women could never lead a real life if it didn't include him at the center of it.

She lifted her chin. She wanted Keeva. She wanted the life that was just out of reach, so close it grazed against the edges of her dreaming mind at night. It was the life that lay just beyond the river. She was this close to having it.

She stepped back. *No way in all the realm I'm letting go of that chance now.*

"No." She pushed him away. He frowned before she swiftly placed her hands on his chest and shoved. He fell back, falling awkwardly over the stump. His cloak tangled around him. Maeve didn't wait. She sprinted for the ash.

"Keep your eyes closed," she shouted. Keeva and Donovan winced, but they both nodded. She was steps away when a hand grabbed the back of her neck. She cried out as the Caretaker yanked her back.

She swung her arms wildly, trying to hit him. She made contact with his cheek, the *thwap* of her knuckles on his chin satisfying. She rushed forward again, tripping over the upturned earth. She cursed her shaking hands as she struggled with the vines around Keeva's shoulders. She felt the Caretaker at her back as she worked. He grabbed her again. "Let go of me!"

He snarled and gripped her tighter below her shoulders, forcing her to face him. She tried to fight out of his grasp, away from his long face, red with anger. Sharp teeth gnashed together as he spat in her face. "Forget her!"

"No!" With her open palm, she shoved his face away and tried to push him off her, but he grabbed her wrists, dragging her to stand on the other side of Keeva.

He shoved her hard against the tree and with his forearm, pinned her chest. The impact against the trunk left her breathless as he shouted down at her, his awful breath choking the air from her lungs. "This is your last chance, Maeve. Forget her now. Forget all of this."

She thrashed, trying to free herself.

"Maeve," Keeva said. "Maeve, fight this."

"Shut up," he roared. Then, with his left arm still pinning her, he reached for Keeva. His long nails sank into her cheek as he forced her to face them. Face Maeve.

Maeve closed her eyes, but a forceful thrust into her chest shot her eyes back open. A vine slithered across her cheek, making her face Keeva.

The Caretaker growled. "Look, Maeve. Look at what happens to those like us. Look at what loving someone does to them."

Keeva was inches from her face. Her fiery locks were speckled with dirt and debris. Her strong arms fought against the vines. Somehow, she still looked like the most beautiful woman Maeve had ever seen. Her will to fight, her drive to never give up broke through the pain searing within her chest.

"No," she managed to say while his elbow dug into her ribs, keeping her pinned. "I'm not like you."

"You are," he screamed. "You're just like me. You're dangerous. A monster. A demon. Just like your mother. None of you are good enough for this realm." He leaned closer, his breath sickening in her ear. "You're alone."

Tears burned almost more than her lungs. Visions of her mother, her grandmother, swam before her. All of them alone. All of them believing it was better that way. All of them forced to live in solitude because of this horrible man carrying out a twisted vendetta, warping them to his wicked vision.

She started at the touch of Keeva's hand on hers. She was still trapped, but she found Maeve's hand between the vines. In her touch, Maeve realized the truth.

She wasn't alone. Not anymore.

The Caretaker roared again, his cloak shaking with his shouts. "Look at what happens." He sounded unhinged. More spit flew as he screamed, "Look!" He dug harder into Keeva's cheek. "Open your eyes, Princess. See the truth. Open them!"

"No," Maeve sputtered, trying to breathe. Her chest felt ready to collapse. The air in her lungs lessened with each strained breath she took. Every time she closed her eyes, the vine pressed harder into her cheek, forcing them open again. "Keeva, don't look."

Tears fell from the corner of Keeva's eyes. "Maeve. It hurts."

"Please, Keeva." Maeve tried to shake the vine loose. She tried to turn her head. It was all too much.

"I'm sorry, Maeve."

His cry tore through them, unrelenting. "Look at her!" His arms straightened along with the vines before a final, merciless shove poured into each of their chests.

Maeve wanted to scream. She tried to close her eyes. She tried to take it back, take everything back, but it was too late. Keeva's eyes flew open. Maeve wondered, just for a second, at the most stunning green she'd ever seen. The thought was brief and terrible but consumed her mind: *a new shade.*

A gorgeous shade of green lay in Keeva's frightened gaze as she stared directly back at her. Keeva's eyes widened; her mouth fell open in a silent scream. It took a moment for Maeve to realize it was her own agonizing wail that filled the fen at what she'd just done to the woman she loved.

Chapter Thirty-six

Keeva couldn't move. Was this what it felt like to turn to stone? *It must be.* Her entire body grew heavy. Her feet, utterly exhausted from kicking against the vines, were like boulders in the river. Her head felt thick with pain radiating from her cheek and shooting down her neck. The roots around her chest constricted like a snare.

She reached for Maeve's hand.

"Keeva?"

She was looking at Maeve. Really looking at her, into her eyes. They swirled with gray and silver, but even more so with fear. "Maeve?"

Her face broke into a tearful smile. "You're alive?"

Hot tears rolled down her cheek. "I'm alive."

Maeve's caretaker bellowed. Her relieved face twisted in pain when he grabbed Maeve, throwing her across the fen. She tumbled into the chopping stump and fell, motionless.

"No, Maeve!"

"Keeva." Donovan wriggled next to her. "My sais." She looked down to find the end of his sais poking between the vines. Straining, she reached for it, using all her remaining strength to fight through the vines and yank it free, keeping her gaze on Maeve.

"Get up," the Caretaker shouted, kicking Maeve's legs.

Keeva's fingers burned with spell-fire. The vines, to her surprise, slackened at her saol. Could it be because he was distracted, no longer focused on them and the tree? She didn't care. She tugged harder and pulled the sais free. Within seconds, she was slashing through the rest of the roots until, at last, she landed gratefully on the ground.

"You lied," Maeve was saying, trying to stand. "You lied to all of us. To everyone."

"Fear is the most powerful weapon." He snarled, walking a slow circle opposite her, his back to Keeva. "People believe what they want to. I only needed to plant the seed."

Maeve shook her head. "I can't believe I trusted you."

"You need me, Maeve. You wouldn't have survived without me and my love."

Maeve straightened, and Keeva couldn't hide a smile at her retort. "This isn't love. You don't know what love is." For a second, Maeve's gaze found hers over his shoulder.

Keeva's heart swelled at the look in them. Donovan fell beside her, finally free of the vines. She took a steadying breath, motioning to him. *You go left, I'll go right?*

He gave the sais a twirl. *Absolutely.*

Maeve's caretaker lunged. Before she or Donovan could do anything, a flashing ribbon of silver sprang from the grass.

"Rowan!"

Maeve's caretaker gave a strangled cry as Rowan lunged, fangs bared, at his neck. They all stared as Rowan's teeth sank into his flesh, pulling him down. The Caretaker reached for him, both hands wrapping around Rowan's body, trying to pry him off. Rowan had wrapped himself tightly around his slight frame, and Keeva's stomach turned as his jaw clenched tighter.

Maeve hurried to her. The three of them stood together, watching the predator twist deeper into his prey. Feathers sprang from the Caretaker's neck. The smooth black seemed at war with darkened blood. Other parts of his body followed suit; feathers springing up, nails stretching into talons, desperate to transfigure. Rowan wouldn't relent, though. A strangled, pained caw mixed with the Caretaker's scream. More blood pooled around them. Finally, after one more sickening *crunch* into his neck, Rowan tugged himself free, unraveled himself, and slithered over to her.

They all watched the Caretaker's breath heave. From where he lay, his dark eyes fixed on Maeve, one hand reaching for her. A final surge of blood sprang from his neck as his limbs shrank and twisted.

White talons speared his boots as his frame shriveled, withering to bones. Maeve turned, and Keeva held her close until all that was left was a knotted pile of flesh, feather, and bone.

The fen was quiet. Maeve cried into her shoulder. Keeva held her tight. Rowan sang a satisfied hiss as he slithered between their legs.

Donovan muttered, "Tacari." He ran inside as Maeve stepped back.

Keeva looked into her eyes. "It's done," she said.

Maeve nodded, more tears falling. "It's done."

Chapter Thirty-Seven

Maeve had seemed frozen in shock outside her door. They'd collected what was left of the Caretaker and thrown it into the fire. Maeve was still staring at the flames, a brown handkerchief in her hands.

Keeva stood with one arm around her when Donovan had called to leave. "I'll be back," she said.

Maeve nodded, transfixed by the flames. "Go. Go see her."

Keeva kissed her. She could hardly look at Tacari, frail and limp in her brother's arms. His pale face was slack.

They nearly flew back to the castle. Along the halls, the guards gawked. "Call the herbalist," Keeva ordered a young woman openly staring at where Tacari was weak and unconscious. She could only imagine what she looked like: red burns from the vines across her arms and neck, dirt and blood on her tunic and boots.

In their parents' chamber, the room was filled with maidens and castle staff. But as soon as Keeva and Donovan entered, Tacari in his arms, a hush filled the room.

"Leave," their father said. The room cleared; it was only the five of them. Keeva quickly arranged a pile of bearskins next to her mother's bed where Donovan laid Tacari.

"What happened?" their father asked, not moving from where he sat clutching her mother's hand.

"A fight in the wildlands. Tacari…he was coming to get me. To bring me here."

She helped lay him down, her gaze fixing briefly on the deadly gash in his throat. "He lost a lot of blood."

"Too much," Donovan said, shooting her a look.

Pulling a blanket over him, Keeva moved to stand next to her mother.

"It's time," their father said gruffly, trying to clear the emotion from his voice.

"But yesterday," Keeva said, looking from her father to Donovan. "She was fine."

He nodded sadly. "The herbalists say that can happen. A final push of life, they call it."

Donovan was already crying. He'd been crying since they'd left the fen. Now he sat shoulder to shoulder with their father, tears flowing unabashedly.

Keeva reached for her mother's hand, hesitating with the fear that they had been too late. They had been too late, and her mother was already gone.

But her mother's eyes opened despite it seeming like tremendous effort to do so. "Keeva, sweetheart."

Keeva leaned down, opening her mother's hand and holding her palm to her cheek. "Mother."

She smiled weakly and slowly turned to look at each of them. "My beautiful family."

Their father visibly shook with sobs. "Asta."

"My love, it's all right." She took a slow breath. "It doesn't hurt anymore."

"But you were all right," Keeva said, hating the way she sounded like a child. "You were better."

"No, my darling. I wasn't. Not really." Her chapped lips parted, straining for more breath. "It's time, sweetheart." Her mother's hand found the neck of her tunic. Keeva helped her pull out the key.

In her mother's tired, clouded gaze, Keeva saw that she knew. Her father was watching her, his knowing eyes fixed forlornly on her necklace.

She turned to Donovan. *You told them?*

He swiped at his nose. *I had to.*

She clenched her jaw. She hated this. She had always hated this. The threat of this moment had loomed in every corner of the castle, in every moment of her life for the last three years. That was why she'd forced herself everywhere else, anywhere but here.

"Keeva, look at me."

The words startled her, and she found her mother's gaze.

"Be here, sweetheart. Don't go. It's all right," she said, and they all waited as she took another struggling breath. "I want you all here with me for this. Don't go," she said again, holding Keeva's gaze.

Keeva started to reply. She wanted to flee. She wanted to run to the wildlands, run to Epona and plead with her for another way. Any way to stop this. But her mother's gaze cleared. In it, Keeva saw peace. And for the first time in a long time, Keeva wept. They all wept as her mother's breathing slowed more. Beside them, Tacari groaned. Donovan moved to kneel beside him. He rested one hand on his chest. The other reached for Keeva's.

Between sobs, Keeva found Tacari's gaze. "I'm so sorry," she said.

His foggy eyes blinked slowly, one side of his mouth opening to speak. "You are a fine princess, Keeva."

She wept. She wept until it felt like she couldn't anymore. Cries racked her body. She was so weary. Weary with all of it. Keeva knew her family was too; she could hear it in their soft cries.

Through the pain and the exhaustion, Maeve's voice came to her. She saw Maeve's eyes. Eyes that held the pain of losing a mother, eyes that knew how to move on despite everything. Eyes that looked back at her with love, that saw her.

Keeva stood. "I'm going to fix this," she said. Tacari turned over, an accepting smile on his lips. She kissed her mother's forehead. "I love you." She met her father and brother's gazes. "I'm going to fix this," she said again. "Once and for all."

Hurrying from the room, she tore the key from her necklace and sprinted to the castle gate. She sprinted for the wildlands, sprinted for Epona.

❖

"Keeva!"

She didn't stop running. There wasn't any time.

"Keeva, wait!" Naela was at her side as she thundered across the trackway. "Keeva, I heard about your mother."

She kept running, but Naela kept pace. "It's time, Naela. I've been foolish. Selfish. It's time to grow up." Glancing sideways, she found Naela's surprised gaze, but a knowing smile told her she understood.

"I'm with you, Keevs."

It seemed like both an eternity and mere seconds by the time they reached the great ash tree. Keeva stumbled to a halt just before the towering trunk. Its bark stood unmoving, no blue-flamed door in sight. Her stomach sank.

"How do we get in?"

Her mind raced as she tried to think of something. Some way to get in. She was about to suggest they find the tunnels from before, though she had no idea where to even begin looking, when the trunk shifted and the door sprang to life.

Through the blue flames walked Brennus.

"Prince Diarmaid," she called, hurrying forward.

"This way," he said, motioning them through the door. Inside, he led them across the vast cavern. They stumbled behind him, the entire chamber still screaming in upheaval. Epona lay trapped before the other door, just as she had been the last time they were here.

"You're still here," Naela said.

Brennus, as transparent as the river in springtime, threw them a smile. "You helped my sister on her passage through Ionad. I had a feeling you'd be back."

Steps away from Epona, Keeva felt very small. The gatekeeper thrashed. Had she been fighting this entire time?

"E...Epona," she called up to her. The gatekeeper's screams continued. Keeva and Naela exchanged looks. Reaching up, Keeva held the key closer. Finally, Epona's face relaxed. Her eyes found the key. They lit up, and she smiled.

As quickly as everything had become upended the last time they were here, the chamber fell back into order. The earth sank, releasing Epona. She fell gracefully down, grabbing the key as she returned to herself. Her cloak fell neatly behind her. Her braid lay nicely over her shoulder. Her face serene, she said, "Thank you for returning this."

Keeva, shocked at the transformation, stumbled back. "Y...you're welcome."

Fire and water shrank and calmed, the walls and rivers seeming to exhale in a great sigh now that the key had been returned to its rightful owner. Behind them, the door twisted to life again. Keeva and Naela stepped back as a line of people marched steadily through. Brennus grinned and fell to the front of the line. The fisherman, Mitre, was behind him. Next, a young girl of only eight. An old woman walked behind her. Keeva started forward when Tacari and her mother walked through the door.

"Mother."

She knew she shouldn't go after her. They stood watching those waiting to cross over walk past them. Epona waited, a patient smile on her face as they strode closer, single file.

Keeva could hardly believe she was crying again, but the tears couldn't seem to stop. Naela, too, sniffled. Epona, meanwhile, led Brennus and Mitre through the opposite gate, pressing her key into it.

Tacari paused at the door. He turned and smiled. Keeva gave a small wave. Naela wrapped an arm around her, both of them crying.

"Wait," Keeva said as her mother stood before the gate, next in line to pass over.

Epona tilted her head. She seemed to analyze Keeva. She studied her. Finally, she nodded.

"Mother?"

Her mother turned. The trance-like state lifted. Blinking, her mother smiled. "Keeva, sweetheart."

Keeva threw her arms around her. "I'm so sorry. I'm sorry I didn't let you go."

"Oh, sweetheart. My darling Keeva." She stepped back, holding Keeva firmly by the elbows. "My strong, stubborn girl. I love you so much."

Keeva swallowed, her head starting to hurt from all the tears. "I love you, too."

Then, her mother kissed her cheek. "I see you, darling. I will *always* see you."

Keeva nodded, her head falling to her chest as she sobbed. Naela found her again, wrapped an arm around her as they watched her mother, Queen Asta Glantor, take one last look at her daughter. Then, she turned and, smiling, passed through the gate.

Maeve was sitting near the fire, a cup of tea clutched between her hands, when she felt it. A pulse swept over the fen. It was brief but strong, like a fairy's prick or an ember leaping from the fire. She glanced up, studying the window. It had happened. She smiled, taking another sip. Keeva had done it.

Closing her eyes, Maeve let the new feeling settle over her. While she could feel the balance restored, feel the scales of life and death once again as they should be, there was something missing.

There was no more raven's caw. No more basket of goods left at her door.

She stared into the fire. She was exhausted, utterly bone-tired from the fight with the Caretaker. She laughed quietly. He'd been anything but that in the end.

Through the steam, the image of her mother sat in the dust-filled chair near the hearth. The brown handkerchief hung neatly tied on one corner. Her mother sewed a patch into an old tunic. Maeve watched her. *Did you know, Mother? Did you know the truth of who he was?*

The small scroll sat on the table. She'd been too afraid to open it. Slowly now, she fetched it. Standing near the fire, Maeve opened it to read. In the middle of the page, a name was circled. *Harbin Andel, aged 62. Deceased – poison.* Beneath that a note had been scribbled: *arum maculatum stains on fingers and teeth. Berry consumption likely; several found scattered nearby.*

Maeve reread the scroll. All this time. All these years, it hadn't been her.

She cried herself to sleep in the aftermath but not for what had happened. She cried for her mother. Cried knowing she was gone. Cried for the life she'd had to live. She cried for the lies that had persisted for so long, the lies the Caretaker had crafted ensuring each of them was alone, like him.

Rowan slithered up her leg, wrapping around the arm of her chair. She ran a hand down his scales. "I'm not alone, though, am I?" He gave a short hiss, his beady eye fixed on her. She looked again to her mother's chair. Her mother looked up from her stitchwork, meeting Maeve's gaze. She smiled.

"No," she said, her mother's vision disappearing. "I'm not alone. Not anymore."

Epilogue

Maeve stood at the riverbank. The summer air was cool, the wind carrying tufts of river spray in its grasp. She shivered, though not from the wind. Anticipation, rather, tickled her shoulder blades. She ran a sweaty palm over the thigh of her pants, careful to balance the tray of acorn bread in her other hand.

Rowan slithered lazily at her heels.

"Well," she said, eyes fixed on the distant village torchlights. "Here we go."

As she made her way along the trackways leading to the higher castle grounds, Maeve kept her gaze lowered. The act was simply habit now. In the aftermath of the showdown with the Caretaker, she'd determined to learn what gorgons were truly capable of. Naela had the idea of using condemned criminals as a test. While Maeve had been wary, her curiosity had driven her to agree. A few days of staring intently at annoyed prisoners had resulted in nothing but dry eyes. It turned out that keen vision and the tendency for reptiles to seek her out were all that differentiated her from other fae. She was, much to her surprise and mild disappointment, plainer than a forest gnome.

The village was alive with people, and she could feel their curious eyes upon her. Firepits had been laid, their tall blazes bright against the evening sky stretching a downy gray over the realm. The orange and reds seemed to spring up from the murky bogs lining her path.

To her surprise, the music playing was light, frivolous, even. Everyone seemed to conduct their conversations in a muted excitement, smiles and kind words exchanged in each circle she passed. The week of mourning had come and gone, according to Keeva's latest note. Tonight, she had informed Maeve, the kingdom of Uterni would honor and celebrate Tacari and their late queen.

"Maeve."

She looked toward the eastern hillside. The great castle stood in shadow dotted with torchlight peeking out like curious eyes from dark windows. Before it, Keeva stood waiting in a fine camel cloak over a forest green tunic.

Maeve's gaze instinctually flickered down to Rowan, who seemed to be trying to take everything in with flicks of his tongue. He startled a teenage villager when he cut between his muddy boots in pursuit of a tree-dweller. Taking a breath, Maeve reminded herself she was safe. They were all safe with her eyes upon them. Smiling, she met Keeva's gaze.

"You made it." Keeva pulled her close, kissing her. It was quick, and to Maeve felt like the most natural thing in the realm. She wondered briefly how she had managed to go so long convincing herself she could go without such wonderful things.

On the hillside packed with court members and castle staff, Keeva led her to Donovan. His arm was around Naela, who seemed to be teasing him about something.

Unsure what to say, Maeve held out her platter. "I made bread."

"Splendid, I'm starving," Donovan said. Naela swatted his hand.

"Donovan," Keeva scolded, taking the plate from Maeve and passing it to a staff member hurrying by. Maeve watched the purple-skinned fae add her dish to a long table packed with meats, breads, and cheese. "After the ceremony."

He gave a dramatic sigh, then leaned back into Naela before saying, "Is it what you expected?"

Maeve looked around, taking in the beauty of the village. Humans, fae, royalty, and villagers all together, everyone a part of the same family. "It's lovely."

Everyone smiled. Keeva slid her arm around Maeve. To Donovan, she asked, "Is Father ready?"

He sighed. "I think he's been ready longer than any of us, whether he knew it or not." Naela nodded, rubbing his arm gently, knowingly.

Their gazes turned to the top of the hill. Four thrones had been arranged, their tall backs to the fading sunlight. The queen's throne was adorned with collections of bright bell heather and bog cotton. The silence that fell over them wasn't heavy, though. Rather, Maeve noticed it was one of acceptance. One of love.

"Is there any word from the East?" Naela asked, bringing their attention back to their group.

Donovan shook his head as Keeva replied, "No. Queen Sina's eye is on Venostes. Gods only know how bad things will get for them."

"Do you think they'll make it?" Maeve asked. Keeva had told her about Ionad, about Princess Aurelia and Jastyn, and about the dark force pursuing them.

Keeva shrugged but gave a hopeful smile. "They seemed strong. If they made it through the mountains, I think anything's possible."

"We'll be ready if they call for aid," Donovan added. "Venostes isn't alone. Not if they don't want to be."

Keeva leaned into Maeve. Warmth filled her chest as a cacophony of drums sounded on the hill. In her ear, she whispered, "I love the belt."

Maeve blushed, her fingers reaching for the frayed strands lining her waist. "Thanks."

"I'll get you a new one, if you like," Keeva said, planting a gentle kiss on her cheek. "But it's up to you."

Maeve nodded, trying to contain her smile.

"It's time," said Donovan. He met their gazes in turn. "Let's go say good-bye." He led Naela toward the thrones where a great funeral pyre had been constructed.

Maeve swallowed to quench her dry throat. She felt nervous. Rowan had returned. He slithered past, following Donovan and Naela toward the hilltop.

"Ready?" Keeva asked, her hand out to Maeve, green eyes shining. Maeve wondered at the look coming from them. Her heart sang in her chest. She looked around, looked at everyone, at the entire kingdom there, together. She was a part of something more. She smiled and took Keeva's hand. "Ready."

Hand in hand, they walked together up the hill.

About the Author

Originally from Dallas-Fort Worth, Ledel now resides in Denver, Colorado. She is a proud Returned Peace Corps Volunteer and has worked in education for eleven years. She was a 2019 Goldie finalist for her debut novel, *Rocks and Stars*. She is currently working on her next novel. To learn more, visit www.samledel.com.

Books Available from Bold Strokes Books

Bones of Boothbay Harbor by Michelle Larkin. Small-town police chief Frankie Stone and FBI Special Agent Eve Huxley must set aside their differences and combine their skills to find a killer after a burial site is discovered in Boothbay Harbor, Maine. (978-1-63679-267-5)

Crush by Ana Hartnett Reichardt. Josie Sanchez worked for years for the opportunity to create her own wine label, and nothing will stand in her way. Not even Mac, the owner's annoyingly beautiful niece Josie's forced to hire as her harvest intern. (978-1-63679-330-6)

Decadence by Piper Jordan, Ronica Black, Renee Roman. You are cordially invited to Decadence, Las Vegas's most talked about invitation-only Masquerade Ball. Come for the entertainment and stay for the erotic indulgence. We guarantee it'll be a party that lives up to its name. (978-1-63679-361-0)

Gimmicks and Glamour by Lauren Melissa Ellzey. Ashly has learned to hide her Sight, but as she speeds toward high school graduation she must protect the classmates she claims to hate from an evil that no one else sees. (978-1-63679-401-3)

Heart of Stone by Sam Ledel. Princess Keeva Glantor meets Maeve, a gorgon forced to live alone thanks to a decades-old lie, and together the two women battle forces they formerly thought to be good in the hopes of leading lives they can finally call their own. (978-1-63679-407-5)

Murder at the Oasis by David S. Pederson. Palm trees, sunshine, and murder await Mason Adler and his friend Walter as they travel from Phoenix to Palm Springs for what was supposed to be a relaxing vacation but ends up being a trip of mystery and intrigue. (978-1-63679-416-7)

Peaches and Cream by Georgia Beers. Adley Purcell is living her dreams owning Get the Scoop ice cream shop until national dessert chain Sweet Heaven opens less than two blocks away and Adley has to compete with the far too heavenly Sabrina James. (978-1-63679-412-9)

The Only Fish in the Sea by Angie Williams. Will love overcome years of bitter rivalry for the daughters of two crab fishing families in this queer modern-day spin on Romeo and Juliet? (978-1-63679-444-0)

Wildflower by Cathleen Collins. When a plane crash leaves eleven-year-old Lily Andrews stranded in the vast wilderness of Arkansas, will she be able to overcome the odds and make it back to civilization and the one person who holds the key to her future? (978-1-63679-621-5)

Witch Finder by Sheri Lewis Wohl. Tasmin, the Keeper of the Book of Darkness, is in terrible danger, and as a Witch Finder, Morrigan must protect her and the secrets she guards even if it costs Morrigan her life. (978-1-63679-335-1)

A Second Chance at Life by Genevieve McCluer. Vampires Dinah and Rachel reconnect, but a string of vampire killings begin and evidence seems to be pointing at Dinah. They must prove her innocence while finding out if the two of them are still compatible after all these years. (978-1-63679-459-4)

Digging for Heaven by Jenna Jarvis. Litz lives for dragons. Kella lives to kill them. The last thing they expect is to find each other attractive. (978-1-63679-453-2)

Forever's Promise by Missouri Vaun. Wesley Holden migrated west disguised as a man for the hope of a better life and with no designs to take a wife, but Charlotte Rose has other ideas. (978-1-63679-221-7)

Here For You by D. Jackson Leigh. A horse trainer must make a difficult business decision that could save her father's ranch from foreclosure but destroy her chance to win the heart of a feisty barrel racer vying for a spot in the National Rodeo Finals. (978-1-63679-299-6)

I Do, I Don't by Joy Argento. Creator of the romance algorithm, Nicole Hart doesn't expect to be starring in her own reality TV dating show, and falling for the show's executive producer Annie Jackson could ruin everything. (978-1-63679-420-4)

It's All in the Details by Dena Blake. Makeup artist Lane Donnelly and wedding planner Helen Trent can't stand each other, but they must set aside their differences to ensure Darcy gets the wedding of her dreams, and make a few of their own dreams come true. (978-1-63679-430-3)

Marigold by Melissa Brayden. Marigold Lavender vows to take down Alexis Wakefield, the harsh food critic who blasts her younger sister's restaurant. If only she wasn't as sexy as she is mean. (978-1-63679-436-5)

The Town that Built Us by Jesse J. Thoma. When her father dies, Grace Cook returns to her hometown and tries to avoid Bonnie Whitlock, the woman who pulverized her heart, only to discover her father's estate has been left to them jointly. (978-1-63679-439-6)

A Degree to Die For by Karis Walsh. A murder at the University of Washington's Classics Department brings Professor Antigone Weston and Sergeant Adriana Kent together—first as opposing forces, and then allies as they fight together to protect their campus from a killer. (978-1-63679-365-8)

A Talent Within by Suzanne Lenoir. Evelyne, born into nobility, and Annika, a peasant girl with a deadly secret, struggle to change their destinies in Valmora, a medieval world controlled by religion, magic, and men. (978-1-63679-423-5)

Finders Keepers by Radclyffe. Roman Ashcroft's past, it seems, is not so easily forgotten when fate brings her and Tally Dewilde together— along with an attraction neither welcomes. (978-1-63679-428-0)

Homeland by Kristin Keppler and Allisa Bahney. Dani and Kate have finally found themselves on the same side of the war, but a new threat from the inside jeopardizes the future of the wasteland. (978-1-63679-405-1)

Just One Dance by Jenny Frame. Will Taylor Spark and her new business to make dating special—the Regency Romance Club—bring sparkle back to Jaq Bailey's lonely world? (978-1-63679-457-0)

On My Way There by Jaycie Morrison. As Max traverses the open road, her journey of impossible love, loss, and courage mirrors her voyage of self-discovery leading to the ultimate question: If she can't have the woman of her dreams, will the woman of real life be enough? (978-1-63679-392-4)

Transitioning Home by Heather K O'Malley. An injured soldier realizes they need to transition to really heal. (978-1-63679-424-2)

Truly Enough by JJ Hale. Chasing the spark of creativity may ignite a burning romance or send a friendship up in flames. (978-1-63679-442-6)

Vintage and Vogue by Kelly and Tana Fireside. When tech whiz Sena Abrigo marches into small-town Owen Station, she turns librarian Hazel Butler's life upside down in the most wonderful of ways, setting off an explosive series of events, threatening their chance at love…and their very lives. (978-1-63679-448-8)

Broken Fences by Jo Hemmingwood. Former army sergeant Seneca Twist has difficulty adjusting to civilian life until she meets psychologist Robyn Mason and has a place to call home. (978-1-63679-414-3)

Never Kiss a Cowgirl by Ali Vali. Asher Evans dreams of winning the National Finals Rodeo in Vegas, and Reagan Wilson wants no part of something that brings back the memory of what killed her father. (978-1-63679-106-7)

Pantheon Girls by Jean Copeland. Cassie Burke never anticipated the detour life was about to take when a meeting with a prospective client reunites her with a past love and reignites the star-crossed passion they shared twenty years earlier. (978-1-63679-337-5)

Roux for Two by Aurora Rey. For TV chef Chelsea Boudreaux and hometown boy Bryce Cormier, love proves as tricky as making a good pot of gumbo. (978-1-63679-376-4)

Starting Over by Nance Sparks. Jennifer has no idea if she can mend Sam's broken soul after the sudden loss of her wife, but it's never too late for starting over. (978-1-63679-409-9)

The Accidental Bride by Jane Walsh. Spinsters Miss Grace Linfield and Miss Thea Martin travel to Gretna Green to prevent a wedding, only to discover a scandalous passion—for each other. (978-1-63679-345-0)

Three Wishes by Anne Shade. A magic lamp, a beautiful Jinni, and a cursed princess make for one unbelievable story. (978-1-63679-349-8)

Undiscovered Treasures by MJ Williamz. For Cyl and her friends Luna and Martinique, life's best treasures often appear when you're not looking. (978-1-63679-449-5)